Dedication

∞∞∞

Serenity,
May you always follow your dreams and know that your mom be-
lieves in everything you do. You are the bravest person I know.

Acknowledgements

This has been my dream since I was a little girl with a book obsession.
The support of my friends, family, and readers means the world to me.
Thank you to my husband, Mark, and my daughter, Serenity.
I know I have been slight neurotic during this process, and
I appreciate you sticking with me and cheering me on. I love
you both more than I can express in words.
Thank you to my parents, Gregg and Sherrie. Thank you first and
foremost for instilling in me a love of reading. Thank you for reading
the book as a reader and encouraging me thorough the process. Thank
you for also reading it as editors, seeing it through tougher eyes.
Thank you to my sister, Alyse, for providing the beautiful
pictures for the cover, the first page of the book, and at
the heading of each chapter. I'm amazed at your talent and
think everyone who reads this should check out her website
www.mountain-roots.com as well as her social media.
Thank you to my brother, Bret, for serving our country and providing
the inspiration I needed to represent families like you in my book.
Thank you to his beautiful wife, Shante, for being strong when he
is gone as you take care of my nephew, Cayde, in his absence.
Thank you to all of my advanced readers/editors. Angela, I promise
I will someday get the concept of comas! Abi, thanks for cleaning
it up and I'm sorry I made you cry. Bonnie and Autumn, you
are both too sweet and are fantastic cheerleaders. Sally, thanks
for motivating me to move forward and take a risk.
Thanks to all the rest of you for your reading and letting
me share it with you before anyone else read it: Chloe,
Beth, Kristin, Jen. I love you all!
Thank you to my beta readers, Lindsay and Emily. I appreciate you looking at my final drafts!
Thanks to all of who are taking to time to read my book!
It's a vulnerable thing to put yourself out there! I wrote this
for myself during a time I needed a healthy outlet, and this

was what I needed. Pass it on to someone else when you're done, maybe it will speak to them like it spoke to me.

"Flowers always make people better, happier, and more help-
ful; they are sunshine, food and medicine for the soul."
LUTHER BURBANK

Part 1-Begonia- symbol of fear

∞∞∞

~Premonition about misfortune or challenges

~Dark and unpleasant thoughts

~Need to be cautious in new situations

1

E leanor heard the crisp clink of the ice cubes against the whiskey glass all the way from the bathroom as if her ears were hypersensitive to this very sound. Her heart sank as she instantly knew that there was no escaping an outburst later.

She tried to remain calm. She tried to slow her suddenly rapid heart as well as her breathing, trying not to appear anxious as this would most likely not help the situation. She attempted to prolong washing her hands, trying to let the warm water soothe her as she stared at herself in the mirror, breathing deeply in and out. She wondered if she could just feign tiredness or claim to have picked up a shift for the next day. She asked herself if she could avoid what felt inevitable.

She turned the water off and stared intently at her reflection, willing herself to be sucked into an alternate universe on the other side of the glass. One where she wasn't another statistic, one where she felt strong enough to leave, one where she felt happiness instead of numbness, one where there was no fear.

"Eleanor, what is taking so long?" She heard on the other side of the bathroom door, snapping her out of her trance. She wondered how a voice that had previously brought her nothing but joy could now bring about fear. She thought about the fact that her body used to react with tingles and excitement at the mere sound of his voice.

She thought about how her body now responded and how it all started with the sound of ice in a glass.

With one final deep breath, she steeled herself as best as she could and opened the bathroom door.

2

*J*ingle jingle, rang the chime of the bells on the front door announcing the arrival of a customer.

Stacia looked up from the roses she was trimming, glanced at the door and muttered under her breath "Asshole, at 12 o'clock."

Rachel looked up from the greenery she was arranging and said quietly, "You know that confuses me every time. I literally have no idea where to look." Stacia looked at her sister and rolled her eyes.

Rachel, ignoring her sister, plastered a customer friendly smile onto her face. She turned around to greet the person standing directly behind her; the customer that had been the recipient of Stacia's asshole comment.

"Welcome to Bee's Flower Shop, how can I help you?" Rachel asked in greeting.

"Welcome to Bee's Flower Shop," Stacia mimicked under her breath as she set aside the bouquet she'd been working on, temporarily placing it in a plastic wrapper. She turned around to assist her sister with Kai. Kai, who happened to be one of the very few customers who made her skin crawl.

The women considered Kai one of their regular customers. He came in at least twice a month, and sometimes more regularly to buy flowers for his fiancé. He looked around sometimes but always walked away with the same arrangement of a dozen long-stem red roses and a card.

It wasn't that Kai was a blatant asshole, working in a family-owned retail shop they saw their fair share of tourist assholes. It was more that there was something a little off with him. The Bee sisters prided themselves in connecting with their customers and usually producing at least one smile per customer, per visit, with their friendly manner and witty banter. With Kai, they'd never gotten anything resembling a smile. He always seemed put-off by having to speak to either of them.

Kai's dark-gray power suit didn't have as much as a single wrinkle or speck of lint. His sleek Italian leather shoes were impeccably cared for with nary a scuff, and his smooth black hair was perfectly sculpted in place. His physical presence alone exuded power. He gave a curt nod of greeting to the sisters as he walked to the flower cooler and started his routine critique of the flowers.

"Shouldn't these look crisper?" He commented.

Stacia shot Rachel a somewhat discreet look of annoyance as they walked behind Kai to the cooler to give him the usual Bee sister's flower lesson.

"We just got those in today," Rachel started, "fresh from our supplier." They were, in all honesty, very fresh with no flaws to speak of. Kai just seemed to need something to complain about.

Kai looked at them both without a hint of emotion.

"Kai, my man," Stacia said in an attempt to crack the stone facade, "remember all you have to do is gently squeeze them at the bottom of the rosebud to test for squishiness."

Rachel grabbed the arrangement Kai had been referencing, and gently applied pressure to the bottom of the ruby rose's base. It remained firm, reinforcing the fact that it was a worthy choice.

"See, no squishy," Stacia interjected. "Which means it's fresh as can be. If you still don't believe it's fresh, put your nose up in there and take a big whiff, they smell amazing!"

Kai didn't crack a smile but did nod in accession. He seized the bouquet and briskly walked to the register. He grabbed a blank card and began to write.

Rachel walked behind the cash register and started to ring up the purchase. Stacia walked back over to her previously abandoned arrangement and began to fine-tune it, trimming and snipping and arranging flowers and bits of greenery. Kai paid for his purchase and headed towards the exit.

"Remember to have your fiancé clip the stems down about halfway at a 45-degree angle for freshness," Stacia said in a sickly-sweet customer service voice as he neared the door.

He didn't say anything or even bother turning back around in her direction, but once again gave a small nod as he pushed open the door and exited.

"Bye Felicia! And good riddance!" Stacia said as soon as she heard the telltale farewell of the bell and heard the door click in place. She turned to look at her sister, who was usually quick to reprimand her when she was loudly and blatantly verbal about her thoughts about customers. They had an unwritten rule that if you said something you had to wait at least two full minutes until after the customer left and all comments had to be spoken quietly and discreetly. She noticed that Rachel had a slight frown on her face.

"What?" Stacia asked.

Her sister wrinkled her forehead as if deciding whether or not to say anything; "I managed to look at the card he was writing while I was ringing him up, not for the first time. On every card I have snooped on, there was some variation of an apology."

"What's so abnormal about some bro buying flowers to apologize to the poor beauty queen he has cheated on?" Stacia scoffed, taking another sip of coffee.

"Granted, I did read it upside down, but I believe it said something like 'I'm sorry that I got angry. I love you, and it will never happen again." Rachel stared at her sister; lips twisted in a sideways smile of concern.

"That is odd," Stacia agreed. "I just don't really know what we could do about it other than continuing to watch it or like

Facebook stalk him and make sure his fiancé is okay. I know that sounds harsh, but I don't really know what to do with that."

"I know," Rachel said, "I think we just need to make a note of it and file it away. Maybe next time we can try to ask him about her or something. I really don't know, either. I just get a vibe that a little something is going on that we need to pay attention to."

"It does make me wonder where all of our flowers go. The reason people get them and give them and the story surrounding all of it," Stacia commented as she went back to her task of bouquet making.

3

E leanor couldn't remember the last time she felt she'd truly been touched from a place of love. When she first met Kai, it had all been loving touches and soft glances. She could recall a time where all it took was a brush of his hand on her hand for her heart to soar and flutter.

Lately, his hands caused mostly fear, disappointment, and pain. It had all changed eight months in, shortly after they'd moved in together when Eleanor had met a coworker, after their shift, on a particularly emotional day. They'd found out that one of the pediatric neuroblastoma patients was going to be put on hospice, and they both needed someone who understood that grief to talk to. Eleanor was still a new nurse and needed some extra support.

Eleanor had been emotional during the discussion, and by the time she thought to look at her phone, Kai had texted several times, worried about where she was. She'd come home less than an hour late to a very intoxicated Kai.

He'd struck her across the face so hard the moment she entered their apartment that she stumbled back and smacked her head on the door. She instantly saw stars from the blow and from the pain. Her first thought was that it had been an intruder as she didn't think her smart, sexy, and wealthy fiancé was even slightly capable of that kind of betrayal.

"Where in the hell were you?" Kai growled; the scent of whiskey heavy on his breath. "I was worried, and I don't want to have to worry about you."

Eleanor had been in shock, "I just needed to talk to a co-worker about a patient of ours who will probably pass away soon. This is the first time I have been through something like that, and I got sad. I texted you, you knew I wasn't coming straight home after work."

As if he had not heard a word she'd said he started speaking, "For an hour I have been sitting here thinking you were not okay," Kai grasped her chin. Eleanor could not tell if he was trying to be harsh or if, in his intoxicated state, he didn't realize how hard he was gripping her face.

"That hurts!" Eleanor exclaimed looking into her fiancé's eyes with shock. What had happened to the man she knew that she was planning on marrying someday?

"My heart hurt for the entire hour I could not get ahold of you," Kai said, barely releasing the pressure on her chin. "I did not even know if you were alive!"

"I'm alive," Eleanor had replied quietly, slowly backing up until her chin fell out of his grasp, tears streaking down her sore face.

The next morning, she'd woken up and wondered if she had imagined last night. It had been so out of character for Kai. He sometimes had a cold demeanor, but that was part of his lawyer personality and the way he interpreted things. She sat up in bed and felt the throbbing in her head and knew that she'd not imagined any of it. The first thing she thought was, if it happens again, I will leave.

"I am so sorry," Kai had said late in the morning when he'd finally woken up hungover, the scent of whiskey still coming out of his pores. "I was so worried when you didn't answer the phone, and then I drank more so I could deal with being scared, and then I just lost control. I don't honestly remember all of what happened, but I can promise nothing like that will happen again."

Eleanor had nodded and reluctantly allowed him to hug and kiss her. She was upset but felt that one incident could be forgiven, especially if he claimed to not really remember what he did. Later that night he'd gone out for groceries and come back with a dozen beautiful long-stem roses and a card asking for forgiveness.

It had not been a one-time incident. Now, six months later, Eleanor was no closer to feeling like she could leave than she was the first time it happened. As time went on, she had, however, learned a few things: it only happened on days he worked, and only when he was intoxicated. Hiding alcohol or watering his drinks down helped prolong the little bit of happiness she got with him before he reached his breaking point on those days where a break down seemed inevitable. On the good days, she felt like he was the man that she'd clicked with, that she'd agreed to marry. On the bad days, she tried to remember the good times they had and the history behind their relationship.

She'd first met Kai when she was a barista at the local coffee shop down the street from his law firm. He'd come in at least every day and sometimes twice a day. It had not taken long before she'd gotten his order down pat. She memorized it so much so that one day he came in and she parroted the order right along with him, "Americano, extra hot, almond milk instead of cream to a dark khaki color."

He'd smiled at her with his perfect white teeth, and his chestnut colored eyes and she knew from that point on that he would be her kryptonite. Eleanor understood that her schedule was beyond full. Even with nearing the end of nursing school, which she'd heard could be compared to boot camp, she worked full-time hours at the coffee shop. With all that was on her plate, she didn't have the time or the energy to take something else on, but once she'd seen how his eyes shown when he smiled, she couldn't resist him.

Their romance had been a whirlwind of dinners with his law partners, bike rides, hikes in the Rocky Mountains, brewery tours, and study nights. They'd connected so quickly and completely that sometimes Eleanor felt like it was all a dream. He'd shown so much concern with her needs and putting them first, which Eleanor had never really experienced before.

Those nights when they'd been at home alone had been her personal favorite of all their activities. Relaxing at home usually entailed Kai showing up at her apartment with her favorite Thai takeout and rubbing her feet while quizzing her on exam questions for school. He'd been so confident in himself and so sure of what Eleanor could be in the future. She felt challenged, supported, and most importantly, loved.

He would always come up with the funniest analogies and scenarios for her to remember for her state licensure test that she'd had a hard time not reenacting the scenes in the testing facility while taking her NCLEX test a few months after she graduated. His acting out of a person in respiratory distress, breathing so quickly while asking her to act out interventions that would save him had caused him to nearly pass out. So, when Eleanor saw a respiratory distress question on her test, thinking about almost having to revive him helped her answer the question with ease.

When he proposed to her at her apartment four months into their relationship, after a particularly grueling finals week at school, Eleanor said yes with enthusiasm. The ¾ carat sapphire ring he got her fit her perfectly, both in size and in style.

"I knew that you were not a diamond girl because there is nothing basic about you," Kai had said as he slipped the engagement ring onto her left ring finger while kneeling in front of her. That night in bed, after they consummated their engagement, Eleanor once again felt a love that she'd never felt before. After all, love wasn't something she was exactly used to.

Eleanor had been born to drug-addicted parents in Denver, Colorado. They'd attempted to get clean and make it work to raise her, but one day they'd dropped her off at her grandmother's house and never returned. Mama J had legally adopted her granddaughter shortly after.

Though she didn't doubt that her grandmother loved her

dearly and did as much for her as she could, she had to work harder to take care of Eleanor, and her fatigue showed. Her grandmother had obviously not planned on being a parent a second time around, but she took it in stride. Mama J worked extra hours to give Eleanor the basics. She'd remained active since her second husband had died and even after Eleanor moved in, she had activities that she didn't give up, meeting friends for Bunko at least once a week and playing on a bowling league. From a young age, Eleanor had gotten used to the solitude that came with her life.

Mama J had been a psychiatric nurse at Denver Health. Witnessing her grandmother taking care of people who often had no one else to fight for them had been inspirational. It was in seeing her grandmother rarely give up on her patients, the people who everyone else had given up on that had taken Eleanor down the nursing path.

Mama J had lived long enough to make sure that Eleanor had gotten into a good nursing college. She succumbed to lung cancer three months before Eleanor graduated high school despite never having smoked a day in her life. Eleanor had finished high school with the support of a few close friends from her gymnastics team and a few teachers who had always cheered Eleanor on. Mama J had left Eleanor her house, which Eleanor promptly sold. The house was slightly too large for one person, and Eleanor hoped for a fresh start. She used the proceeds from the sale of the home to purchase a tiny condo near her nursing school.

Almost four years later, her journey with Kai began as her nursing school journey was ending. When they'd decided to move in together, it had been easier to move Kai in with her as she already owned her condo and he'd been leasing his. It also happened to be close to both of their jobs, making commuting in Denver traffic slightly better.

Eleanor was just putting the finishing touches on the baked salmon and pilaf that she was cooking in the oven when she walked by the reflective glass on the overhead microwave and caught a glimpse of herself in the reflection. She could see that the heavy makeup that she'd used to cover the bruising on her cheek was fading a little bit. Eleanor had just fished the compact that she now carried with her out of her back pocket and just finished gingerly applying another layer of color when she heard the click of the lock in the front door, signaling Kai's return. She quickly returned the compact to her pocket before he could see what she'd been doing.

She heard the crinkle of cellophane and knew before she saw them that he'd purchased roses for her. She'd previously loved roses, but now the sight of them made her feel ill. They represented insincere apologies from Kai and a lack of self-care on her part. Even their sweet scent made her a little nauseated.

Being a granddaughter of a nurse and a nurse now herself, she knew how cliché it all was. Loving Kai, when stressed at work, had too much to drink and became angry Kai who hit her and then apologetic Kai who brought her flowers coated in false promises. Repeat.

"Good afternoon," Eleanor said as he entered the room. "How was your day?" She presented her left cheek, which was the least sore, and allowed him to kiss her hello.

"Work was work. Nothing worth reporting. I brought you these," Kai said almost robotically as he presented her with the flowers. Eleanor accepted them with a crater-size hole in her gut. Once again, she thought of where they would be had she either only gotten the one apology bouquet from him, or better yet, never gotten any flowers that coincided with an apology. After all that had happened, she would be happy never getting flowers from him again for any reason.

"Thank you, they're beautiful," Eleanor said quietly, choking back the disgust that lingered in her mouth. She suppressed the nausea that had engulfed her as she caught a whiff of the floral scent. Inside she chastised herself as she always did for not saying more; for staying.

"The flower shop girls told me to remind you to trim them before you put them in water," Kai commented as he grabbed a vase from under the sink and placed the flowers onto the counter. He handed her the card that was attached, and he started to trim the flowers as she read:

I am so sorry my anger got the best of me again. I love you, and I can't wait to plan the rest of our lives together. It won't happen again. I promise.

All of my love,

Kai, your future husband

"I really am sorry Ellie," Kai said, a somber look on his face as he filled the vase with water and placed the roses in the vase, arranging them to near perfection. Every time he said these words, he looked nothing but sincere. He genuinely seemed sorry, and that was always the hardest part.

Eleanor hid the internal battle going on inside as she nodded. She hated the word promise now almost as much as she hated roses, "It can never happen again."

She didn't know how many times they'd danced this very dance. How many times they'd said the same variation of this over and over; like a morbid waltz. She believed that he had some remorse every time it happened, he just didn't have the follow through and self-control to stop, mainly because alcohol and stress were involved, and she didn't have the self-esteem or energy to leave. They were caught in a vicious cycle, and neither of them seemed to have the ability to break it.

Kai gave a brisk nod as he headed to the bedroom to change out of his suit and into some more comfortable clothes. While he changed, Eleanor got the salmon out of the oven and put it on the dining table. She'd purposely left the whiskey and wine glasses off the table in the hope that out-of-sight, out-of-mind would be effective tonight. After last night she didn't know if she had the energy, and she'd told him it could not happen again.

Kai sat down at the table and began dishing out salad for them both. "How was your day today?"

"Well, my favorite little patient was admitted again for pre-bone marrow transplant maintenance. Not only did she hug me when she saw me, but we got to work on our handshake, which is more of a few handshake-like moves with a lot of attempts at the latest modern dances," Eleanor said as she started dishing out the salmon. "She taught me how to floss, which is a dance I definitely don't understand whatsoever, but it's funny to try it. I love hearing her laugh while I attempt it which makes making a fool of myself worth it. Depending on how she feels tomorrow we will try to work on our handshake again."

"Are you sure working on the Bone Marrow Transplant Unit is where you want to be? I don't know how you can deal with all that stress and sadness. What could be sadder than kids with cancer?" Kai looked at her with concern.

Eleanor contemplated her answer as she finished chewing her bite of salad. Even though he was sober currently, she didn't want to answer the way she wished she could. They'd currently had a decent night, and she didn't feel like triggering anything. In a perfect world, she would be able to answer that him defending people in court that were most likely guilty and getting paid well for doing so was sadder than cancer. She felt, sober or not, he would not handle that comment well.

When she was done chewing her food and contemplating her response, she replied, "I agree that my chosen profession has some challenges and sadness, but what I go through is nothing compared to what those kids go through. They inspire me always to try harder, and they challenge me to be brave. Let's not forget that I also worked my ass off to get into Children's Hospital's Nurse Residency Program, and I'm not going to just give that up. It was super competitive to get into, and I could not handle knowing that someone didn't make the cut so I could be hired there and then quit the minute things got challenging."

Kai again nodded briskly, "I just want you to realize how sad it will be when you lose your patients, especially when you get so close. That is what I worry about. Your heart can be too big sometimes. Too big for your own good. Are you sure you want to deal with sadness?"

"I know what sadness looks like, and it has done nothing but make me stronger," Eleanor retorted, immediately regretting her choice of words, quickly trying to backtrack. She decided if she added more to her comment it would not seem to Kai like she was speaking about them and their current situation. "Case in point. A. I'm pretty much an orphan, B. I don't have many friends, and C. I may have over-cooked the salmon. That all seems sad to me."

Kai's face contorted into a smile when she mentioned the overcooked salmon, and again for a brief second Eleanor saw a hint of the man she fell in love with. He took a bite of his salmon, "This salmon is superb. Actually, I would say it is not even slightly overcooked."

Eleanor smiled back, glad to be onto less serious subjects. They finished their dinner mostly in silence. Eleanor cleaned up after they were done and packed her lunch for work the next day. She got her scrubs pressed and ready to go. She changed into pajamas and started preparing herself to settle down so she could get to bed at a reasonable hour as she had to be at work at 6 am for a twelve-hour shift.

She'd just sat down to watch some television, her guilty pleasure, Naked and Afraid when she heard the freezer door open and heard the gut-wrenching sound of ice cubes clinking in a whiskey glass.

Once again, Eleanor's heart sank.

4

Scarlett looked out of the kitchen window at the colorful array of reds, yellows, violets, and deep oranges attached to stems swaying in the light Colorado breeze. She exhaled forcefully as she put the last of the dishes in the dishwasher.

She could always count on the beauty of the outdoors to center her if only temporarily, the earthy scent of the outside lingering on her clothing for hours after. She could have her mood changed in a matter of seconds just by looking at flowers, smelling their blossoms, putting her fingers through the dirt while planting seeds in their neat little rows. She loved the cycle from seed to seedling, to plant, to death. She also loved the fact that it repeated, thus providing an opportunity at a new life again and again.

She purposely planted perennial flowers for every season in her garden that would produce colors from the beginning of the spring through the fall just so she could always have something blooming. When Colorado winter took over, and her blooms succumbed to the weather, she started little seedlings inside just so she could be around something alive and green.

She loved that being outside could make her forget if only temporarily, the touch-and-go of their life recently and the difficulties they'd endured the last two years: her sick child, distance from Louisiana and her family, and distance from her husband, despite residing together. She knew the forgetting was always temporary, but a temporary reprieve was still better than none.

She'd just started to turn from the window when a beautiful cobalt colored blue jay flew by the window landing on the bird feeder outside. She ran to the bedroom, grabbed her camera and snuck out the back-porch door zooming in on his beauty and the contrast of the bird's blue body against the red and orange of the fall chrysanthemums.

The bird was startled away when her cell phone beeped loudly. She set down the camera and looked at the new text message: *Good morning mommy (followed by 15 variations of smile emojis)!!!!!!!!!!!!!!!!! Daddy said you guys were switching soon, and I can't wait to show you my new tricks!*

She took a deep breath, the smell of flowers light on the air before heading back inside to pack a bag for the overnight hospital stay. She had to get back to the reality of their lives.

5

"Watch this move," Stacia said as she turned around and wagged her butt in rhythm to the Rihanna song blaring over the loudspeakers of the shop. It was 15 minutes before the shop officially opened at 8 am and Rachel and Stacia were known to blare Rihanna or Taylor Swift at full blast as they danced their way through their opening duties.

Dance parties were just one of the many ways they knew their family was just as much about having fun as it was about business. When they found out that dance parties were not a regular part of most people's family routine, the Bee family tended to find it a little odd.

Bee's Flowers had been started by their grandmother, Elizabeth Bee, shortly after she'd graduated from high school. She'd received a little money from her grandfather after graduation and used that along with years of hoarded babysitting money to purchase a little cart that she displayed her flowers on. She would always laugh about the fact that she became successful by pushing the cart up and down the streets of Denver following couples on dates. She claimed that she used her passive-aggressive nature, stalking qualities, and a calm smile to guilt the men she encountered into buying her wares for their girlfriends.

Betty had been so successful that she'd purchased the tiny storefront just before the Colorado winter of her second year in business and it had been in the family ever since, eventually expanding to not only showcase flowers but merchandise as well. Betty still worked about 10 hours a week and participated in the morning dance party as often as possible.

Their grandfather, David, had met Betty when he was on a particularly lousy first date and Betty had stalked him relentlessly trying to get him to purchase flowers for his date. "I will buy your flowers," David had said after about ten minutes of Betty's persistence, "but I will be giving them to you while I ask you to dinner." Betty had been flustered but accepted the offer as David's date had stormed off. They'd been together ever since.

All of the Bee girls from Grandma Betty on had kept hyphenated Bee names to stay true to the Bee's Flowers namesake. Grandma Betty and Grandpa David were now getting closer to retirement age, and they'd recently developed an overwhelming urge to travel. They'd been so passionate about it that they'd purchased an RV with the license plate TRVLBEE. Their Grandpa David had not been too keen on the license plate, but Grandma Betty insisted as she stated it was thanks to her flower shop, they were even thinking about retiring on time. Grandpa David had worked as a teacher, which had obviously been a very respectable job but didn't rake in as much money as Grandma Betty's business, particularly after they'd branched out into the world of wedding flowers. He'd counteracted her comment by mentioning the fact that he'd worked for the flower shop for free every summer. He'd lost the argument.

The maiden voyage of the TRVLBEE had been three months ago, and they'd now taken it on a few week-long trips here and there. The sisters were pretty sure their grandparents just wanted to make sure they had an excellent grasp on the business side of their store before leaving on a broader scale. The Bee sisters took it as a challenge, wanting nothing more than their hard-working grandparents to retire in style.

Rachel looked at her sister's dance moves and mimicked them by turning herself around, feather duster in hand, and shaking her butt in time to the music, occasionally using it as a microphone to sing along to the lyrics. They both shimmied over to each other and did a few hip bumps before they became aware of a loud knocking on the side entrance door that led into the alley where they received their shipments. Through the square glass pane at the top of the door, they both looked at the amused face of Marco, their flower supplier. He was nodding his head in time to the loud music with a sideways smile on his face.

Stacia blushed as she grabbed the music remote out of her Bee's Flowers apron and turned the volume down, "I can't believe he just saw that."

"I see that blush sis. Though based on the fact that he is smiling, I'm pretty sure that he likes what he sees." Rachel said quietly, nudging Stacia with her elbow as she headed to the door to let him in.

Stacia's blush deepened as she walked out of their line of sight to the back-stock area where she manually fanned her sweaty red face. She did a quick armpit test and then tried to look casual as she walked back into the main display area.

Marco was the epitome of handsome with dark curly locks, skin the color of caramel, and eyes as blue as the peaks of the Rocky Mountains on a sunny Colorado day. Not to mention the fact that he had a South American accent and was also an incredibly nice, smart, business savvy man. Stacia, who liked to think that she was a strong independent woman these days, with a pretty great sense of humor, felt like she became a bumbling fool around him.

"Hi Stacia," Marco said as soon as she walked back into the room.

"Hey-o," Stacia said somewhat awkwardly in return. As if the awkwardness wasn't bad enough, she also became incredibly clumsy when she was in his presence. Today this fact was confirmed immediately when she casually leaned against a card display causing it to hurtle towards the floor. Marco rushed forward and caught the card tower in the nick of time before falling completely to the floor, but not before the rack expelled almost every single card that it held. Stacia looked from her sister to Marco and then looked down sheepishly at the floor now littered in card stock.

"Weren't you thinking of reorganizing these anyway Rach?" Stacia, cheeks even redder with embarrassment, joked sheepishly as she glanced at her overly organized older sister.

"Yeah, you just took care of half of the work, thanks for your consideration." Rachel retorted as she walked to join Marco and Stacia who had both begun scooping up cards from the floor.

They heard the jingle of the bell followed by the entrance of a late twenty-something woman. The woman paused at the door, gauging whether she should enter after witnessing the mess all over the floor.

"Oh goodness, is now a bad time?" she asked in a light Southern drawl. "I was just grabbing some coffee from next door and heard the music from outside. I figured I had always wanted to check out the store and I thought now would be a good time. I mean who can resist Rihanna?"

"There is never a bad time for a customer at Bee's Flowers," Rachel stood up and handed the card stock in her hands to Stacia. She brushed her hands off on her apron and walked over to the woman, leaving Stacia and Marco alone to clean up the rest of the card stock.

"In full disclosure, we were having a dance party to Rihanna, but then my sister had a clumsy moment after a bout of excessive blushing due to the handsomeness of Marco over there, the dimply one," Rachel said jokingly. "Since you appreciated our music, we would be extra happy to help you in whatever way we can."

The woman chuckled, "I do love me some Rihanna, and I think that there is never an occasion that isn't made better with dancing. I did happen to see y'alls dancing through the window, and you were rocking it I must say." The woman again let out a quiet chuckle, "Thank you so much for letting me in early. I would love to get my daughter some flowers."

"Well, that I can help you with, what sort of flowers are you interested in?" Rachel asked as she motioned for the woman to follow her as she started off in the direction of the flower cooler.

The woman held out her hand to stop Rachel, "I can't get her real flowers, even though I would love more than anything to be able to," she said sheepishly.

Rachel looked at her quizzically. "Um, ok, that is not a problem. We have other selections of gifts over..."

Rachel was interrupted by the woman. "I'm so sorry, it may be easier if I explain the situation, my daughter has a form of leukemia, and she is currently in the hospital which means she can't have any real flowers because they may carry bacteria, she has always helped me garden since she started walking and shares my appreciation of flowers. She has a "garden" in her hospital room, but it does not have any real flowers in it, I take pictures in my garden so we can put them up on her wall."

Now it was Rachel's turn to blush, not out of embarrassment, but because she was unsure what to say, "I'm so sorry, I can't even pretend to know how hard that must be." She paused for a moment, trying to think of the perfect gift, "I do think there is an alternative that may work. A different type of flower, in fact. It would add a little variety to your existing garden."

Rachel walked away from the flower coolers towards the merchandise area gesturing for the woman to follow her. They walked over to a display shelf where a variety of books were shelved.

"I'm just about as passionate about books as my sister is about flirting with Marco over there." Rachel said with a wink.

The woman smiled and chuckled at Rachel's remark, glancing at Marco and Stacia who were putting the remaining cards back in place. Stacia giggled at something Marco said, and then immediately blushed.

"I know you are probably wondering why I'm showing you a display of books when I just promised you a flower alternative." Rachel said as she pulled out Dr. Seuss's *Green Eggs and Ham* from the shelves. She opened it displaying some torn out pages.

"I was wondering a little but didn't want to offend you quite yet as we just met," the woman said with a smile and a wink.

Rachel paused for a minute, "I'm Rachel, by the way."

"And I'm Scarlett," the woman said in her slight drawl as she offered out her hand for a handshake.

Rachel shook her hand with a smile, "I knew we would get along just fine the minute I found out you were drawn in by the sounds of RiRi." She paused and gestured to the top of the bookshelf. "I turn the pages into flowers."

Scarlett looked to the top of the shelf where there was a variety of black and white and colored book pages that had been cut and glued together, transforming into paper flowers. The flowers were displayed in either little glass boxes or vases. Along with different colors, there were different paper flower variations which ranged from open or closed roses to daisies, to small succulents.

"You can pick one already made, or you can pick a book, and I work my magic with the hot glue gun, which takes about five minutes. Or you can pick up to five flowers for a bouquet, and I put them in a little vase or tie them with a ribbon. If you are interested that is, I won't be offended if you want to look around more."

Scarlett smiled as she traced the binding of the books on the shelf with her fingers. She stopped on James Matthew Barrie's *Peter Pan*. She pulled it out and flipped through it for a moment.

"I absolutely love this idea. We have always been big readers ourselves. I saw these once on Pinterest and thought they were so neat," Scarlett said as she continued to flip through the book lovingly. "Can I get five from this book, please? I have read this one to Molly for years. We have been using a line from this as our motto these last two years, '*The moment you doubt whether you can fly you cease for ever to be able to do it.*'"

Rachel grabbed the book gently from her hands, internally holding any tears from leaking out of her eyes, "Give me five minutes."

Rachel walked to the back, plugged her hot glue gun in and waited for it to warm as she pulled five pages from different sections of the book. She carefully cut three of the pages to fit the open rose mold and two of the pages to make closed roses. While arranging and applying the hot glue, Rachel couldn't avoid thinking about how hard it must be to have a sick child; to even find the strength to smile every day. She could not imagine her daughters even being sick enough to need to be in a hospital.

She popped her head out to ask Scarlett a question and spotted Stacia leaning against the doorframe, holding the door for Marco and giggling like a little girl. Rachel rolled her eyes but inside she was excited to see her sister shedding some of her sarcastic, protective exterior. Stacia had been through a bit of a rough patch in the last year, and Rachel knew that some of her sister's attitude was due to this fact. If Marco helped melt some of the attitude away, Rachel would embrace it, even if Stacia was ignoring her opening duties. She also liked Marco and saw no harm in her flirting with a nice man.

"What is your daughter's favorite color?" Rachel asked as she peeked out from the storage area where they'd a little extra space and could work on projects and floral arrangements for weddings. Scarlett was looking around at the other books.

"Molly loves teal, but she is eight, so it changes pretty frequently," Scarlett answered.

"I have eight-year-olds, so I know all too well about the frequent mind changes. I will make teal the main color but will throw in some extra colors, just in case," Rachel said as she grabbed a spool of teal, gold, and iridescent white ribbon from behind the sales counter and took all three to the back room. She cut loops of ribbon, interweaving the streams of ribbon down their paper stem and then tying them snugly around the bouquet. She placed the arrangement in a jar and covered the jar with a swath of shiny gold and black polka dot fabric for a little extra pizzazz and contrast. Finally, she added the finishing touch, a small placard stating that the pages had come from *Peter Pan* that she hot glued onto the fabric.

Rachel walked out with the arrangement and headed towards Scarlett. Rachel held the non-floral floral arrangement out for

Scarlett to inspect, "Here you go. I really hope that Molly likes it."

Scarlett smiled as she reached out and grabbed the jar, inspecting the roses, "I have a feeling she will love it. I love it!"

"It was so nice to meet you, Scarlett. I really hope you come back and see us soon. I truly hope you have a great rest of your day as well," Rachel started to guide her towards the exit.

"Wait, what do I owe you?" Scarlett asked with a look of puzzlement on her face.

"The first bouquet is on me, please. I'm a mother, and I would love to give you this small thing from one mother to another," said Rachel solemnly before trying to lighten the mood. "Plus, you may or may not be scarred for life after having to see me and my sister's dance moves."

Scarlett couldn't help but chuckle, "I thought the rump-shaking wasn't bad, and the hip bump move was on point! I really would prefer to pay y'all for your time and effort."

Rachel shook her head, "It took me five minutes, and it prevented me from having to watch my sister giggling. Giggling! You actually did me a favor. I'm just happy we were able to find something that Molly could enjoy."

Scarlett chuckled again, "I must admit, y'all seem like a pretty fun family. I appreciate the gesture."

Rachel smiled in agreement, "You should see when my grandma joins in the dance party. Her hips don't lie."

"Until next time then," Scarlett headed towards the exit door but stopped and turned around one last time before pushing the door open. "Thanks for the smiles and the kindness. I needed it more than you know."

With that, the jingle of the bell, as well as a friendly wave from Rachel to Scarlett, signaled Scarlett's exit. Rachel took a minute to compose herself, thinking of her two children at home who happened to be Molly's age. Rachel thought about how lost she would be without them. How could a mother face potentially losing her child already in eight short years? She was interrupted in her thoughts by another giggle coming from her sister's direction.

Rachel rolled her eyes before heading towards Stacia, who was still holding the door open for Marco. Rachel walked until she was parallel with the door so Stacia could see her, but Marco couldn't. She looked in her sister's direction and batted her eyelashes relentlessly until she got her sister's attention and then crossed her eyes as she mimicked a kissy face in Stacia's direction. She snapped back to a regular face when Marco started to walk back inside the door.

"How are things with you Marco?" Rachel asked.

"Things are going well. I really can't complain," Marco replied.

"You mean you are too nice to complain," Rachel said knowingly. "Don't take this the wrong way because you know we really enjoy working with you, but are you planning on delivering flowers forever? I have seen the pictures you take; they are absolutely stunning! Also, the writing pieces that go with the pictures are amazing. Who wrote them?"

Marco looked slightly embarrassed, yet proud, "I wrote them. I have always liked different facets of art."

"Well, that is impressive!" Rachel exclaimed before asking, "Is the photography business going well or are you on a hiatus?"

"Well, I have to continue delivering flowers because what would my life be without seeing the Bee sisters every morning?" Marco gave a sideways glance at Stacia. "Honestly, business is fine. I could have more photography jobs, but I have become a little pickier. I almost always refuse to do weddings anymore because I had to deal with so many bridezillas that made the experience less than desirable. Now I'm just promoting my online store with the print shop and doing family and senior portraits. My dream job would be to branch out and do photography books or something of that nature."

"Photography books would be cool!" Rachel said, nodding in agreement.

Stacia chirped in, "We know all about the joy of these bridezilla creatures and their family members. Remember last week when we had to put in for the urgent delivery of roses?"

"I'm pretty sure I still have PTSD, and by that, I mean Petal Tint Stress Disorder!" Rachel commented.

"Oh my goodness that fits so perfectly! It all came about because the bride's mother said that the pink roses were too pink. Then when we got the new shipment, she decided she liked the first roses better. Thank God we had kept the original ones in the cooler and could easily use them," Stacia shook her head, "Some people have too much time on their hands."

"I hope never to spend that much time comparing pinks ever again!" Rachel exclaimed. "Seriously though, let us know if you ever want referrals from us. We promise we would only get you in contact with the best behaving bridezillas. We would do anything to help you out until you start your big book career." She glanced at her sister, emphasizing the help you out portion.

Stacia blushed again but managed to cover it up by heading towards the alley door, "I bet we could really help Marco out right now by helping him unload our shipment."

The bell sounded three times as they all headed towards the alley to unload.

6

Scarlett usually reserved her tears for the way home from the hospital, but today, as she sat in her car, in the parking lot of Children's Hospital, she could not stop the steady stream from coming.

After the diagnosis two years ago when Molly was six, they'd decided to try to live life as normally as possible despite cancer, despite having to uproot their lives and move states away for her care. She'd felt normal for a few minutes in the flower shop, surrounded by living things and carefree laughter.

She'd felt like they'd been so focused on Molly for the past two years, that anything that temporarily allowed her to forget often brought tears as well. She didn't know if the tears were because of guilt for enjoying an experience away from her daughter, or because of a chance at a release she wasn't used to allowing herself. In between all the chaos of cancer, she tried to find the beauty and joy in the little things, like a blue jay in the backyard and laughter in a flower shop.

She was again pulled out of her thoughts by the text notification on her phone: *You almost here babe? I was hoping to see you for a few minutes before I head out. Molly had a pretty long nap this morning and has WAY too much energy. Maybe she got into my jellybean stash, jellybeans for lunch at least means she is eating, right?*

Scarlett replied: *Jellybeans could count if they tasted like lunch maybe? Possibly a popcorn, a pear, and a fruit smoothie one? You are correct, if she ate those, at least she is eating. I'm on the way up. See you soon! Xoxo*

Scarlett took a few cleansing breaths, took out her compact from her purse and did a quick revamp of her makeup. She'd switched to waterproof mascara two years ago after the realization that grief could and would hit when you weren't expecting it. Therefore, she only had to do one swipe of the mascara on her lids and one swipe under with a tissue. She grabbed her overnight bag, her coffee, and the jar containing the paper flowers and headed towards the hospital.

She entered the lobby and took in the familiar sight of the hospital, red wagons and children with their parents throughout. Children's Hospital, Scarlett, Tevin, and Molly's home away from home.

The sounds of children filled all the empty spaces in the hospital corridor. Scarlett tried to send every parent subliminal messages: *don't sweat the small stuff, hug them constantly, enjoy each and every moment.* She hoped that every child there felt loved and would make it out okay; she wholeheartedly wished this the most for her own. She hoped that this wasn't selfish, but she'd become a mom through and through the minute she found out she was pregnant, and this feeling became even stronger when Molly entered this world.

She rode the elevator up to the seventh floor, the unit with the most security, the most caution; the Bone Marrow Transplant Unit. She stopped in the side room after using her temporary visitor badge to gain access. She washed her hands thoroughly for the recommended two minutes and then washed them for two more.

She entered the unit, passing the familiar faces of the nursing and ancillary staff. She waved across the hall to Eleanor, Molly's primary nurse. Scarlett knew that Eleanor would give them all a few minutes alone before coming in to say hello. Eleanor had gotten close to the family in the last few months, but she always respected that sometimes family connections came before medicine and that tiny gesture alone made Scarlett feel so much more normal.

"Mom!" Came Molly's excited squeaky voice as Scarlett entered the room. "I'm totally whooping Dad at Mario Kart."

Molly was perched on her hospital bed with a bright green wig on and a pair of polka dot pajamas. She was clutching a Wii remote as if her life depended on it while staring at the television screen above her bed. Scarlett's husband Tevin was just as precariously perched on the front of the fold-out futon chair also clutching a Wii remote so tightly that his knuckles were white.

"Whoop me never!" Tevin exclaimed as he shimmied his Wii remote right and left at a rapid pace, his Mario character sat on his Go-Kart swaying right and left on the screen.

Molly took the momentary distraction to throw a turtle shell at Mario causing him and his vehicle to careen off the track, allowing her Yoshi to stream across the finish line in first place.

"I. Am. The. Champion. For once in my life!" Molly screamed excitedly as she tossed the remote down onto her bed in football spiking style. She then stood up on the bed prancing around and raising her arms in a victory dance, green hair tossing this way and that with each hop.

Scarlett went over to her daughter and went in for a hug. She couldn't remember the last time she'd hugged Molly without fear. Fear that she would transfer germs to her daughter, fear that she would breakdown crying, fear that she would squeeze so hard she would break her daughter's frail body, fear that it would be the last hug.

She straightened Molly's green wig and looked at her daughter's pale face. Before Molly's diagnosis, she would never have been able to pick out a leukemia patient on the streets, but now all it took was a glance at the pale skin and slightly gaunt appearance for Scarlett to diagnose strangers on in public in her head.

"Mom, you will never guess what I found out from The Discovery Channel today!" Molly beamed up at her mom, "the cells in your body replenish every seven years! That means that we only have five more years until all my cancer cells will be gone!"

Scarlett felt a sob catch in her throat, she quickly stifled it, not wanting to worry Molly, "Wouldn't that be so amazing." She glanced at her husband with worry in her eyes. They'd always promised to try to live as normally as possible, but they'd also promised to still be honest with each other and with Molly no matter how hard or heartbreaking that may be.

"I can't wait to tell Dr. C and Eleanor! It will be sad though because I'll obviously miss them when I don't see them anymore." Molly explained matter-of-factly as Scarlett and Tevin eyed each other again from across the room.

"Honeybuns, we can always try to have positive thinking, but those cancer cells don't really cooperate the way normal cells do. You have to think of them like bully cells or robber cells or bad guy cells that won't obey the law." Tevin said, stopping when he saw his wide-eyed wife draw her hand across her neck, indicating that now was maybe not the time or place for this discussion. Tevin put his Wii remote down and headed towards his wife, putting his arm protectively around her back.

Molly stared blankly at her parents for a moment before she rolled her eyes, "Seriously you guys, it was on The Discovery Channel. Those people know everything."

Scarlett was just scripting a reply in her head when there was a light knock on the door.

Eleanor peeked her head in, "It's almost time to hook you up, Ms. Molly."

"Eleanor!!!!! We need to show my mom our handshake first!" Molly climbed off the bed with the assistance of her father and headed towards the door.

"Well of course," Eleanor said as she headed inside the room. She entered the room wearing a yellow disposable gown she'd first donned over her scrubs before walking towards the room's sink. She washed her hands for a few minutes, allowing them to dry before placing a pair of blue gloves on both her hands. Her face was, as it always was in her patient's rooms, covered from nose to chin with a yellow surgical mask to help protect her patient's compromised immune systems even further.

Molly bounced from foot-to-foot near the bed, having waited impatiently during the cleaning routine, anxious to show her parents their new handshake. Eleanor walked over to Molly, "Ready!"

First Eleanor and Molly faced each other and started to countdown, "Five, four, three, two, one."

They both put their hands together in a praying position bowing to each other while never breaking eye contact. They stood simultaneously and slapped their palmed hands together, slapping one hand above and the one hand below, "Now spin," shouted Molly as she turned the side of her palm facing Eleanor around allowing Eleanor to guide Molly towards the ground in a somewhat clumsy salsa dancer spin. "Now shimmy," Eleanor said as she used her free hand to grab Molly up from the floor and hands clasped together, they shimmied their shoulders back and forth. "Now floss," said Molly as she let go of their hands and both started threading their arms alternatively in front of and behind their hips, moving faster and faster.

Eleanor burst out laughing at her own attempt at the new dance move. Molly collapsed on her bed in mock exhaustion hand to her forehead in a true diva move. Tevin and Scarlett clapped, both their faces beaming with smiles.

"I'm not quite as coordinated as you Molly," Eleanor said as she assisted Molly from the bed and together, they performed a mock bow and curtsy.

"We'll work on it, but you will have to practice at home," Molly said with typical eight-year-old bossiness. "We're going to keep adding and adding and adding to it until it's probably like at least thirty minutes long."

"Oh, I may get pretty tired after thirty minutes, but I will practice whatever we add. I can't wait to see the next part!" Eleanor exclaimed with a wink over her mask in Scarlett and Tevin's direction. "I'm just going to grab your medicine Miss

Molly, and we will get you hooked up."

"How long is this one? I wanted to go to the playroom with my mom later." Molly stated.

"You'll have time to play later," Scarlett said. "We can do some school stuff while your medicine is running, and if we finish with your school stuff before it's done, we can always walk with your pump to the playroom."

"Fi-ine," Molly said, somehow making the one syllable word into two. She climbed into bed and moved the right side of her shirt aside in preparation for Eleanor to return and hook her chemotherapy to the central line that was implanted under her skin.

Even two years into the journey, Scarlett was always amazed at how quickly these children became somewhat accustomed to something so horrific. It was a typical sight here to see children playing with each other while their central lines hung out of their clothing infusing chemo drugs. She'd been told that children were brave and resilient, and she had proof of this fact daily.

Tevin went to the fold-out futon and grabbed his overnight bag and laptop. "I have to check into the office pumpkin." He moved Molly's wig aside and placed a kiss on her peach fuzz scalp.

"I love you, daddy. Don't forget to pixie dust your dreams tonight," Molly gave Tevin a giant hug.

"After all," said Tevin, as they embraced "'*The moment you doubt whether you can fly you cease for ever to be able to do it.*'"

Molly chimed in with him, getting most of the lines from the *Peter Pan* passage correctly.

"That reminds me, Molly close your eyes!" Scarlett exclaimed as she remembered her trip to Bee's Flowers. Molly, knowing that if she peeked, she would possibly miss out on a present, obeyed. Scarlett went over to the counter and grabbed the colorful jar with the paper flowers.

Scarlett took them over to the bed and tapped Molly's arm, "You can open your eyes. I got you flowers."

"Mommy, flowers are not allowed, because..." Molly started to say before she opened her eyes and gasped.

"They are so beautiful Mom. The other kids are going to be so jelly!" Molly let go of her shirt and grabbed the vase from her mom. She gingerly fingered the paper petals. "They look like the roses from your garden but made of books! I miss the garden, even though I have a fake garden here. How are the flowers? Oh, and the ribbon is teal, and there are polka dots!"

"They are beautiful Molly." Scarlett acknowledged before addressing her daughter's multiple exclamations. "You don't like to make other kids jealous because you are a nice girl. The garden is not as beautiful as it could be with you helping, and I told Rachel at the flower shop that you loved teal, but she guessed that you liked polka dots and was correct. Rachel also found out how much we liked *Peter Pan*, so she used pages from the *Peter Pan* book she had. She put this label on the vase so you would know that was the book she took the pages from."

"Rachel sounds super nice, but won't she get in trouble for ripping out book pages?" Molly asked seriously, a look of concern on her face.

"Well, baby," Scarlett said reassuringly, "Rachel owns the books. She understands that beauty in books can take on different forms. Sometimes you receive joy from reading or hearing the words. Art in its many forms gives us joy in different ways. Do you like flowers? Do you like books?"

"I love them both," Molly said enthusiastically.

"Rachel just combined them for you in one pretty package that you are allowed to have in here. I would say that is pretty special."

Tevin came up behind Scarlett and gave her shoulders a squeeze, "I love you," he kissed the back of her head, "We will talk later, about the cells," he whispered into her hair quietly so Molly would not hear. He was obviously as concerned as Scarlett was about the seven-year cell comment and the potential for false hope.

Scarlett turned around and gave him a bold kiss on the lips.

"Ewwwwww," they heard Molly exclaim from behind them.

"What?" said Tevin, "We love each other, so what!" He faked a noogie on Molly's head as she giggled.

It was true, Scarlett did love her husband. There was no doubt that having a sick child put a strain on a marriage. It was hard to find alone time, and on the rare occasion they tried to sneak away on a date, they were so consumed with concern about how Molly was doing that they usually ended up leaving early. Through it all, they'd clung together and were always figuring out how to make it work.

Tevin worked for an operations consulting company that he'd worked for in Louisiana. They happened to have a branch of the office in Colorado and the company had been nothing but supportive, allowing him to work some office days and work from home as needed. Scarlett did private bookkeeping for various companies, always from home, so they'd lucked out in the work situation. They both knew a lot of families were not as lucky in that regard.

One of the two of them liked to be there with Molly, so they'd found that rotating through every 12 hours was the easiest way to do it. Scarlett would bring bookkeeping work with her to the hospital and work on it while Molly was doing schoolwork, or while she was sleeping.

"Text me later?" Tevin asked, waggling his eyebrows up and down, which Scarlett knew implied a hope at more than just texting. Having so much time apart they'd been forced to get a little creative in the intimacy department.

She discreetly swatted him on his butt as he walked out of the room, briefcase in hand. "Where do you want to put the flowers?" Scarlett asked as soon as she and Molly were alone.

"You should put them by my wall garden!" Molly answered excitedly, "But I'm still looking at them, so can we wait for a while?"

"Of course, baby," Scarlett answered as she looked at the "garden" she'd made for Molly from photographs of their real garden at home. She'd taken pictures of the garden in different stages of bloom and season and collaged them together, so it appeared that there was a magazine garden on the walls. She thought about the blue jay picture she had taken that morning and how great it would look in the picture garden once she had it printed.

Eleanor came in with the chemo, ready to deliver poison into her baby's veins in the hopes that the cells wreaking this havoc on her little body would be destroyed while leaving her healthy cells well enough to keep her alive.

"Eleanor, I got flowers!!!! But don't you worry, they aren't the germy kind! They are made from *Peter Pan* book pages but don't worry. It isn't illegal or anything because it's art and it makes our hearts happy, which is never a bad thing."

Scarlett chuckled under her breath. "You got it, baby, happy hearts are never a bad thing."

Molly assisted Eleanor in moving her shirt aside, exposing the catheter she would receive the chemo through. Molly hummed quietly, fingering the flower petals once more and smiling.

7

Stacia was getting better at focusing on the positive and getting rid of the negative. After everything that occurred last year, she'd grown accustomed to covering up the hurt with fake smiles and sarcasm.

Now she was working on letting the smiles reach the corners of her mouth and meaning it. She was getting better at using sarcasm as a means to be funny and not as a deterrent to keep others at bay, afraid to let anyone get too close.

She'd been feeling like it was time to move on for a while like it was time to lick her wounds and get on with her life. She was sick of letting the situation get the best of her; they'd moved on, and she felt like she should too. She'd been working on healing herself one day at a time, and though that was working well, she felt like she needed to cleanse the anger away, sage for the soul so-to-speak.

She felt conflicted; could she get rid of the photographs of them all together, the pictures she constantly critiqued to figure out when the shift had occurred, without destroying evidence of her childhood? She knew that she held all the memories in her mind, but if the friendships were beyond repair, weren't the memories enough?

She opened the closet door and on tiptoe fumbled around on the top of the shelf until her fingers brushed a large shoebox. She was attempting to pull it down when it flew out of her hands, causing all of the contents to spill onto the floor.

All it took was one glance at the spilled contents for her heart to squeeze inside her chest. She knew she had to deal with the contents of the box, but she had hoped to deal with one picture at a time, not all of them at once. She knew she probably should just throw the whole box in the fireplace without having to look at a single item, but part of her wanted to remember what was behind each picture, burning the memory in her brain before she burned away the evidence.

She closed her eyes, trying to gather courage. She took a step forward and felt something crush under her foot. She peeked an eye open and saw what she suspected she had stepped on, the dried remnant of a rose. She thought it strange that the flower was just as disintegrated and torn as her relationship was now with the two people who used to mean the most to her. She took one more deep breath, willed herself to be strong, and opened her eyes completely.

8

"*R* *ing"*
"*Ring*"

Stacia was in the back of the store freshening up a bouquet in the cooler. She looked up to see who was walking into the store to offer assistance to the customer.

"*Ring*"

She kept hearing the ring of the bell, but no one was there. She put the bouquet back into the flower cooler and shut the cooler door. She started walking to the front door to see if the bell mechanism was broken. She got to the front door and opened it to find a basket with a newborn baby in it on the doorstep.

"*Ring*"

Stacia opened her eyes and was hit with the realization that her cell phone was ringing. She tried to calm the beating of her heart from what she now realized was a dream, it had felt so real.

"Hello," she said, still caught in the in-between stage between the dream and reality.

"Well," her sister said from the other side of the phone, "I was going to see if you could pick up coffee this morning, as you are never without it. But since you are obviously still sleeping, I will get my own coffee."

Stacia rolled over in bed, "What time is it? Do we work today? Coffee, I do need coffee."

"Anastacia Dawn Bee!!! Are you freaking kidding me?!" Her sister shrieked in an octave higher than her normal voice. "Please tell me you are messing with me right now. The shop opens in one hour, and we have a delivery today that we need to put away before the Perkins' wedding consultation at nine! From the ten minutes I talked to the mother-of-the-bride, they have a lot of money to drop on their flower budget, and we do not want to blow it!"

Stacia groaned as she willed herself out of bed. She never forgot to set her alarm, but after last night, she must have been so emotionally drained that she forgot to set it. That or the two glasses of wine she had consumed to give her the liquid courage she had needed to go through the Luke/Amber memory box.

She went to the mirror and looked at her puffy eyes. She should have at least put some cucumber slices or a cold washcloth on her eyes before she went to sleep, but she hadn't been prepared for the outpouring of emotion that had slipped out last night. She usually wasn't an emotional person, but once again, this could have resulted from the task of eliminating photographic evidence of a large portion of her life coupled with too much Pinot Noir.

She threw on her Capri-length jeans and black shirt along with a pair of TOMS. She grabbed her Bee's apron from a hook in the kitchen and grabbed a protein bar. She was about to rush out the front door when she saw out of the corner of her eye a piece of photograph lying near the fireplace. She walked over to it briskly and snatched it off the brick mantle. It was a picture of her and Luke near the pier at Pacific Beach in California. Amber had taken the picture for them. Conveniently, his face was partially burned away while hers remained.

"Looks much better now," she said quietly to herself before running out the door.

Stacia lived in a small one-bedroom apartment not too far from the flower shop. She loved the walk to work as it allowed her to pass by all the unique shops in their area. On average days, when she wasn't running incredibly late, she loved to stop for breakfast and a cup of coffee next to the flower shop at The Bean Juice. Hopefully, Rachel was going to be a kind big sister and grab her a cup of coffee.

Stacia double-timed it to the store trying to focus on what she needed to do today and not on last night's memory of burning away remnants of her and Luke's life together...and Amber. She'd been doing reasonably well at ignoring Luke and Amber's existence until yesterday when she'd glanced at the local newspaper while inside The Bean Juice and stumbled upon their engagement picture. Seeing the photo must have been the last straw; as of that moment, Stacia felt 100% certain that she was ready to cleanse herself of the past and move on.

In Amber and Luke's engagement picture, they were positioned in the typical engagement pose on the stairs at Red Rocks with a view of the amphitheater's rock wall behind them. Luke was standing a stair above Amber with one arm on her shoulder. Her left hand was resting on his hand, showing off her engagement ring. It was just an extra harsh stab in the back that they chose to do their picture at Red Rocks, as the venue had been where they all loved to go to concerts together.

Amber and Luke, Amuke, or Luke and Amber, Lamber. She at least held some comfort in the fact that they both had basic names and a horrible couple name and would likely have a very basic life together. She knew that was petty, but it helped to be petty right now.

After reading in the announcement that the couple currently resided in Denver, she had confirmation that they'd officially moved back to Colorado. Now that she'd done a nice burning ceremony to cleanse herself of the past, she just had to hope that neither Luke nor Amber ever stepped foot into their flower shop. She didn't even want to think about their baby or the baby dream from last night.

Stacia arrived at the shop and heard the sounds of Taylor Swift's newest pop hit coming from the door. She hadn't realized how loud the music was from outside. It had seemed to work in their favor earlier that week, bringing in a new customer, and it was a great way to start the day. Her mood was instantly elevated at the thought of a dance party with her older sister, hopefully with ample amounts of caffeine, even though there was bound to be a little scolding for her tardiness.

"I'm here and ready to shake some booty," Stacia shouted as she entered the door, aggressively bobbing her head in time with the music.

"Oh, hello sister," Rachel said, one eyebrow raised as she took in her sister's slightly disheveled appearance. "You're just in time to help unload the flowers." Stacia could see that her sister was trying to send her subliminal messages with her eyeballs. Rachel aggressively tilted her head in the direction of the alley.

Stacia stood there, not quite sure if her sister was truly implying something about Marco and the flower delivery, or just dancing badly, very badly.

Rachel again tilted her head, motioning towards the alley. When Stacia didn't visually appear to grasp what she was implying, she added a couple rapid eye blinks. Stacia shrugged her shoulders. At this point, Rachel looked so ridiculous Stacia decided she was going to carry this on as long as possible, even if she had figured out what she was indicating from the get-go. It was her duty as the little sister to mess with her big sister after all.

Stacia decided to taunt her sister a little more to see how long this charade would last, "Is there a bee swarming around? Or did all of the monkeys from the Denver Zoo escape and are now hanging in our alley? Or......"

Rachel rushed over to her sister, "Let me help you tie your apron." Quietly, under her breath, she said: "Okay smartass, Marco is here and asked for you to help him unload alone. He asked for you personally! This would have gone seamlessly any other day, but today you happened to be late and currently have mascara streaks down one side of your face, your hair is sticking up like a lion's mane, and, dear God did you forget to brush your teeth? It smells like roadkill in your mouth."

Stacia suppressed the joke in her head about how her sister

would know what roadkill smelled like after it had been eaten when she saw Marco's shadow passing by the alley window. Stacia finally understanding the importance of Rachel's pseudo seizures grabbed the stick of gum and rubber band her sister was discreetly handing her and dashed to the employee bathroom before he entered the store.

She splashed some water on her face, rubbed some water over her teeth, put the gum in and messily threw her hair in a bun. Stacia knew that she didn't need to worry about pinching her cheeks for color as just being around Marco brought color to her cheeks. She walked out of the restroom and received a nod of approval and a thumbs up from her sister. She went to the back where Marco had already opened up the back of the delivery van.

"Good morning," she said as she already felt the hint of butterflies in her stomach. Marco just rattled her, and she liked that after a year of not allowing herself this, she was feeling all of the feelings... whether she wanted to, or not.

"Good morning," Marco smiled making his blue eyes shine, and his dimples pop out.

Stacia's stomach fluttered again as she couldn't help smiling in return, a warm blush creeping from her cheeks to her ears. He just simply did things to her without much effort.

Stacia walked over to the open back of the truck and started grabbing brown paper wrapped packages. She attempted to make small talk, "It's kind of cold out here."

Marco came up behind her and held out an offering, "Sweatshirt?"

Stacia accepted it, though she had not been very cold, just trying to not appear super awkward in the silence.

"Thanks," Stacia said as she slipped it on, heart and stomach fluttering increasing even more after catching a whiff of his cologne. "You have a lot of deliveries today?"

"I have two more today, so it shouldn't be too bad. Rachel said you guys are going to screen the Perkin's family for possible bridezilla psychosis and recommend me if they fall low on the psychosis scale," Marco said as he grabbed a large plastic bin of vases and other merchandise.

Stacia giggled as she tried not to glance at the biceps peeking out of his shirt. She chastised herself for being so focused on the physical part of him and for giggling so much. She'd never been the type of girl who laughed at everything as she was usually the one making the jokes. She couldn't tell if she was giggling because he was funny, she was flustered, or because they were attracted to each other.

She'd been successful in blocking anything resembling romantic feelings from the moment she found out about Amber and Luke, instead focusing on the anger and the hurt and the need to protect herself from further pain.

She knew that this had been slowly fading since she met Marco. Based on her one romantic relationship, she'd learned that romantic feelings could lead to disaster, to heartache and pain that you could feel like a rock in your core, weighing you down to the point of submersion. She couldn't remember the last time she hadn't thought of love without it being synonymous with fear.

She composed herself, taking a few deep flower-scented cleansing breaths, "You may have to help us define levels of bridezilla psychosis, so we are on the same page. I would hate to cause you any unnecessary bridezilla-related stress, especially since you were trying to take a break from all that." They started walking towards the store with their merchandise in tow.

"Last year when I had an emergency room visit after the wind smashed the back of the trailer onto my hand, the doctors and nurses kept asking me my pain level on a scale of one to ten with ten being the worst pain imaginable. Maybe we could try that scale?" Marco chuckled.

"Ok, so if we use a one to ten scale for our flower portion, one could be 'I want specially ordered tulips.' Ten would be 'I want specialty ordered organic tulips from Denmark that are the exact color of puce as the bridesmaid's dresses, and I need them to have the exact same number and shape of petals, and I want it tomorrow.'" Stacia said, playing along.

"Ok, ok, so one in the photography world would be 'I want an hour of pictures before and after the ceremony.' Ten would be 'I need individual glamour shots of each wedding patron which I want you to photoshop until every attendee looks straight out of the pages of Vogue. Not only that but I want a separate photo shoot for the pets in attendance, all while keeping with the 'Pirates of the Caribbean' theme which you will be expected to participate in,'" Marco contributed with another dimple-ridden smile.

Stacia laughed, again! *What the hell is with all the laughing?* She thought to herself. Rachel had mentioned the other day that she'd also noticed a giggling issue with Stacia when she was around Marco and, dammit, if her sister wasn't correct. Once again, she felt that this was proof that maybe she was ready to move past the pain of Luke and Amber's betrayal. Maybe it boiled down to all three possibilities: he was funny, she was flustered, and they liked each other.

"I would say that is an appropriate ten." Stacia was still laughing, picturing it all in her head as they entered the storage room where Rachel was waiting for them to bring her the merchandise so she could put it all away in the proper places quickly so they would be ready when the Perkins family arrived.

"What are you two laughing about?" Rachel asked as she grabbed the paper packages from Stacia and began to get the flowers out of the moist cloths and into vases.

"We were developing a universal scale of bridezilla psychosis using a one to ten scale," Stacia answered.

"That way we are all on the same page when you filter potential clients for me," Marco chipped in. He set the container of merchandise he'd brought in and set it near Rachel, "T. Swizzle today?"

"It's a T. Swizzle day for sure," Rachel answered. "Not to rush you fine folk, but the Perkin's consult is in less than one hour, and we need to have at least one or two sample pieces for their mountain-theme wedding before they get here."

"I think there are just one or two more things in the truck. Do you still have time to help me, Stacia?" Marco asked.

Stacia nodded, and as they headed towards the alley door, he turned and winked at Rachel and mouthed the words "Thank you," before holding the door open for Stacia allowing her to walk out first.

Stacia walked to the back of the truck and was slightly confused when he went to the passenger side of his truck instead of the back. She'd just grabbed the last paper-wrapped flower parcel when she saw him coming from the passenger side of the truck carrying a bouquet of sunflowers wrapped in fancy brown flower paper and tied with a rope ribbon.

"That's kind of strange that they didn't wrap those. It looks like somebody already arranged them too. It's weird, but Rachel does the ordering, so who knows," Stacia said, quickly rearranging the parcel she was carrying so she could carry the bouquet in by hand.

Marco looked at her, slightly flustered. "I was hoping to ask you to dinner tomorrow night. These are actually for you."

Stacia stood frozen in place. She tried to process all of the thoughts running through her head. The idea of her moving on was new enough that she felt she needed to do everything at a snail's pace. Obviously, she'd been thinking about Marco and his relationship potential. She really liked his personality, and it obviously helped that he was so handsome. He made her laugh, he was so nice to Rachel, and he seemed to understand their need as sisters to have fun and play around with each other.

She wasn't sure how long she stood there blankly eyed before she was jolted back to reality by a dejected-sounding Marco, "I really hope I have not been misreading all of our interactions. We laugh nonstop when we are around each other, you make flirty jokes at my expense, maybe that is normal for you..."

"No, no, no. Oh my goodness the flowers are beautiful. Sunflowers happen to be my favorite. I'm so sorry that I just sat there like a bump on a log just then. At the risk of laying out a bunch of baggage and scaring the shit out of you, I feel like you need to know what you are signing up for, and that is the only reason I paused," Stacia said as she reached forward and accepted the flowers from Marco.

"In a nutshell, I moved to California with my ex-fiancé and best friend. I found out they were sleeping together. My best friend ended up pregnant, and I ended up back in Colorado, and it all happened about a year ago."

"Shit," Marco said, a brief look of horror flashing on his face.

"Yeah," Stacia said, "To keep this honesty train going down the tracks, I saw their engagement photo in the paper yesterday, and last night I burned all of my pictures with them. I'm in the process of cleansing my thoughts and space of them so I can hopefully make room for someone else. I would prefer to make room for someone like you if I didn't just scare you off."

Marco sat there for a second, lost in his own thoughts as he tried to process Stacia's statements, "Do you feel like going through all of that made you who you are now?"

Stacia nodded her head, "Yeah, but it has kind of made me into a slightly jaded, yet slightly funnier version of my old self."

"Good," Marco said matter-of-factly, "That is the person that I feel I connected with and want to take to dinner. Your baggage is maybe pushing a three on the dinner deterrent scale for me." Marco winked at Stacia causing Stacia's face to erupt in a grin.

"Dinner it is. Ten out of ten on the yes scale for dinner," Stacia said as she felt a blush and butterflies at the same time.

"How about we come at this with no pressure, we'll start with one dinner and go from there," Marco said as he got close to her and gave her a quick peck on the cheek. "Your sister already got my phone number last week when she helped me with your favorite flower. I have to run, so I'm not late for the next delivery. If you just want to text me this afternoon, we can work out the details."

Stacia stood there watching him drive down the alley. She waited for his truck to disappear before doing a quick happy dance in the alley, sunflowers in hand. They were absolutely beautiful and genuinely were her favorite.

"Rachel you traitorous wench!" Stacia yelled when she got back inside, immediately grabbing a vase for her sunflowers and handing off the remaining merchandise to Rachel.

"I plead an amendment of some sort. You know whichever amendment that means I'm sworn to secrecy," Rachel retorted as she continued to unpack and load the flowers into the cooler. "I couldn't stand the giggle-slash-flirting-slash-eyelash-batting that you have been up to since you met him without interfering! Plus, it was making you awfully clumsy, and I honestly was becoming fearful for the well-being of the store."

"I also looked like crap on a stick this morning Rachel!!! You could have at least called and warned me last night or given me a courtesy text this morning."

"I did help you clean up the crap as best as I could. He wanted to surprise you, and I wanted to respect that. Never in a million years did I think this would be the one morning you decide not to set your alarm!" Rachel grabbed a few flowers from the parcels Stacia had just begun to unwrap.

"All sarcasm aside Rachel, I'm scared! I gave my heart fully to Amber as my best friend through my entire childhood and then gave my heart fully to Luke as my boyfriend, and they were sneaking around behind my back, not just one time, they were doing it for years! Now they have a baby and are getting married! I had a dream someone left a newborn baby at the front of the store last night after I burned all the items in my hate-filled Amber/Luke shoebox!" Stacia exclaimed starting to arrange her own samples for the Perkins family.

"I'm about to be really honest with you Stacia. Can you handle that right now?" Rachel inquired.

"Yeessss?" Stacia questioned, unsure if she was up to doing this right now but placating her sister anyway.

"You were so young when you and Luke became a couple that you never really got to figure out who you truly were as a person, an individual. Everything revolved around what Luke wanted to do. He was nice enough, but he didn't push you to be a better you at all. Though your sense of sarcasm and overall bitchines has increased in the last year, which can be annoying as hell as your older sister, I can't be mad because you are at least thinking and feeling for yourself. I'm super proud of that actually, even if, as I mentioned, it's annoying sometimes," Rachel dodged the paper wrapping Stacia balled up and threw at her.

"One more honesty point for you again as your older and wiser sister: in life, I have learned you shouldn't always put your best foot forward. Sometimes you need to be the worst version of yourself, and if someone can love you even at your worst, they will fight that much harder for you. I can tell you all about it someday if you want, but I'm advising this only because I have been there," Rachel said contemplatively.

They turned off the Taylor Swift and put on some Vancouver Sleep Clinic, which was nice and mellow. They grabbed some more vases and flowers and continued arranging as Stacia pondered her sister's thoughts and advice.

"What if it doesn't work with Marco?" Stacia asked after a few minutes.

"Then it doesn't work out, and you will still be okay," her older sister advised. "It's just dinner with a nice and very handsome gentleman with the dimples of a Greek God."

Stacia nodded in agreement, "Just dinner with Marco and Marco's dimples, though technically he is a Guatemalan God. Just dinner, dimples, Guatemalan God, got it."

They let the music relax them as their hands arranged roses and baby's breath and greenery into tall flowery works of art. They'd just finished the last sample piece when they heard the jingle of the door.

Stacia who was facing the door muttered under her breath, "Judging a book by its cover here, but I'm guessing that we are at least a level seven on the psychosis scale."

Rachel gave her sister a glare but chuckled lowly before turning on her professional face, turning around to greet the customers, "Hello, welcome to Bee's Flowers, you must be the Perkins family."

9

Rachel sometimes missed him so much that it took her breath away. She stayed so busy during the day at the shop and caring for her girls that she noticed his absence the most when she went to bed next to the space he used to occupy. She would often roll over in bed reaching for him and feel nothing but the sharp realization that came from crisp, cold sheets.

She slept with an old t-shirt of his that still had his scent on it, and that helped, but it wasn't at all the same. When the pangs of loneliness hit her extra hard, she would put the shirt next to her nose and nuzzle it, even when the scent of him had worn away with time she was comforted just knowing it had touched his skin at some point. It made her feel as if she was in some way touching him, and he was in some way touching her back.

She thought of airplanes, of how their life together had begun unexpectedly on a plane almost ten years ago and how their life now revolved around him leaving on airplanes and hopefully, soon, returning on an airplane. Returning to her meant returning whole both physically and mentally; not in pieces, not in a coffin, and not with a mind riddled with trauma.

She knew that this was what she'd signed on for, but that didn't make her miss him any less. She knew that families all over the world had to make these same sacrifices and she did appreciate it, but she wanted and needed her husband. She needed him for the serious things; she needed him for mundane things. She needed him for the laughter and the tears, the sickness and the health, the good times and the bad times. She just needed him.

She was glad that she had her family close by, that she and her sister came from a line of incredibly independent, strong women. She was delighted that she had her job and the chance to work with their grandmother and sister who kept her smiling. She was thankful, most of all, for their daughters and the fact that they were strong and independent as well.

Nothing entirely filled that void. Nothing quite took the fear away. She glanced at his picture by the bedside and tried to think of all the things they would do together when he returned, if he returned. She fell asleep with a hole in her heart and tears on her pillow.

10

Rachel was awoken by a scream so loud she was surprised the windows didn't shatter.

"Mom! She took my brush again!" Stella screamed from down the hallway.

"Well, I had to take your brush because I couldn't find mine after you borrowed it yesterday and your side of the room is a BIG MESS!" Marie screamed in return.

Rachel shut her eyes for a minute, willing resolution to occur, so she didn't have to get out of bed. She wished Chad was here to assist her in moments like this as the twins were daddy's girls for sure. Sometimes he could connect with them better, especially when it came to conflict resolution. Often all it took was him saying the words, "Now girls," for them to quit what they were doing.

Rachel didn't hear anything else for a minute, and a little spark of hope that all had been resolved appeared but was quickly snuffed out when she heard another blood-curdling wail. She raised both of her arms in the air before thumping them on the bed. Rachel glanced at the clock, of course, it was twenty minutes before her alarm would go off so she would feel slightly cheated of that extra twenty minutes of sleep all day.

She couldn't believe the girls had woken up early. It was usually a bit of a struggle to get two girls and herself ready in the amount of time they had without scrambling and almost being late to every activity.

"Moooooooommmmmmm! Stella, let go of MY HAIR!" She heard another scream.

Rachel jumped out of bed, threw on her robe, and ran towards the twins' room before the fight led to 8-year-old bloodshed. Stella was currently standing on the bed holding the brush as high as she could while keeping her sister, who was standing on the floor, at bay by her hair, preventing her from moving at all without her hair pulling. This wasn't the first time either sister had used hair in a hostage situation. Rachel swiftly stepped forward like a ninja and grabbed the brush before Stella had a chance to move it out of the way.

"Please let go of your sister's hair immediately," Rachel commanded with as much vigor as she could muster first thing in the morning.

When Stella hesitated, she gave her the most severe mom stare she could dish out without coffee coursing through her bloodstream. It must have evoked a little bit of fear because Stella reluctantly lessened her grasp, so a few strands at a time slowly left her hand. Marie was visibly uncomfortable but appeared to be trying to hold it together for the moment, so her sister didn't know how badly it was hurting her.

"All the way Miss Stella," Rachel said deepening the mom stare and the voice full of vigor.

Rachel could see the wheels in Marie's head turning. Based on what she knew of her girls, she could tell that Marie was plotting revenge on her sister as soon as the last strand of hair left Stella's tight grasp. Rachel jumped between the two of them, again like a ninja, as they attempted to paw at each other with animal-like noises coming from their small little bodies.

"Enough!" Rachel shrieked loudly. "You are going to lose everything that you care about in the next five seconds if you do not each take a step back and put your hands behind your backs. In fact, I need you to stand at attention like you have seen your daddy do. Though I do appreciate that you somehow woke up early today, I feel slightly robbed of 20 minutes of sleep. I have also not had a drop of coffee enter my body yet, which you may not understand now, but you will when you are older. Let's just say you are both on very thin ice."

Both girls took a step back and put their clasped hands at their sides in perfect imitation of their Air Force father.

Rachel had to pull the corners of her mouth back to avoid laughing at their determination to do it correctly. The sheer cuteness of her two bedraggled daughters with their dark springy curls sticking straight up and their pajamas full of wrinkles from a night of sleep would have been cute enough. With the added state of dishevelment from their recent struggle, the fact that they now were trying to look like perfectly pressed military personnel was humorous at best.

She'd known that she and Chad were going to have a heck of a time with twin girls the minute they found out she was pregnant. The girls in her family had a history of being strong-willed, and this tradition had been carried on to both Marie and Stella from the minute they were born crying and screaming into the world of Bee women. Marie had been born one hour after her sister; she was so stubborn. They'd been independent then and had never stopped.

Her girls cleverly disguised their sassy, strong wills with their cute exterior. Both girls had their dad's coffee-colored skin and beautiful ebony black curly hair. They had Rachel's hazel eyes speckled with brown, which just made them more beautiful. Strangers were constantly commenting on how angelic they were with their contrast between their skin and eyes, which caused Rachel to smile and nod in appreciation while internally thinking of how non-angelic they could each act.

"Okay," Rachel said with some authority, still attempting to channel her husband, "I want you to start in separate areas today. Stella, you may start in the bathroom by washing your face and brushing your teeth and hair. Marie, I will..."

Rachel was interrupted by Stella, who was feigning innocence, as she commented under her breath, "How am I going to brush my hair first if you still have my brush? I'm going to need my brush back please, mother."

"Young lady," Rachel said, switching to a drill-sergeant cadence, knowing this situation had the potential to continue spiraling out-of-control if she didn't get a handle on it soon. "You need to give me five jumping jacks."

Marie giggled at the thought of her sister being handed a physical punishment by Mom, the Drill Sergeant. Marie pointed at her sister, "Ha ha, naughty naughty!"

"Now you can also give me five jumping jacks," Rachel ordered in Marie's direction.

Both girls attempted five jumping jacks but were equally uncoordinated with their attempts. Both girls were clapping both their hands up while their legs were jumping out, both of their hair flopping in their faces in its currently frizzy state.

Rachel again tried to contain the laughter that was threatening to spew out. How come no one had told her that parenthood would be so hard and so humorous at the same time?

After each girl had finished their five clumsy jumping jacks, she gave them another mom stare. "Are you guys ready to behave? Or do we need to add some push-ups?"

Without another word, Stella politely grabbed the brush her mother was holding before she headed into the restroom while Marie stayed in their room and started putting together her clothes for the day. Rachel gave the outfit of leggings, a t-shirt, and a sweatshirt a nod of approval. She tried to provide the girls with the independence to pick out their own outfits, but sometimes they were not appropriate for the temperamental Colorado weather.

She walked to the bathroom, got out some curl product and handed it to Stella who was carefully combing through her curls. Rachel helped her apply some of the hair cream, and they secured a front section into a rubber band. The girls then traded, and Rachel repeated the outfit and hair routine with Marie.

They all walked down to the kitchen together and, in walking by the calendar, Rachel noticed a star on today's date on the calendar.

"Do you know what day it is?" Rachel asked as they entered the kitchen and she began pulling out various breakfast food items for the girls to pick from. She appreciated that Chad from afar was providing them with something that would reset the whole morning.

"Is it Daddy gift day?!" Stella shrieked jumping up and down; Marie, seeing a nod from Rachel, joined in the celebration.

"Let's start eating, so we aren't late for school. I will go grab the box, and we can start looking at it while we are eating," Rachel said as she helped Stella pour her cereal and put a bagel in the toaster for herself and Marie.

Once they had breakfast in front of them, Rachel went to the pantry and closed the door. She stood on a step stool and grabbed the box marked October. Behind the October box was a box marked November and one marked *tentative December. She smiled at her husband's optimism. She tried to completely ignore the box that had been shoved far back in the corner, the box marked ominously "IF" on it.

She couldn't remember the last time she'd glanced at the IF box without fear that she would someday have to open it. IF she had to open this box, it meant he was never coming back. The details of that box filled her with a multitude of horrible feelings she hoped never to have to address.

She went back into the kitchen and together they opened the October box. Inside were three manila envelopes with each of their names on the front.

Rachel helped each girl open their envelopes. Inside each envelope was a picture of Chad with each of the girls, a gift card to TCBY and a movie gift certificate. There was a letter addressed to each girl as well. Rachel let the girls look at them first so they could practice their reading, and then Rachel proceeded to read them each aloud.

Stella (aka Stella Phant),

Hello beautiful girl, I'm writing this as always to say that I love you and I miss you. I know that it's hard having me gone, but since you just opened the October box that means that there should only be one or two more boxes to open, this can always change, but I am staying positive. That means I should hopefully be seeing you soon. I still think of you all a little bit extra on gift box days!

I hope that you are being kind to Marie and helpful to your mother. They both need some extra hugs from you.

The fun goal for this month: go to a restaurant and pay for someone's meal. Pick someone who looks like they maybe had a bad day or someone alone. Add the pictures to the goal book for when I get home. I love you, princess!

XOXOXOXO Daddykins

Marie (aka Missy Marie),

Hello beautiful girl, I'm writing this letter because I love you always and miss you every day. I know that everything is harder without me being there every, but I know you guys are tough and have it under control. I always think about you all opening the box on these gift box days, and I smile when I picture you all seeing the treats and reading the goals. I really hope this is one of the last two boxes.

Please be kind to your mom and obviously your sister as well. Make sure you are all giving each other some extra hugs. You all need each other during this time.

The fun goal for this month: go to a fancy bakery and get some fancy cupcakes. Take them to the nursing home down the street and ask if you can pass them out to people. Offer them a cupcake, and a hug if they seem okay with that. Take a picture and add it to the goal book. Love ya missy moo!

XOXOXOXO Daddy-O

Rachel let each girl examine the contents of their envelopes further as she opened her envelope. Inside were two books. One was a novel she'd been talking about reading, and the other was a single hardcover book with a matte black cover. Rachel opened it, and her letter was written on the inside jacket.

Rach,

My queen. I miss you so much it hurts. Before I met you, I didn't know that you were missing. Now that I know how amazing life can be with you and the girls, not seeing you and Stella and Marie leaves a void in my life. I know how much you love flowers, but I didn't think you would appreciate me sending you some (as you see your fair share of them each day) so I thought this was a good alternative.

Each section has a flower meaning, and I picked flowers that fit the feelings I got when looking at the images on the pages. Make sure you look at it with the girls.

Until I see you again, know that I miss you and can't wait to hold you again.

Fun goal: Take all of the flowers that are about to spoil and hand them out to the homeless people that hang out near the Denver Mission, take Stacia. She will love doing it and will kick someone's ass if needed. Put the pictures in the goal book.

Love always,

King Chad ;)

P.S. Has my shirt lost its scent yet? I'm pretty sure there is a ripe one still in the back of my truck in my gym bag. Proceed at your own risk.

Rachel felt a tear slip down her cheek as she laughed, feeling multiple emotions at one time. Since they'd started their relationship, they'd always had this great banter back and forth. He wasn't only her husband, but he was her best friend. Rachel walked over to the couch and put a girl on each side.

"What is this mom?" Marie asked as they all cozied up next to each other on the couch.

"We will just have to see," Rachel said as she turned to the first page where there were a variety of pictures of the family at the park this last summer before Chad deployed. Cut-out pictures of daisies were glued all over the page. There was a piece of paper with Chad's handwriting that said: **Daisy- purity, true love, new beginnings**. Rachel let another few tears run down her cheeks as she turned to the second page.

"That is so cute!" Marie exclaimed while Stella stared at the pictures of all of them together. Rachel started laughing at the next page, it was one of her favorite photos of the girls. They'd been at a water park that day, and towards the end of the day, the girls had grown impatient with each other. They'd all had a great time, but by the time they took the picture the girls were equally exhausted and irritated with each other, so they'd sat back-to-back to rest against each other with their towels on. Both girls had identical glares on their sun-kissed faces as they stared at the camera.

"That day was so fun," Stella said as she fingered the photo of her and her sister at the water park. In her head, Rachel thought about how neither girl looked like they were having fun by the end of the day but decided to let it slide, happy that Stella had chosen to remember the good parts of the day.

On the following pages were pictures of Rachel and Stacia together at the store mid-dance move and Grandma Betty and Grandpa David standing by their RV. The flowers covering this page were snapdragons. Chad's inscription read: ***Snapdragon-strength (Lord knows you Bee girls have no shortage of this)***.

Rachel and her girls spent the next twenty minutes admiring the pages. They teared up at some, they laughed at some, they reminisced at all of them. When Rachel's phone alarm rang, they reluctantly put the book down.

"Time for school girls."

Part 2 –Iris– symbol for hope

∞∞∞

~Wisdom

~Faith

~Hope

11

Eleanor woke up every morning with hope. She would open her eyes, fresh from sleep, and it would always take her a few seconds for her to bring her life into clarity, for her to figure out the haze between reality and nightmare; to figure out the difference between how her life was behind closed doors versus the outside appearance. Who would guess that a successful nurse and a prestigious lawyer had such terrible secrets?

Some days she would wake up and feel sore from head-to-toe. Her initial hope was always that the soreness she felt was from a gym workout and not a result of Kai's anger. Sometimes she was relieved to remember that she'd merely pushed herself too hard at the gym, but sometimes she was hit with the horrible memory that her fiancé had hurt her again the night before.

As each day started, she tried to focus on hope. Hope that today was a fresh start, not just for her but for her fiancé. Hope that they could each be stronger in the things that needed to be fixed. Hope that this was all still somehow a bad dream. She hoped for courage; courage to stay and try to change the state of their lives or the courage to leave and start fresh.

Having something so troublesome in their relationship had made Eleanor feel like she was hyper-focused on all the negative things; she was aware that the situation was bad enough that she could not disclose it to anyone, though she knew that she should. She had a hard time focusing on anything positive that occurred in the day-to-day routine though she could recall some snippets of quality time between her and Kai.

She hoped that she would continue to be successful in her career. She hoped to be the best nurse possible and put her focus on her patients. She hoped that her patient's strength would, in turn, make her stronger. She hoped what she was going through would never impact her ability to take care of the patients and their families because she sometimes feared that it could.

She hoped that Kai's work would be less stressful and that maybe he could quit drinking and find a way to deal with his anger. She knew that all the things that he was going through at work triggered him though he didn't like to discuss it with her. She wished each day that Kai would wake up with the same desire that she had. Desires for hope-in-action, realization, contemplation, self-reflection, and ultimately, change.

It seemed lately that she found herself putting more of her time and energy into focusing on her own hope and less on hoping for his sake. She hoped that this would make her a stronger person. She hoped that someday soon there would be a solution, an answer to all of this. For right now, she felt like each day was the same and that in continuing this way they were living the true definition of insanity.

12

Until last week, on her days off, Eleanor had woken up before Kai to fix breakfast for him before he left for work. They would eat at the table together so they could have some time with each other before he had to go. When Kai had first moved into her apartment, she'd done this out of love. After he became abusive, she'd started doing it out of fear.

Last week, she'd reached a breaking point. All had been going reasonably well in the last several months of their relationship, meaning that it had been almost a month since he'd laid a hand on her in anger. He'd even consumed less alcohol during this time and somehow managed to keep his temper under control. She'd hoped that maybe something had changed for him.

She couldn't remember the last time her hope had grown wings and taken flight; become something true and real. Eleanor had started to let love creep back in slowly and steadily over the last month. She began to think that maybe she could forgive him for lashing out and in turn maybe forgive herself for allowing it by staying. Eleanor also thought that maybe with some extensive couples and individual counseling there could be hope for a quality life and a real future.

Then last week, he'd abruptly snapped over an empty saltshaker on the dinner table. It was a polished granite shaker, and there was no way to tell whether or not it was empty until it ran out. He'd seemed a little edgy when he'd returned home after an extra-long workday but had not given her any warning that would have indicated that he was that close to the edge.

Eleanor hadn't been scheduled to work that day, so she'd wanted to make him a nice dinner. She'd decided on prime rib, potatoes, and carrots and she'd tossed it all into their Instant Pot shortly before he got home. He'd been attempting to salt his meat and vegetables when he discovered the salt shaker was empty. Without any indication, he'd thrown it at her face, full force. It had crashed into her right cheek causing her to cry out in pain immediately and causing her to see stars, yet again.

He'd instantly looked panic-stricken as she'd for once glared at him as she pushed her chair back and walked away from the table. "I'm not going to do this anymore," she'd said seething with anger as she looked directly in his eyes before fleeing to their bedroom and locking the door, for the first time, not allowing him in. She'd gone into their en suite bathroom and used a cold compress to try to minimize the swelling. For once instead of feelings of fear and sadness, her body was overflowing with anger.

She allowed a few angry tears to escape before she became frustrated and swiped them away. She'd been through a lot in her life: born to addict parents who flitted in and out of her life wherever it was convenient, raised by a loving but somewhat unavailable grandmother, always slightly fearful of connecting with people.

She'd finished high school solo and had gotten through nursing school while working her ass off. She'd done a lot on her own, sometimes with minimal to no help from others. She wondered how she could be so smart and yet remain with Kai, which was anything but smart.

Eleanor had changed that night. It was like a switch that had been slowly turned off after the first abuse had abruptly been turned on full force. She'd decided to be the one in charge of putting her hope into action and see if Kai would follow suit. She chose to make hope a verb instead of an adjective. If he could not handle it, then she would need to move on.

In fact, after that night, she'd started to retake small steps towards independence in case she needed to leave, and if it got bad enough, possibly abruptly. She'd switched her direct deposit so each week a more significant percentage of her check went into a savings account that only had her name on it. She figured if he discovered it, she would just lie and say it was savings for their wedding.

The night of the saltshaker incident he'd pleaded from the other side of the heavy oak door, banging on it with his fists as he argued his case, "Eleanor, please listen to me. This isn't me. You have no idea what is going on, please let me explain. Eleanor, I love you. Eleanor, I want to change. Eleanor, Eleanor, Eleanor, Eleanor."

When neither Eleanor nor the door bent to his demands, he'd slid an apology note underneath the door, promising he would get help, saying that he would go to counseling, that he would join Alcoholics Anonymous. When his attempts at niceties were unsuccessful, he texted her angrily, saying that she was the cause of his extra stress.

When she still had not acquiesced to his demands, the texts had become softer and more manipulative: *If you open the door, everything will be better. If you loved me, you wouldn't put me through this. If you cared, you would let me apologize.*

Eleanor had ignored his pleas and had instead put her earbuds in her ears and turned on a white noise app until over the sound of rain in her ears she eventually heard the door to the guest bedroom close.

Eleanor knew that the minute she woke up the next day she was going to be a new person. She was going to be a stronger woman and hope that it worked out well for her.

13

 oday, Eleanor woke up an hour after Kai left for work, now leaving him to figure out his breakfast. Being a nurse, she worked three twelve hour shifts a week, which resulted in four days a week to get things around the apartment done but also resulted in a lot of free time.

She was trying to focus on doing things for herself. She was no longer feeling guilty for not waking up and cooking Kai breakfast. She was preparing what she wanted to eat or not cooking at all. She wasn't staying home to see him, especially on her days off and after work. Because of this, she was making more plans with coworkers, which as a result had ended up making work even more enjoyable. She was finding that the more she attempted independence, the more she felt she was gaining back the confidence she'd started to lose when the abuse began.

He'd purchased not one, but two dozen roses the day after the saltshaker ordeal and she'd thrown them into the trash in front of him. She'd ripped the card in two, without reading it and had also thrown that in the garbage. Her heart had been beating at triple speed. She'd hoped he would not lash out at her, would not harm her after her insubordination.

Instead, after she'd thrown the roses and the card in the trash, he'd looked at her sad and defeated. For once he looked like the one who had been wronged — harsh words in her mouth and hard lines on her face she'd laid it out for him.

"I do not need you. I have never needed anyone in my life. When I first met you, I wanted you as my boyfriend and friend first. As I got to know you, I wanted you as a lover and then my fiancé. You have not done what you promised to do in caring for me, and I'm no longer going to put what you want and need first. I'm going to work on myself, and if you care to do the same to keep me, then great. If not, Kai, I will move out and move on with my life." Eleanor had said this again with a frightened heart but with a hard exterior. Her face had shown the strength and seriousness that she'd forgotten existed for the last several months. She'd left all emotion out of her statement, trying to be matter-of-fact so he would be more likely to hear what she was trying to say.

"I understand," Kai had replied, and for their sake, Eleanor hoped that he truly did understand. Eleanor had reached the point-of-no-return. She was looking towards the future, and she knew that she needed to heal from the past but not dwell on it.

Her change seemed to be working, for now, not only in herself but in eliciting a change in him. Sticking up for herself had deflated him somewhat. He now seemed to be working fewer hours, not drinking, and had even signed up on his own to see a counselor. She'd found a pamphlet for Alcoholics Anonymous next to their bed, and she was hopeful that he'd started attending meetings. Eleanor had been putting 100% of the focus on herself and had made a point of not giving him a bunch of praise. In the back of her mind, she felt that he'd caused this rift in their relationship, and she should not praise something that should have never been an issue in the first place.

Today Eleanor had made plans to meet a coworker at a coffee shop downtown for brunch before going shopping in the area for another coworker's baby shower gift. Eleanor got herself ready and arrived downtown thirty minutes early. She'd found a place to park a few blocks from The Bean Juice, where they were meeting, and decided to window shop. There were a few cute clothing boutiques and consignment stores on the way, and she admired the merchandise from the window, not entirely up to a full-blown shopping excursion before shopping for the baby shower.

She passed by a quaint-looking shop, and the display of wind chimes, fairy gardens, and various glass containers of succulents and air plants caught her eye. She looked up at the name of the flower shop, and her blood curdled for a moment as she realized the name of the shop matched with the light-yellow inscription that was on every card she'd received from Kai with her roses; Bee's Flowers.

Eleanor stood outside for a moment. She thought again about her hope for herself and the changes she was making. The timider Eleanor of a few weeks or even a month ago would not have braved going into the store that she felt was synonymous with the abuse she'd experienced, even though at a glance it looked right up her alley. She didn't hesitate for another second before pushing the door to the store open.

"Welcome to Bee's Flowers. I'm Betty. How can I help you?" Betty appeared to be in her late sixties or early seventies. She had a kind face and kind eyes, but Eleanor noticed something about her that she'd always noticed about Mama J, the look of a hard worker.

"I was just walking by and was drawn in by your window display, it's super whimsical," Eleanor said honestly.

"My granddaughters did that. I was pretty impressed myself. My husband and I just got back from a trip to the Grand Canyon in our RV, and they were running the show. They did such a great job that I decided to give them a surprise day off before my husband, and I leave again for a month-long vacation in Lake Tahoe starting next week."

"That sounds like a lot of fun! How great that you all get to work together," Eleanor said as she started browsing the shelves nearby. Inside she felt that tiny twinge of sadness that came with not having a family presence in her life. Would things have been different had she had a parent, grandparent, or sibling to help her through the Kai debacle? Had she had a close confidant;

would she have ended up in this situation?

"Nothing tests sisterly bonds like being stuck together all day, every day, especially when there is a seven-year age difference." Betty said to Eleanor with a knowing smile before asking, "What are you in the market for today?"

"Anything but roses," Eleanor blurted out before she could stop herself.

"I hear you, sister," Betty agreed, "I spent the first several years of my career pedaling rose petals, so to speak, and there were days I thought if I never saw or smelled another rose it would be too soon. It's nice that nowadays the floral business has expanded to more than just the good old rose. Well, let me ask, was there something specific in the window display that caught your eye?"

Eleanor paused for a moment to think about the window, "I think that the fairy gardens are adorable," she admitted. "What child at some point in their life doesn't think and hope that fairies are a real thing?"

Betty smiled in agreement, "I agree. I was tickled pink the first time I saw one of those fairy gardens. They can be as simple or as elaborate as you would like, and they are so easy to care for. All you need is some moss, rocks, decorations, accessories and a few succulents or air plants if you would like. The succulents and air plants hardly need watering. The hardest thing about them is that they are so easy you sometimes forget that you have them."

"Honestly, you had me sold at decorations and accessories, I work with pediatric patients and I feel like a lot of my time with them is talking about things like that," Eleanor said as she allowed Betty to lead her over to the selection of fairy garden supplies. "You'll just have to let me know what I need to do from here."

"First you need to pick a container of some sort to plant all your items in. Then you can grab some living accessories. We have tiny flats that have a variety of succulents in them that you can use," Betty instructed. Eleanor selected a flat of succulents and a glass hexagon that had a few inches of raised glass all around that already had a tiny fairy-sized tree planted in it. Betty and Eleanor took the plants to a small work area in the back, and Betty assisted Eleanor in putting her succulents into the dirt using some miniature shovels.

"That looks great!" Betty exclaimed, "My granddaughter Rachel orders all the inventory. I'm going to have to let her know that I approve of those fancy vases!"

Eleanor thanked her for her praise, also loving the way it looked so far.

"Now you can just pick some decorations, and you can arrange them here or at home," Betty said, once again motioning to the fairy garden section.

"I have to meet a friend in a few minutes next door," Eleanor admitted. "I think I'll just grab my decorations and put it together at home. Thanks for the offer though."

Betty nodded, "That isn't a problem. Please just come find me when you're ready to ring up or if you find anything else you need assistance with." She then went back to her dusting.

Eleanor perused all of the different fairies and their accessories and decided to do an outdoor patio theme as she currently lived in an apartment that only had a balcony for outdoor access. Her grandmother's house had had a small flagstone patio out back that they'd spent a fair amount of time enjoying. Sitting outside and enjoying the sun or looking at the stars was one of the few things that they found time to do together from the time Eleanor was little until before Mama J passed.

Eleanor selected a bag of tiny rocks to make a stone patio with, a small fire pit, some chairs, a hammock, and a tiny open tent that had little fairy lights that lit up. She purchased a few fairies and garden gnomes. She couldn't believe she was so excited about putting the fairy garden together. It was such a simple activity, but she was excited nonetheless.

She found Betty and paid for her merchandise. Betty carefully wrapped all the items for her so nothing would break during her shopping trip.

Eleanor left, excited that the shop was no longer tainted in her mind. Maybe a few trips in here and her feeling on roses would change. She walked next door and into The Bean Juice.

14

Scarlett could not sleep. She was too filled with hope that tomorrow they would get the all clear to go home. She wasn't naive enough to think that their journey was even close to being over, but she hoped that they could at least fight this disease together while under the same roof.

She hoped that Molly's body would co-operate. How was it that someone's own body could wage war against itself? She hoped that Molly's cells would squash out the potentially fatal invaders and replenish the competent cells that had been depleted by both cancer and chemotherapy. She hoped Molly would fight like hell from the inside out.

She hoped that her daughter would be able to enjoy the comfort of her own bedroom again. She expected that the last walls her daughter would see would not be the walls of a pediatric oncology unit. She hoped she got a chance to sit in the garden with her daughter again, warmth on their faces, the scent of lilacs in the breeze, laughter in the air and sweet iced tea in their bellies.

She hoped to reach every milestone with her daughter, her transition from a child in elementary school, to a teenager in middle school and high school. She hoped to help her move into her first apartment and have a beer with her on her 21st Birthday. She hoped to see her walk down the aisle with a partner of her choosing. When she and Tevin were long gone and buried, she hoped her daughter lived to be one hundred with bright purple hair and fifty great-grandchildren.

She'd felt hope in the past for benign things like promotions and general well-being, but she'd never known how vital hope was until after her daughter's diagnosis. Hope takes on a whole new meaning when it is a matter of life or death.

She not only had hope for her daughter but hope for her and her husband. Hope that they could focus on being a couple first instead of parents of a sick child… only feeling like a couple at a distance. Only getting to act like husband and wife when time and place aligned. She hoped that if Molly passed away, that they had what it took to remain together despite the grief.

She'd started to compare cancer to a game of poker where the wager wasn't money, but the life of her child. The cards had been dealt, and there was no changing what they would read. The stakes were high, but she couldn't change the outcome no matter how much she hoped and prayed that she could. Her ability to play the game well having no bearing on the results. There was no cheating or bargaining in the game of life.

For now, she merely hoped she could sleep.

15

Scarlett had gotten a whopping two hours of rest. She'd realized at 3:45 a.m., after hours of tossing and turning, that there was no hope for another wink of sleep. She'd planned on running outside, but the crisp fall Colorado air was a little too chilly for her Louisiana blood. She'd instead run seven miles on her treadmill in their basement, opting for a fast interval run in the hope that she would burn off some of her nervous energy and also possibly get herself tired enough that tonight she could sleep no matter what Dr. C had to tell them today.

Scarlett had loved how excited Molly had been when she received her paper flower from Bee's Flowers and had intermittently stopped in since then. Scarlett decided to go to The Bean Juice for a relaxing breakfast and coffee before zipping over to Bee's for another gift for Molly. Tevin had stayed with Molly last night, so he just planned to meet her at the care conference.

Scarlett had taken the time to sit and enjoy her breakfast. She enjoyed each bite of her spinach and cheese quiche, eating the savory dish slowly to thoroughly enjoy it. She'd slowly sipped her spicy chai latte, letting the cup warm her hands. She'd brought a paperback book in, one that had nothing to do with cancer or self-help, and she'd read it as slowly as she'd eaten and enjoyed just being in the moment.

She knew enough about herself and about what she'd been through the past few years to know that taking care of herself first made her into a better mother and wife capable of taking care of Molly and Tevin. She wanted to be in the right mindset before this morning's meeting so she could calmly and collectively take on the day, whichever way it went.

After breakfast, she'd gone next door to the flower shop where Rachel and Stacia assisted her with another paper flower, from a colorful Dr. Seuss book this time, and a little glass terrarium with a Tinkerbell fairy and a few accessories that she could admire. She was hoping that Molly would be able to come into the store herself in the next week if she was released today to pick out some living plants for her set-up. She knew that Molly would get a kick out of helping pick out all of the materials for a little Tinkerbell habitat as Tinkerbell was by far her favorite Peter Pan character.

Scarlett had been greeted by name by Stacia as soon as she entered the store, "Hey Scarlett. How's it going today?"

"I'm doing okay. How are y'all doing?" Scarlett didn't know if she'd the wherewithal to delve into the stress that she was under at the moment, knowing that it may be a lot to lay on someone she only knew superficially.

Rachel came over a moment later to join them in the next paper flower mission. While they'd been looking through the Dr. Seuss pages and gluing the flowers together, the sisters had decided to fill her in on Stacia's and Marco's two dates.

"My blushing is becoming less of a problem," Stacia had said proudly as Rachel had raised an eyebrow as if she was worried she might inadvertently hear some scandalous reasoning behind this.

"Calm down Rach," Stacia had replied to the eyebrow raise, "As we have discussed, we are taking things slowly. There has just been one smooch per dinner for a total of two. Two smooches, can you handle that Rachel?"

Rachel had answered her sister with another eyebrow raise and an older sister glare, "Just make sure you tell me to cover my ears if there is anything I should not hear."

"I was under the impression that we were all adults around here," Stacia said as she attempted to help her sister with the hot glue gun. When she instead hot glued her fingers together, she'd hurled out an impressive string of expletives. She'd looked at Scarlett and then at Rachel, obviously afraid that she may have offended their customer.

"That must have hurt like a bitch," Scarlett said innocently in her Southern drawl, winking at Stacia.

"I knew I liked you before, but I like you even better now," Stacia said as Scarlett assisted her in unsticking her fingers. "I would never have expected a curse word to come from your sweet Southern mouth."

After she left, Scarlett thought back on the fact that the sisters had recognized her immediately, which had caused her spirits to soar. They'd asked how Molly was doing and had even given her hugs of support when Scarlett had reluctantly verbalized that today was a big day for them.

Despite the stress, Scarlett felt like it had been a good day, and she hoped it would continue that way. She could not remember the last time that hope had seemed so close at hand rather than a vague and far away concept that was just outside of her reach.

Once she'd paid for her purchases, which she felt the sisters had significantly discounted, she headed to the hospital for their care meeting with Dr. C and the bone marrow transplant care team.

16

Scarlett entered through the main entrance of the hospital and performed her usual lobby routine, just slightly sped up as she was anxious to get upstairs. She quickly sent parents kind thoughts and smiled at the children who looked anxious to be there.

She texted Tevin from the elevator: *On my way up. Please don't start without me.*

Her cell phone dinged in return: *I'm heading in that direction. I think the care team is already in there but don't worry, we won't start without you. We are doing this together. Don't forget, "All the world is made of faith, and trust, and pixie dust."*

Scarlett thought about the fact that they really could use some pixie dust right now. They could use any amount of luck they could get in reality. She got off the elevator and performed the usual routine with hand washing and extra hand washing for good measure. As she rubbed her hands aggressively together, creating soap suds, she kept saying the same mantra over and over in her head: *let her be okay, let her be okay, let her be okay. Please let me bring my baby home, please let me bring my baby home.*

Molly had been admitted ten days before the bone marrow transplant. They wanted to get her as healthy as possible beforehand and had kept her there for hydration and medications as well as the surgical insertion of her central line which would be used to administer her chemotherapy.

Molly had felt pretty well during those ten days so it had been quite a feat to keep her contained and calm while still allowing her to burn off some 8-year old energy knowing that fairly soon she would not be feeling well at all.

They'd not stored any cord blood when Molly was born as in their worst nightmares, they could have never imagined that cord blood could be needed, that this would end up being the state of their lives. Thankfully, Tevin had been a match for bone marrow donation for Molly, which had been a relief as sometimes not even relatives were a match. Because they didn't have to use The Bone Marrow Registry, they were able to proceed relatively quickly with the transplant. This would be their second, and last, attempt at transplant.

After all of the procedures, Scarlett had felt that she had two people to check on and care for: Tevin and Molly. They'd taken the bone marrow from Tevin's hip, using a needle biopsy method. It was a relatively minor procedure, and he only complained of some mild soreness, but Scarlett could tell each time that he was uncomfortable. He'd covered it up with concern for his little girl; they both knew that she was the one that would have to do all the real hard work.

They were now at day 25 post-transplant and day 35 of hospitalization. That meant 35 days of Scarlett and Tevin seeing each other only in passing, 35 days of fear and hope, 35 days of empty space at their house without Molly there at all, and 35 days of not quite feeling like a family unit.

At day 15, post-transplant, at their first care conference, they'd been told Molly would need to stay longer as her cell counts were not where they needed to be. Not only that, but they'd gotten quite a scare when at day 5 Molly had gotten a fungal infection. She'd almost died. The team had caught it and treated it quickly, but she knew it was in the back of everyone's minds going into this care conference.

She went straight to the meeting room as she knew if she went into Molly's room, even for a minute, it would not be easy to sneak away again for both her and Molly. Upon entering the room, she recognized the care team which consisted of Eleanor, Dr. C, and his physician's assistant, Stephanie, Robbi, the social worker, Blake, the dietician, and Samantha, a nurse practitioner, and bone marrow treatment specialist. Each member of the care team shook Scarlett's hand and reintroduced themselves.

Tevin was already sitting down, and his face externally showed the stress that Scarlett felt internally. She was sure if they looked at current photographs of them and made a side-by-side comparison from three years ago the age progression would be unreal. It was crazy what stress like this could physically do to a person.

After she'd taken her seat, Tevin grabbed her hand under the table and squeezed it three times, their unspoken communication for "I love you." She'd squeezed it back three times in return and didn't let go after the third squeeze needing him and his touch.

Dr. C started the meeting, "I know you are both extremely nervous, which is understandable. We are all here as a team, and we want Molly to be home almost as much as you do. We kind of want to keep her here because she is such a little ball of spunk and sass. We will all miss that." There were nods of agreement all around the table.

Scarlett and Tevin both laughed nervously. "Wait, does this mean she gets to go home today?" Scarlett asked, processing what he'd inadvertently told them.

Robbi, the social worker, answered the question, "We feel that as of today she can go home, and we are all here to get you the tools you need to keep her as healthy as possible."

Scarlett and Tevin looked at each other with grins from ear-to-ear and hearts full of happiness and gratitude. Scarlett looked around the table and saw that everyone was smiling. She felt so lucky to have had people that genuinely cared about the well-being of not only their child but her and Tevin's well-being as well. She was having trouble containing her excitement, feeling like she had so much happiness inside her at the moment that she could scream and jump up and down.

"I want to scream and jump up and down," Tevin said quietly in her ear as he guided her towards him for a quick hug.

"I was thinking the same thing, I actually dare you to do it," Scarlett whispered in his ear, putting a hand firmly on his leg after he started to call her bluff by pretending to start to stand up.

The care team gave them a few moments to celebrate and let the news sink in so they would be better equipped to hear their discharge plan. Samantha, the nurse practitioner, opened a folder that held Molly's most recent blood work as well as her most recent chest x-ray. "Her platelets went up, which was what we were hoping to see. Her chest x-ray was also clear, so we are not working with any underlying pneumonia."

The physician's assistant Stephanie spoke about the papers she had in tow. "Her vitals have been stable with no fever to speak of. The infection appears to have cleared up with the antifungal medications she was receiving here. We will send you with some antifungals to take at home just for some extra coverage at the beginning."

"You will obviously want to refrain from any travel as we want you in a close radius if you need to return," Dr. C advised. "You will want to have her stay masked in public at first and watch her closely for signs of infection. She will need to take her medications to prevent her body from rejecting the transplant every day. Blake here will provide some information on diet at home to help with all the medications she will be taking as some can wreak havoc on the body, as you well know."

Robbi, glancing at Scarlett and Tevin, smiled. "I know you are pros at all of this two years in, but I also know that you are excited to get Molly home. Obviously, all of this information will be in the discharge packet. Can you think of anything else that you may need from us?"

"If y'all could just help pack her up and get us a date for the first follow-up appointment?" Scarlett asked with excitement.

17

Stacia was slowly replacing the steadily thinning layer of self-protection with hope. Hope that she could successfully learn from the past while also learning to move on. She hoped that she was whole enough now to be a good addition to someone, not half a person who was dependent on a significant other to define her or her level of happiness. She hoped that her codependency in her past relationship would never happen again. She hoped that in being vulnerable while remaining strong, she could possibly find love again.

She tried to go through the day without putting too much thought and effort into the fact that she was dating again, hoping that this would help protect her from potential hurt in the future. She hoped that by taking things nice and slow, whatever was meant to bloom, would bloom.

She couldn't remember the last time she'd hoped for her own wants and needs first in a relationship. When she'd been in her previous relationship, there had always been hope that HE was satisfied, hope that she was being a good enough girlfriend, hope that when he promised forever that he meant it, hope that she made him happy.

Now the hope she had was in growth for herself, with or without a man by her side. She hoped that she could be loved while being independent and healthy. She hoped that the person she ended up with would love her for her and not always try to change her or change what she wanted for the future.

She hoped she would never again have to hide the person she was on the inside, she hoped that she could allow her true self to shine, she hoped she could be unapologetically Stacia, coffee obsession, sarcasm and all.

The truth of the matter was that for the past year she'd just been going through the motions in the hope that she would heal and gain some of her old self back. She hoped that by being surrounded by the Bee women in her life, she would flourish and grow. She hoped to be an example to her nieces and a support system for them, as well as for her sister. She hoped her grandmother would gain the faith in them that she needed to retire and enjoy her freedom.

She hoped to find her unconditional love someday, but for right now, she hoped just to enjoy herself and let fate take it from there.

18

"We should have probably been Broncos cheerleaders," said Rachel as she admired their dance moves in the glass reflection in one of the displays. Today they'd opted to put their music on shuffle so they could dance to a broader variety as they performed their closing duties.

"I think I would prefer to be a Broncos kicker," Stacia replied as she mimicked drop-kicking a football and punting it. "More money, a possible entourage, more street cred, cute uniform with football pants or leggings or whatever they are called. I'm pretty sure football leggings would make my legs look pretty hot."

"You are already cool enough with a constantly inflating ego. I could not imagine you in football leggings with a larger ego than you already have," Rachel retorted. "I may not be able to handle being in your entourage."

"Who said you would be invited to be in my entourage?" Stacia said with a sassy shake of her head.

"I'm pretty sure you would need me to run your crew. I have seven more years of expertise and more knowledge of nineties gangster rap, which is a necessity in any entourage." Rachel replied matter-of-factly.

"How about we compromise and settle for showcasing our dancing skills on the Ellen Show," Stacia said with a laugh. "I'm pretty sure if she saw Grandma Betty dance with us, she would want to hire us as permanent dancers on her show."

Rachel held out her hand, "Deal! Ellen Show for the compromise."

Stacia opened up the cooler door to the flowers and plucked all of the flower petals that were starting to droop and pulled out any stems that didn't pass her test. As Grandma Betty had often said, they were not okay with selling subpar merchandise at Bee's Flowers.

While Stacia deadheaded the flowers, Rachel straightened up the merchandise and balanced the cash in the register. Their grandmother had agreed to update to iPads at the beginning of the year. Because of the update, the girls were able to reconcile credit cards from home, which had decreased the amount of time it took to close at night. Tonight, Rachel was going to do the reconciliation while she was at home with her girls since Stacia had another date with Marco.

Tonight, would be date number four. They'd so far gone out for Pho, to a movie, and bowling. For this outing they were going to a nice quiet restaurant for a fancy dinner and a few cocktails. They'd been having fun, but Stacia was a little more nervous about tonight as it seemed like more of a romantic date than the others had been.

On their previous dates they'd brushed over all the typical first-date stuff; family, friends, likes and dislikes.

Marco: father from Guatemala, mother from America, met while working together for a tour group. They'd moved here when Marco was 13. He still had friends and family that he visited in Guatemala every few years, but most of his current friends were from his indoor soccer (futbol) league. He liked dogs, mountain biking, soccer, and craft beer. He disliked cheesecake and was allergic to cats.

Stacia: born to high-school sweethearts who were kind and attentive but had become more interested in being a couple since Stacia and Rachel had finished high school. They currently lived in an over-55 community in Florida where they played golf pretty much every day while also selling real estate. Stacia was working on rekindling some high-school friendships since she'd moved back a year ago but thoroughly enjoyed hanging out with her sister and nieces in the meantime. She liked coffee, running, and was constantly redecorating her apartment. She disliked bacon and "people acting like asshats."

Stacia knew that their superficial brushing of the surface was all in an attempt to give her time to adjust to the pursuit of romance and she was trying to enjoy not being too serious. Marco was being so patient and kind about the whole thing, and she was beginning to realize that he was doing it because he liked her and didn't want to scare her off. While taking it slowly, Stacia was starting to realize that she really liked Marco as well, and that feeling increased with every interaction.

She'd felt so comfortable on their excursions. Marco was fun and witty and didn't take anything too seriously. On their bowling date, he'd knocked over a total of maybe ten pins. Instead of getting frustrated and angry, he'd allowed Stacia to wrap her arms around him from behind to help him guide the bowl towards the pins better. He'd assured her that he was better at other sports, but bowling had not been he and his friend's game of choice while growing up in Guatemala.

She was used to dating Luke, whom she'd known since childhood. There had not been anything particularly new or exciting towards the end of their relationship. They'd been in their early twenties and already stagnant. Discovering how Marco dealt with situations and the mystery of what could come next was new and exciting. Stacia discovered with each interaction she was becoming less and less scared, and more and more hopeful. It had been many years since romance and hope had coincided in her life.

Stacia and Rachel finished closing the shop, and Rachel gave a few parting words of advice, hoping that they would have another great date.

"I can't wait to hear all of the details!" Rachel said. "Unless there are naked details, in which case you are going to need to censor yourself, sister. Remember earmuffs!" Rachel had thrown her hands over her ears as Stacia had swatted at her.

Rachel left, and Stacia locked herself inside the shop. Grandma Betty was big on safety and required them to secure themselves in the store when they were alone. She'd also purchased security cameras as soon as her granddaughters had taken over the bulk of the work there, "I want to make sure you girls are working hard enough." Grandma Betty had said, but both girls knew it was because she wanted to make sure they were safe.

Stacia changed quickly in their break room. She slipped into a cream-colored long-sleeve maxi dress that was covered in bold red and orange poppies, slipped on some tights and a pair of wedge boots. She fixed her bun, so it was a little less frizzy and put on some extra mascara and a layer of lip gloss. She'd just finished when she heard a knock from the alley.

She could see Marco standing outside of the door. He looked incredibly handsome in a pair of khakis and a blue button-down shirt that accentuated the blue in his eyes.

"Hey there," she said as she opened the door.

"Hey beautiful," Marco replied with a smile, handing her a single bright yellow Gerber daisy. He reached out his arms and enveloped her in a big welcoming hug. He planted a kiss on the top of her hair. "You smell like plumeria."

"We were putting some centerpieces for the Atkins' wedding together, and they happened to have plumeria as the main staple. You have a good nose there. Thanks for my flower, Gerber daisies also happen to be one of my favorites."

"When you drive in a van full of flowers you quickly learn which ones are worth smelling," Marco said in reply. "And you can thank Rachel, she provided me with a pretty long list of your favorite flowers before I asked you on our first date."

"So, you're saying my sister does listen to me?" Stacia said with a smile, quickly putting the single flower in a tiny vase and leaving it inside the store. Stacia entered the passcode to the alarm box by the door and locked the deadbolt. "I'm ready if you are. I'm starving, but that isn't really a new thing. I'm pretty sure you have realized that I love to eat by now."

Marco chuckled in reply, "I'm glad you eat more like a Guatemalan woman than a lot of picky American women. I want a woman who enjoys the taste of food and drink, who doesn't think a side salad and two oyster crackers count as a meal." He threaded his fingers through her fingers and guided her down the alley. They walked the two blocks to the restaurant, making small talk the whole way there.

"I have an indoor futbol game this weekend if you are interested," Marco said as they walked.

"I would love to come," Stacia replied. "I played soccer myself in high school and college and miss it sometimes. I was kind of a beast."

"You should totally play with us sometime!" Marco exclaimed, "They are coed leagues. I remember how quickly I became afraid of the women when we had our first game. At first, I did the typical male thing and was trying to be all tender until some girl kneed me in the face without apology. They do not mess around."

"No, they don't," Stacia admitted. "Have you ever seen the YouTube videos of soccer players reactions to being injured? I'm not at all sexist, but I must say the men in a few of the videos could win Oscars for their dramatic falls."

"Have you seen the one where the girl doesn't stop playing despite a broken nose?" Marco asked.

"Yes, it's beyond awesome. Homegirl literally has blood dripping down her face, and she has this total nonchalant expression. I had this pretty intense girl on my team, and rumor has it that this one time she made a girl bleed, then she swiped some blood off her face and licked it, just to psych out the other team," Stacia said.

"Wow, I hope never to encounter her," Marco retorted as they arrived at the restaurant.

Marco was a perfect gentleman, holding the door open for her as they entered and pulling back her chair when she sat down at their reserved table. Stacia had always told herself that she was too independent for typical "nice-guy behavior." With Marco, it was clear that he was a gentleman because he cared about her. He wasn't doing these things because he felt she was incapable of taking care of herself. For him, it was just one more way he had of showing Stacia he was interested in her and Stacia appreciated that.

They'd ordered drinks while they looked over the menu. After perusing the drink menu, Marco had ordered a Left Hand Milk Stout and Stacia, making an effort to expand her craft beer palate, ordered the same.

"What do you think?" Marco asked after the beers had been delivered and they'd ordered an appetizer.

Stacia had been unsure of what to think when the waiter first set it in front of her as the beer was coffee-black in color. She'd never really tried a dark beer before but often heard people asking for any beer but a dark one. She took a tiny sip and let the flavors linger on her tongue for one moment, as she'd seen Marco do.

Stacia placed her fingers together on her temples and then made them explode, making a mild explosion sound, mimicking her mind being blown as she sampled another taste of the beer. "It tastes almost like coffee with a hint of mocha. It's absolutely delicious! To think until this very day, I was afraid of dark beers; I've been living a lie! I guess I'll let you help continue to change my mind about beer."

"We do live in the Mecca for craft beer here in Colorado," Marco said as he sipped his beverage again. "If you are up to the challenge, I will continue to share my beer snobbery with you."

"Well, if you keep feeding me beer like this, I will totally accept your offer," Stacia replied.

"Does this mean you are interested in continuing to spend time together?" Marco asked, steering the conversation in a more serious direction.

"I really like spending time with you, more than I can say without possibly scaring you off," Stacia replied honestly, following his lead. "As you found out from my word-vomit explosion the first time you asked me to dinner, I'm scared to death of liking you, and your dimples, and your blue eyes."

Marco smiled at her typical attempt at humor to diffuse the potential seriousness of the conversation. "If it makes you feel any better, I'm scared too. It's normal to be scared when there is a potential to like, or possibly love, someone."

"Love scares the shit out of me," Stacia blurted out before she could stop herself. She took a breath and reassessed what she was trying to convey to Marco. "I think that my last relationship was a relationship of comfortable love. If I could be that hurt by someone I had known practically my whole life, who I wasn't unconditionally in love with, how could I survive falling in true love?"

Marco reached across the table, grasping her hands in his: "I can't promise that what happens between us will never hurt. I can't promise that there won't be tears amongst the laughter, and the fun, and your sarcastic comments. I can promise always to be honest with you. I can promise you that we can take these baby steps together. I really like you, Stacia, and I have, from the moment I met you. Which I remember quite vividly as the time I scared you as you were turning the blind corner in the shop and you punched my arm harder than a heavyweight professional boxer. Give me a chance, give us a chance."

"I really want to make a joke about the punching comment, but I will refrain, mainly because you are so sweet and, as I already said, I like you too, Marco." Stacia squeezed his hands back in reassurance. "If you can just be patient with me and know that sometimes you will just have to rein me in, I'm willing to give us a chance. I want to be your girlfriend, if it's time for an official title, that is."

Marco stood up, ignoring that they were in a closed environment and gave her a swift but sexy kiss on the mouth, followed by a giant hug. To bystanders, it probably looked as if they'd just taken their relationship to a serious level as if they'd just gotten engaged.

"You're gonna be my girlfriend," Marco singsonged quietly in her ear while her head was pressed to his chest.

Stacia beamed with excitement. Then they became aware of their surroundings and the people gawking at them adoringly. They timidly retook their seats.

"Maybe if they think we got engaged they will bring us a free dessert," Marco joked until he saw the look of horror on Stacia's face at the word engaged.

"Would you feel comfortable telling me some of what occurred with your ex-boyfriend?" Marco asked, quickly changing the subject. "If not, I completely understand, but I want to be able to move forward together with an understanding of each other's past."

"I can appreciate that," Stacia nodded slowly in agreement. Their dinners came, and they both began working on their meals, taking time to sample each other's dishes before Stacia started to speak about Luke and Amber.

"I grew up in a neighborhood with only two children my age, Luke and Amber. I had Rachel of course, but she was the older sister and, therefore way too cool to want to hang out with me. We were all inseparable. Sometime around 9th grade, Luke voiced an interest in me, and we took it down the relationship path. The biggest issue now, looking back, is that I think he probably wanted Amber the whole time."

The waiter appeared again to check on them, and they ordered another round of stouts, this time poured on nitro, which Marco explained was smoother without all the bubbles.

"Continue, please," Marco coaxed her as soon as the waiter was out of hearing distance.

"Luke was very different with Amber. Amber had kind of a submissive personality by nature whereas I have, believe it or not, always been a little mouthy. She would do what he asked without hesitation, whereas I would give him pushback. I feel like maybe at first he liked me because he wanted a challenge, but he could never get me to conform completely, and I think that bothered him. I always felt like he was never 100% satisfied with me as a girlfriend. Because of this, I tried way too hard to please him. I wanted to stay in this area and work at the flower shop while going to college. But he asked me to marry him right after graduation. I said yes because my heart felt like it was right, but my head kept telling me it was a dumb move."

Stacia paused to take a few sips of her nitro beer before continuing. She smiled at the taste of this one as well, "Luke wanted to be in California, so we moved to San Diego for college, and Amber came with us. Amber and I rented a tiny apartment together, and Luke was obviously there quite a bit. As I mentioned before, I didn't really want to go to school out there, but I felt that I had to just so I could be around them. About six months into our sophomore year I came home to them sitting on the couch together, holding hands. Amber was crying hysterically. They told me that Amber was three-months pregnant and that they'd been sleeping together since we got to San Diego."

"Wow," Marco commented, again grabbing her hand for support, "What did you say?"

"Well, I'm pretty sure I dropped several F-bombs before throwing the ring at them in temper-tantrum style before I ran out of the room. Honestly, I was so mad and blindsided that the rest of that night is all a blur of anger, tears, and a little relief if I'm being honest. I stayed with a friend that night and called Rach to tell her what had happened. Rachel drove overnight without any hesitation and helped me get my things the next day and then we promptly left for Colorado. I've been here since."

"That is intense, I can't imagine how painful that was," Marco said.

"It was painful." Stacia agreed. "But as time goes on, I have come to realize that I'm actually thankful that it happened. When I look back at our past, they truly do fit better together. I had to change to be what he wanted and needed, and that is never the girl I wanted to be. Plus, they now have a baby to take care of and have to adult 24/7. I get to be out to dinner with a handsome man while they are at home changing diapers and wearing spit-up on clothing."

"You didn't even mention dining with me and my dimples," Marco joked before becoming serious again. "I'm happy to hear that you found a way to look for the positive in all of this," Marco said. "I'm also happy you threw a few snarky comments into the story. I was getting a little worried about your state-of-mind having gone with no sarcasm for a whole five minutes. I'm obviously the happiest that I got to meet you and that I get the privilege of sitting here on a beautiful fall night with a funny, snarky, intelligent, beautiful woman."

Stacia felt warmth travel from the pit of her navel towards her face and down to her groin. She extended her hand and promptly knocked over a glass of water, which Marco quickly caught, causing only a tiny spill.

"Here I was getting all cocky, thinking I was getting less clumsy," Stacia joked as she mopped up the water spill with her napkin.

"Right now I feel like we are a well-oiled machine. I'm here to catch any potential falling objects while you are in my presence," Marco joked.

"You ready to get out of here?" Stacia asked.

Stacia insisted on paying this time, and they walked hand-in-hand back to Bee's, where they sealed the night with a kiss that made Stacia tingle from her head to her toes with desire, excitement for the future, and the hope for more good things to come.

19

Rachel hoped that he was looking up at the stars, as she was, and thinking about her at that very moment. They'd made a promise to each other to look to the sky in their times of sadness knowing that they were both there, somewhere, looking at the same sky. She had a revitalized sense of hope each time she did this, knowing that somewhere, under the same atmosphere, was her husband.

She hoped that he was healthy, she hoped that he was at peace, she hoped he was safe. She hoped that he knew that he was loved and missed. She hoped he had times to laugh amongst the stress. She hoped he was developing new relationships and that they were all able to help support each other.

She hoped for contact with him; a letter, a call, FaceTime, a text. She was never without her phone on the off chance he was able to get ahold of her. Instead of turning the volume down at night, she turned it all the way up so if he called she did not miss it.

She thought about how it felt right now, being a single mom, without the permanency of being a single mom. She hoped that this close to the end of his deployment that he would remain free of harm. She could not imagine being this close to the end and having to then face losing him and becoming a widow with two small children.

If he were there for the day-to-day tasks, no matter the situation, it would all seem better. She hoped that when he returned, they would all slip back into reality with minimal effort, but she knew that this was neither healthy nor realistic. She hoped that their love would grow and thrive despite the distance. She hoped for a normal life with her husband by her side.

She shivered, looking at the stars in the sky before going back inside to her cold bed.

20

"You and Marco are still coming tonight correct?" Rachel asked as she ran the hot glue gun over a paper flower. She was currently making some into Christmas ornaments as it would soon be time to update the display for Christmas. They'd been selling so well she wanted a stockpile of ornaments to hang up on their little display tree that would go up in the merchandise window.

"We are still coming. That hasn't changed in the forty-five minutes it has been since you last asked me," Stacia grumbled.

"It's just important to the girls and their teacher, as the girls keep reminding me," Rachel said in reply. "The fact that both Stella and Marie have a singing part in the program is amazing. Their teacher last year didn't really do any sort of holiday program like this, so they are just beyond excited."

Stella and Marie's teachers had decided to do their holiday program the second Friday in November, in the hopes that families would not be so stressed with the hustle and bustle of the holidays. Doing it early, per the music teacher, would make it more enjoyable for families, freeing them from one less responsibility before Thanksgiving and Christmas.

"I really wish Grandma Betty and Grandpa David could be there," Stacia mentioned. "I get that they are just sunning it up at Lake Tahoe, but you know that they get a kick out of things like this."

Rachel nodded in agreement, "Mom and Dad would have also loved to come, but it doesn't make sense for them to fly out here twice. By the way, we should call them soon to figure out holiday plans and where they want to stay and all that good stuff."

"We can allow them to witness all of tonight with this little thing we call technology. We have recording devices on these here smartphones, you know, the little pocket computer thingamabobs." Stacia said jokingly whipping out her cell phone from her apron. "It's a big bummer that my apartment is too small for me to accommodate any additional guest. Bu-umber."

"Shut up smart ass. You are extra sassy tonight like maybe you had too much coffee or something," Rachel said as she made a menacing gesture with her hot glue gun.

"Wow," Stacia joked in return, "What, are you threatening me now?"

"Marco would still be crazy about you even if I used this glue gun to mark that pretty face of yours. I have seen the way he looks at you all goo eyed."

Stacia shook her head at her sister's comment, suddenly becoming serious, "I think I'm falling for him."

"Anastasia Dawn, I could tell from the moment you bragged about punching him that all of that was a possibility. He brings out the best in you; you act like your true self when you are around him. Have you guys done the deed yet?" Rachel waggled both of her eyebrows at her sister.

"Rach! I thought you didn't want to know all of the earmuff worthy details!" Stacia exclaimed. "But since you're asking, and I have been dying to talk to someone about it, I should probably fill you in."

"Fill me in then for Christ's sake before I change my mind!" Rachel persisted.

"Well," Stacia began as she started arranging a little Christmas fairy garden that would also go in the display window, "I don't know if you have noticed that Marco is extremely handsome."

Rachel glared at her sister, "Really…it would not take a genius to come to that conclusion. Let's get to the good stuff!"

"Ok, ok, sheesh. His last relationship was similar to mine with Luke in the fact that Marco felt like he could not be himself. He was dating this big-shot Denver lawyer, and she used him as a trophy piece. They actually broke up because he refused to wear a skimpy speedo banana hammock-type swimming trunks on vacation with her firm because she wanted to use him and his abs to impress her coworkers. He confronted her at the resort after he discovered that she'd slipped the trunks into the bag after he said he would not wear them. She then told him if he didn't wear them, he would be on his own the rest of the trip. He promptly dumped her and spent the rest of the time scuba diving, avoiding the hotel room, taking pictures, and meeting people from different countries around the resort. He said he felt used physically, and long story short, we are trying to wait before we get more physical though everything we have done has been amazing, so it will just be that much more amazing when it does happen."

"Wow," Rachel said, "I don't think it's cool that Marco was treated like a prized bull, but good for you guys for really taking it slow. That is rare these days."

They were interrupted by the ringing of Rachel's cell phone. Her breath halted, and her heart buzzed rapidly as she saw that it was from an unknown number. "Hello," she said breathlessly.

"Rachel, My Queen!" Came Chad's deep voice from the other line.

Rachel broke into tears, attempting not to let him hear the sobs through the phone. She wanted to be strong, to get past the rush of emotions she was feeling at hearing his voice. If he was able to call her, that meant he, for the moment, was alive and safe.

Stacia immediately came to her side and grasped her hand in support, "Hello there handsome," Rachel replied shakily, "You have no idea how happy I am to hear your voice."

She heard a sniffle on his side of the line, and she knew that he too was trying not to let the emotion overtake him. "I'm over the moon to hear your voice too, believe me. I get to come home baby, I'm on my way home."

Rachel, no longer able to hold it all in, started sobbing into the phone, "I'm so proud of you and what you are doing, but I need you in my life every day. You deploying was hard when we barely knew each other, and it has been the hardest thing I've ever been through with children and with how in love with you I am now. I need you in my life everyday Chad."

"I'll be home soon baby. I need my girls, and I need you too. We make a pretty good team all of us, and I love you all more than you will ever know. I'll be able to call tomorrow so make sure you have your phone on you. Please tell the girls I'll see them in the next few days. I want them to know I'm close."

"I love you too Chad, and if my sister were not here, I'd say more about what our first night together will be like. You will have to just use your imagination for now," Rachel smiled as she heard Chad laugh in response on the other side of the line.

"Bye Stacia, love you Rach!" he said loudly enough for both of them to hear before hanging up the phone.

Rachel let Stacia hold her as she cried tears of joy. All that she hoped would happen was happening. Chad, for now at least, sounded like his usual self, and he was coming home to her and the girls.

"Let's get out of here. You need to see the girls after the news you just heard, and I need to eat something so Hangry Aunt Stacia isn't the one attending the program tonight." Rachel nodded in agreement, and they made plans to meet at the school in two hours so they could get some seats together before the event.

Rachel grabbed the girls from the after-school program at school, grabbed a take-and-bake pizza from a nearby pizza place and headed home to frantically get the girls fed and dressed. She could not wait to have him back by her side for the normal day chaos.

She'd told the girls in the car on the way home that she'd

spoken to their father, but she told them he was headed back without any definite time mentioned. She could not handle getting her own hopes up and possibly crushed; she could not fathom putting the girls through a false sense of hope if something didn't work out. The girls had been excited, screaming as loudly as their mother would tolerate in a moving vehicle at the thought of possibly talking to him on the phone the next day and maybe seeing him soon.

They got back to the school right in the nick-of-time, and Stacia and Marco were already in the cafeteria awaiting their arrival. The girls went to the back to prepare with their class while Rachel, Stacia, and Marco waited with the other families for the doors to open so they could take their seats.

The doors opened after ten minutes of small talk, and families began to stream into the auditorium. The girls' music teacher, Mrs. Wren, stopped them before they got inside. "I don't know if anyone mentioned to you that we want the families of the students who have solos to be in the reserved area up front. We just know that moments like this are special, so we sectioned off a spot for easy recording on your phone."

"No one mentioned it," Rachel said as Ms. Wren began leading them to the front of the auditorium. Stacia discreetly elbowed her sister in the arm as they walked down the main aisle, giving her a guilty look as they walked to the coveted front seats.

Ms. Wren guided them into the front row and then went on her way, obviously in a hurry to corral the parents into the auditorium so she could then face the task of corralling a bunch of wild elementary school children onto the stage.

"I feel guilty!" Rachel said in a hushed tone, "I'm just hoping that maybe each child gets a turn to sing in a program with their parents up front."

"Kids who don't stink at singing get solos," Stacia whispered so only her sister could hear.

Rachel promptly swatted her on the arm and gave her a glare, "Behave."

"Don't you mom-glare me," Stacia replied with a glare of her own.

"Do I need to sit between you girls?" Marco asked innocently, leaning forward in his seat. He promptly earned a swat on the arm from each sister.

The lights dimmed, and the chatter in the auditorium became dim as well.

The principal, Mr. Cameron, walked onto the stage with a microphone in hand. He thanked everyone for taking the time to come out and support the school and the music program. He then introduced Ms. Wren, who walked onto the stage.

"Thanks, Mr. Cameron, and thank you, families. The theme of the Holiday Program tonight is community. We will be representing holiday songs from all over the world, and before each song, students will do a skit or give some information on some traditions specific to the country of origin and how it portrays a sense of community. Thanks again." Ms. Wren walked up to the podium as one of the other teachers walked off of the stage and ushered the kindergarteners onto the stage.

Stacia whispered a comment to Rachel about herding cats. Rachel promptly clamped her mouth shut, which suppressed her laughter while again shooting her sister another mom glare.

Each kindergartner held a paper menorah that they'd most likely colored. A boy and girl walked to the microphone. "Hanukkah is the Festival of Lights," the little boy said, barely above a whisper. "This is a menorah!!!!" The little girl screamed at full voice, causing titters of laughter throughout the auditorium. The kindergarteners then sang "Hanukkah, O Hanukkah" in English, with one verse in kindergarten level Yiddish.

"If this is how cute the whole program is going to be, I may implode," Stacia whispered amongst the clapping after the song.

The program continued on with skits and props, kids who hammed it up, and kids who were not even moving their mouths along with the words they were supposed to be singing. No one threw up, and no one passed out, which had happened last year twice at the End-of-School Celebration Program.

The girls' second-grade class, according to the program, was to be performing last. Rachel felt a tinge of nervousness as she knew the girls had a singing part. Thinking back, she could not recall either girl practicing at home, but Rachel didn't put it past herself to have been too busy or preoccupied to notice. Plus, the girls liked to sing in their room regularly so maybe they'd been practicing without her knowledge. Rachel heard the applause that indicated that the girls' class was up next. Instead of the class filling in during the applause, the stage remained bare. Once the applause had died down, Ms. Wren went to the microphone.

"This last song is more of a community song and less of a holiday song. We wanted to honor a slightly different tradition that occurs in different countries, the tradition of giving flowers. I would like first to invite Stella and Marie Bee-Harper onto the stage, and I would also like to invite their mother Rachel to come up."

Rachel looked at Stacia in confusion, Stacia shook her head indicating that she didn't know what was going on. Rachel felt a little blindsided, but the moment she saw her girls walk onto the stage and saw them beckon for her, she pushed any hesitation aside and went to join them. One of the teachers pulled a chair onto the stage as another teacher carried a few vases of various sizes and placed them next to the chair. Rachel sat down, and her girls joined her on either side, putting their arms protectively around their mother's shoulder.

Ms. Wren continued, "As many of you know, Chad Harper has been deployed for the last year. The ladies on this stage have made huge sacrifices so we can all have our freedom." Ms. Wren was interrupted by applause. Rachel felt warm tears starting to spill over. She looked in the front row and saw that Stacia was also now crying. Marco had a comforting arm around her shoulder.

When the applause died down, Ms. Wren began again. "We wanted to do something to let you know how we feel. Instead of words, we are going to use flowers, given that you happen to own a flower shop. In different countries, flowers are given for a variety of reasons. They are given to symbolize love, grief, happiness. In Asia, if you give someone a potted plant it should not be red as this symbolizes constriction, and in France, flowers should always be in an odd number, but never give someone thirteen flowers as that is unlucky. Stella and Marie thought we were just going to mention our thanks to them tonight, but they were not aware that the second grade had a secret project, which all you parents know is not a small feat in the second-grade age. The secret project was to bring a flower today that symbolizes something important in a community. Each child will bring a flower on stage and say the meaning behind it while we all sing this next song together."

Rachel felt shaking on both sides of her arms and heard sniffling, confirming that both girls were now crying as well. Rachel could not even tell what song they were singing, she was hyperfocused on each of her children's classmates as they brought up a flower one at a time, stopping at the microphone. She could not remember a time she'd felt so loved and appreciated, and she was in a room full of strangers.

"Strength, togetherness, support, love, happiness." Rachel and her girls placed the flowers one-by-one into the vases right next to them. None of them bothered to cover the tears that were flowing, though one of the teachers did discreetly hand them all Kleenex as she helped guide the students one-by-one onto the stage.

Rachel suddenly heard Stacia gasp from the audience, causing her to glance in her sister's direction. She had a slightly hard time seeing with the glare of the lights onstage, but when she covered her eyes with her hand, she saw both her grandparents and her parents standing next to Stacia. She didn't yet compute what was going on until she heard one of the girls scream.

"Daddy! Daddy!" Rachel felt movement as her girls tore themselves away from her and towards their father, who had just walked on stage carrying three bouquets of flowers. Rachel sobbed as a million emotions traveled through her as she walked towards her husband. She felt gratitude, gratefulness, love, hope, and relief. She had to refrain from flinging her whole body around his as they were in public, instead settling on a giant hug and kiss, nuzzling her nose into his chest, taking in the comforting scent on her husband.

The four of them held each other so tightly that nothing short of a natural disaster could have separated them. In a few moments, they felt additional bodies join their hug as Stacia, Marco, Betty, David, Greg, and Cheryl joined in; holding them together as their emotions burst out.

The transition from the stage to backstage was a blur. Rachel felt slightly in shock and shaky but in a good way, she never in a million years would have guessed that this was how tonight was going to go.

Rachel couldn't let go of her husband's arm. He kept bending his head down to kiss the top of her head. Her family surrounded them again backstage, smiles on all of their faces and tears on all of their cheeks.

Chad's face beamed as he got individual hugs from everyone. Marco was all grins and dimples when he was included in the hug train as Stacia introduced her boyfriend to her grandparents and parents. Grandma Betty in true style commented on his cute dimples, beautiful eyes, and muscular physique.

"Who planned this?" Rachel asked when she'd calmed down somewhat. Someone had handed her a whole box of tissues at some point, and she grabbed a few and passed the box around. The girls beamed up at their parents, refusing to take more than a step away from either of them.

Grandma Betty looked at Chad, and then at Greg and Cheryl. "It was Chad's idea, but I helped fine- tune it, and your parents helped with the airport pickup. Ms. Wren literally planned the whole program to line up with this. She grew up in a military home as well and was fully on board. I helped with the secret second-grade project and with the bouquets. I kind of felt like a drug dealer in the parking lot with all of the second-grade families coming to my car to select a flower for a dollar." They all laughed as they pictured the scene. Grandma Betty added, "All the proceeds will go towards a military charity of your choosing. I brought a lot of flowers, and we sold every last stem."

"I know how you girls all feel about surprises. I couldn't have imagined doing this any other way," Chad said beaming down at his wife. Rachel had always loved surprises. She could hardly handle her excitement at being surprised and liked to surprise others as often as possible. The girls had also inherited their mother's same love of the unexpected. Christmas was always a little intense at their house.

Ms. Wren came backstage at that moment. Black makeup caked to her eyes and cheeks giving her a raccoon-like appearance, "Well," she said, "there is not a dry eye in the audience. Thanks again for your service, Mr. Harper. Thanks for letting us do something to celebrate all of you."

Stacia helped Ms. Wren with her makeup, "Thank you for doing this," Stacia said. "What an amazing surprise. I don't cry, and I can't seem to stop crying."

"Did you notice what was in your bouquets?" Chad asked the twins, gesturing to the flowers he'd brought in with him.

"I was too busy being surprised!" Stella exclaimed.

Marie walked over to the bouquets and examined them. "These look like some of the flowers from the book you made us." Chad nodded in agreement.

"Was the flower thing my grandma's idea? Or your idea?" Rachel asked her husband.

"Well I had to one-up the book somehow," Chad acknowledged.

"I loved it, and I love you," Rachel said going on her tiptoes to give him another kiss.

"How long will you guys be here?" Stacia asked her parents, shifting some of the focus off of Rachel and her family so they could have a few seconds of privacy.

"We have a tee time in two weeks," Greg replied happily, "We missed you, big girls." He hugged each of his daughters before kneeling before his granddaughters. "We really missed you girls too. I need as much Papa time as I can get in the next two weeks."

Both girls hugged their grandfather ferociously. Each had had a particularly strong bond with him since they were born. No one was quite sure how the girls had come to call him Papa but since they could speak that is how they referred to him, and it had stuck.

"Should we grab some dinner?" Cheryl asked as she hugged all of her girls as well.

"Maybe these lovebirds need some alone time for some hanky panky?" Grandma Betty piped in.

"Grand-MA! We are at a school function!" Stacia exclaimed.

"What?" Grandma Betty said innocently, "It is true, isn't it? Don't these kids get sex education at some point in their..."

"As true as it may be," Chad interjected, "I need my family right now. My whole family. But I get to choose where we eat, I have been craving good old-fashioned cheese pizza!"

With that, they gathered up their flowers and slipped out the back so they could all be in the moment of happiness and the fulfillment of hope together.

Part 3 - Lotus - symbol of contentment

∞∞∞

~Emptiness from Desire

~Victory over attachments

~Enlightenment

~Love and compassion

~Self-awareness

~Rising out of suffering

21

9 MONTHS LATER

E leanor now went to bed every night looking forward to the next day. Her day would begin with her alarm going off at 4:30 every morning and she would head to the gym for a kickboxing or yoga class, or she would head to work. Either way, she was content.

She'd become stronger inside and out. Where she used to feel timid and ashamed, she felt herself emitting strength and perseverance. She'd physically gotten stronger. Working the muscles in her body had been a great stress release, had helped build her confidence, and her physique was getting leaner and more toned.

She'd immediately started seeing a counselor after the last incident with Kai and the saltshaker. She'd been working on dealing with the feelings and emotions that came with being abandoned by her parents and raised by her grandmother. She'd been working on dealing with the abuse that Kai had put her through. Her counselor had encouraged her to leave. Though she'd considered it, she was content for the time being. She still felt like she wanted to give him a chance.

Eleanor knew in her mind that staying may not be smart, but he had, for the time being, stepped up to the plate. To satisfy her mind, she'd made an escape plan with the help of her counselor.

She knew she was at a crossroads with diverging paths in front of her. She knew that no matter the road, she would be okay.

She knew in her heart that they loved each other, but she was trying to figure out if they could step out of the unhealthy relationship and completely heal to become two healthy, married individuals. To satisfy her heart, she was putting all her energy into loving herself and loving him with all that she had left.

Eleanor was content with the new-and-improved Kai and the new-and-improved Ellie. She was allowing that contentment to continue to help her grow, but also keep her grounded. She knew that to completely step out of the remnants of the abuse they needed to have some hard discussions, air all of the discrepancies out.

She was hoping, if all the improvements continued, there would be a wedding, a future, a happy life. She could not remember the last time life looked this promising, like it may work out in her favor.

22

"**B**abe, your alarm is going off," Kai whispered. Eleanor grunted and turned over in bed. "Ellie, your alarm." Eleanor opened her eyes slowly after a gentle shake from the other side of the bed woke her up. Through her sleep-matted eyes, it was hard to tell what time of day it was at first.

"Is this a workday or a workout day?" Kai asked as she grunted again before pressing the snooze button on her alarm clock.

"Workout day," Eleanor replied sleepily as she buried herself under the covers again, wanting to stay cozy for a few more minutes before the snooze alarm went off. "You want to come with me?"

"Depends on what you have in mind," Kai replied, snuggling up behind her. "I could probably fit a run in before I head into the office."

"That would be great," Eleanor said, closing her eyes and enjoying the moment.

"Do we have that counseling appointment today or tomorrow?" Kai asked quietly.

"Today," Eleanor whispered in return, suddenly more awake, and nervous thinking about what could happen during and after their appointment. Eleanor had approached him last week about a joint session at her counselor's office to discuss the progress that she'd made over the previous ten months. She wanted to talk about her hope for the future of their relationship. She hoped they could discuss some of the reasons Kai had lashed out at her in the past with the help of a professional. Eleanor had not blatantly told Kai, but this was the final obstacle she needed to overcome before she made a decision to plan a wedding or to put a plan in place to move on.

The snooze -alarm went off, and she pressed the button one last time, allowing them to enjoy the silence and serenity of the new day for just a few more minutes. They laid there, breathing slowly, holding each other for eight whole minutes until the alarm blared again and they, reluctantly, got out of bed.

Kai and Eleanor were at their best when they ran together. It was as if their bodies instinctively knew how to match each other's pounding on the pavement stride-by-stride. They ran together silently, with only the thudding of their shoes on the ground, the beating of their hearts, and the background of the city for company. During their runs, they didn't even feel the need to listen to music or speak. Instead, they gestured with their bodies: turn right, turn left, straight, in a seamless dance.

They ran for an hour, getting in 7 miles. They went upstairs and showered together, now letting the water do the talking; letting the warmth soothe their muscles as it washed away the evidence of their workout. They eventually turned to each other, soaping each other lazily, enjoying the feel of each other's hands before it became more frantic, they then turned to mouths, kissing each other heatedly, until they joined together, the warmth from their rapid breathing and the steam from the shower increasing their coupling until they both climaxed together. Their shower ending with a heavenly release.

"I wish we could just go back to bed," Kai said, sated, as they headed out to the bedroom to dress.

"I could write you a nurse's note," Eleanor said jokingly as she slipped on her robe, wishing herself that he could go back to bed with her.

Kai made them breakfast, him in his suit, and her in her robe, and they sat in silence. He reading a magazine, and her, her Kindle. There was once again comfort in their silence as they sat eating and sipping their coffee. They didn't need to fill the air with unnecessary words as they both found contentment with just sitting, just being themselves, just being together.

Once they'd both finished eating, Eleanor had cleared their dishes and tidied up the kitchen. Kai grabbed his briefcase and came over to give her a farewell kiss, "Thanks for earlier, that was quite literally, steamy." Eleanor laughed, blushing. Kai then asked, "Should I meet you at the counselor's office after work?"

"That would be great," Eleanor nodded. "Do you know where it is?"

"If you can just send me the contact information, I will look it up. 4:30, correct?" Kai asked as he kissed the tip of her nose.

"Yes sir," Eleanor acknowledged, giving his forearm a squeeze.

"See you then, beautiful," Kai walked out of the door, brief-case in hand.

Eleanor got herself another cup of coffee and this time went out to the balcony so she could sit and reflect with the sun shining on her. She really wanted to have her thoughts in order before they had their counseling session today so she could get her point across efficiently and effectively.

She was content in her life currently because she'd found the strength to rescue herself and had thus established her independence without Kai. But she wasn't 100% content in the fact that her heart and her head were still so conflicted.

She thought about all of the growth she'd made over the last 10 months, since the salt-shaker offense. Her showing Kai anger and defiance really had ignited a change in him, but would he change himself forever? She couldn't help but focus on the what if...

She hoped she wasn't overlooking things she shouldn't ignore. She'd lost so much in her young life already, so much so that abandonment was a familiar feeling to her. She knew that if she didn't love Kai that she could and would have left the first time. But she loved him. She felt a connection still, which just made everything even more confusing.

She knew she was smart. She'd been raised by a nurse and was a nurse herself. Because of that, she knew what she would recommend. She knew that if she heard of this happening to a friend, a co-worker, a family member, she would encourage them to leave. She knew that once someone exhibited this sort of behavior; it was more likely that it would happen again. But for some reason, she just felt in her heart that there was more to the story, and she wanted to get to the bottom of it before making a life-changing decision for them both.

Ten months ago, she'd started leaving the house every time she saw him filling a glass with alcohol. He'd eventually, of his own accord, thrown all of the alcohol out. She had her suspicions about Kai being involved in Alcoholics Anonymous confirmed when he started attending meetings and informed her that he would be unavailable while attending.

Kai of the last ten months was the Kai she'd fallen in love with. Since he'd started making an effort to be a better person he'd started laughing more, he'd started wanting to get out of the house more, and they'd seen his co-workers more. Kai had also encouraged Eleanor to do more things that made her happy; especially after he witnessed her asserting her independence.

Kai had always been relatively mum about his childhood, but she knew that his life had not been a piece of cake. His mom had been born in Vietnam and had come to America after marrying his biological father, who was 15 years her senior. Kai's dad had died of a heart attack when Kai was just 12-years-old, and his mom had immediately started seeking her next husband. Eleanor knew that his mom's inability to be alone was in part due to the loneliness of immigrating from her country-of-origin, partly because her culture involved being married and rearing children, and somewhat because being a wife and a mother had always been her dream.

Kai's mother had married his stepfather, Bill, only two months after meeting him at the restaurant where she worked.

Kai wouldn't speak much to Eleanor about what happened after his stepfather moved in, but Eleanor knew that shortly after that he became physically and emotionally abusive to Kai.

Kai's mother had become pregnant in the first year of her new marriage with twin girls. From the moment the twins were born they'd been treated like princesses while Kai was put under immense pressure in everything he did. In school he was expected to get straight A's, excel at sports, expected to be perfect. Not being perfect came with a hefty price.

When his senior year and graduation approached, his parents offered him only two pathway options for college: either pre-med or pre-law. He wasn't fond of blood and gore, so he'd gone the pre-law path.

Eleanor had not found out firsthand about Kai's tainted past. A lot of Kai's childhood trauma stories had been retold to Eleanor by his younger sisters. Even though they were not tortured by their father, they could hear his cries from behind closed doors. They'd been pretty diligent about making sure Kai was doing well and had started checking in with Eleanor for reassurance once their engagement had been announced.

Eleanor's heart had ached when she'd learned of the abuse. She almost wished that he'd lashed out at her in the past for no reason because then it meant that he was just cruel, and not wounded. She could leave cruel eventually, but wounded was a lot more complicated.

Eleanor hoped that the counseling appointment would be a success today. She wanted to start planning a wedding, or she wanted to move on. She'd been putting money aside that she would use either for their wedding or to move away. Not knowing which direction to go caused her some anxiety.

She felt like just getting on the same page would benefit them greatly as would her forgiving Kai and moving on and he being able to forgive himself. She loved the idea of healing from all of it and eventually sitting down with the Bee sisters, who she'd gotten the pleasure of meeting multiple times over the last few months and working out her colors and floral designs for her wedding. She also loved the idea of taking on travel-nursing positions and getting paid to travel the United States if their engagement ended and they parted ways.

Eleanor knew that Mama J would have loved the good things about Kai. She would have wanted to mother him up a little and cook for him and nurture him; especially after finding out about his past. She also knew that if Mama J had seen the marks on her skin, she wouldn't have stood for it. In fact, she would have had a hard time preventing Mama J from leaving marks of her own on Kai's skin.

On the other hand, she knew that Mama J preached about second chances with the patients she took care of on the mental health unit. Mama J had more experience than most concerning the permanent marks that could be left on a person's heart, body, and soul from childhood trauma.

Eleanor looked up and sent a message to the sky in the hopes that from somewhere up in the clouds, Mama J, in guardian angel form, could send her some good advice from up above.

Eleanor got to the counseling appointment thirty minutes early because she was so nervous. She wasn't doing herself any favors at home, running through every possible scenario in her brain. She just really wanted it all to go well. She was pleasantly surprised when she saw Kai in the lobby, also early.

He handed her a piping hot cup, "I thought we would most likely get here around the same time, and I thought you could use a chai latte to reduce your stress."

"You were correct, thanks," Eleanor took the cup from his hand with a slight tremble and sipped slowly, grabbing a magazine so she would have something to do with her nervous energy. She once again reminded herself that no matter how this session went, she would be okay. This mantra, repeated in her head, increased her sense of peace.

They were called into the counselor's office, and Eleanor introduced Kai to Bethany, her counselor. They sat together on the loveseat while Bethany took a seat in a plush chair opposite them, notebook in hand.

Bethany began the session: "I appreciate you coming in today, Kai. I know that it is never easy to be brought into something like this, especially since Eleanor and I already have a relationship established. I can assure you that we will try to make this an open-ended discussion, so both of you feel like you have the chance to speak fairly. I don't want you to leave here today feeling attacked, Kai. I also want to be honest and communicate with you that we have some serious matters to speak about today. With that in mind, Eleanor, why don't you start with what you hope to accomplish today."

Eleanor suppressed the nervousness that her body had become conditioned to feel and instead worked on channeling all the strong women she knew from work, her grandmother, and the ladies at Bee's. She took a breath and looked at Kai, "I want to talk about the abuse that I sustained last year. In fact, I need us to talk about it. From there I want to decide whether we can heal and move on or forgive and move on without each other."

Kai looked at first surprised, and then ashamed. Eleanor thought she may have also witnessed a quick flash of anger; she hoped it was anger at the situation, or at himself, and not anger at her that would be directed at her when they went home.

"What are you feeling right now?" Bethany asked, voice neutral and professional, well aware of the tenderness of the situation.

"Mad at myself for losing control, mad that we are having to talk about it. Mad that I ever put our relationship in jeopardy, and mad that I hurt someone who has shown me nothing but love. Embarrassed and mortified also come to mind," Kai admitted, looking defeated.

"Embarrassed that I disclosed it?" Eleanor interjected, "Or embarrassed that you ever laid a hand on me?"

"If you want complete honesty, then I would have to say both," Kai replied, turning sideways to look at her, eyes lowered. "I was raised to be a cold and private person. I am ashamed that I became exactly the person I did not want to become the second I hurt you. It has taken me going to counseling to get remotely comfortable with talking about my upbringing. It has been hard to learn how to deal with my emotions healthily. It is so far out of my comfort zone; you have no idea."

"I have an idea of what it takes to step out of your comfort zone," Eleanor replied with a hint of sarcasm before continuing, "I have been through a lot in my life. Getting not only the confidence, but also the drive to make a future for myself has taken a lot of work and dedication."

"If I may, I want to keep us on track here," Bethany interrupted. "Kai, was there something going on in your life around the time the abuse started? From what I understand from Eleanor, this all seemed to start abruptly about 8 months into the relationship, and it lasted on and off for about six months, with the last time being around ten months ago. Was something different at work? At home?"

Kai paled a little. "I can tell you exactly what I was doing when things unraveled, it is so ingrained in my mind. I was working on a horrific case. I am still bound by attorney privilege, but I will say that I had a person I was defending that was very similar to my stepdad in his words and in his actions. I helped him get off on horrific charges." Kai paused for a moment before continuing, "Growing up the way I did, I did not learn to feel or deal with my emotions. I learned how to suppress them, and during the trial, I realized I felt better when I drank. The day his charges were dismissed was the day that I last laid a hand on my fiancé in anger." Kai turned towards Eleanor again. "Part of me wishes that you had left me the first time I hurt you, so I didn't have to feel this shame and guilt every day. I don't know how to get over what I did to you."

Eleanor's heart sunk as she started to think through the cases that she'd known he was working on around the time their relationship had taken this horrible turn. After a few moments, her head took her to the Pierce case. She knew that Kai's boss had passed the case onto Kai as it wasn't typically the type of case Kai customarily accepted. Mitchell Pierce had been accused of breaking into small businesses around town around closing time, sexually assaulting women, then beating them sense-lessly and robbing them, and their place of business.

Mitchell happened to have wealthy parents who continued to take care of him, although he was in his early 50s. The per-petrator always wore a Halloween mask, gloves, and a condom, so there had not been conclusive DNA evidence. There had been two witnesses, a married couple, who had seen him in the back-parking lot of a clothing shop minutes before his last crime. Eleanor remembered Kai saying that he believed that one of his client's parents had possibly paid off some witnesses. The last victim, at the consignment clothing store, had actually succumbed to the injuries, passing away in the ICU a few days after the crime. When the two witnesses recanted, there had not been sufficient evidence to continue the trial, and it was dismissed.

Eleanor looked at Kai, in that moment she knew that she was correct. She could not remember another time when the events of the past had seemed so clear. She could see that he was obvi-ously trying to hold his emotions in, visibly upset.

Eleanor looked at him as she extended her hand towards him, "I will never think that you laying a hand on me was okay in any way, shape, or form. I can at least appreciate what you were going through and how it correlates to what you went through growing up. I realize this case could have been a trigger for you. I wish that you could've talked to me about what was going on, but I know talking hasn't always come easily to you." Eleanor let that sink in before continuing. "I also must say that I don't know how you could have prevented the outcome if his parents were paying people off and enabling him despite the appalling nature of his crimes."

A few tears slipped out of Kai's eyes despite his attempt at control. "I'm so sorry, Ellie, I hope you know that this is me, not the other person. I was so caught up in being successful in the trial that I compromised my belief because I wanted to impress the partners. I think that since I have gotten into counseling and dealt with the alcohol issues, I have felt more like myself. I am learning, I am trying. I really am trying."

Eleanor squeezed his hand. "I need you to know that I see the work that you have been doing, and I think that it has helped. I do need you to know, however, that I do not need you."

Kai looked at her somberly and said, "I know, believe me, I know."

Eleanor replied: "I do love and want you, but I have no problem leaving you if you touch me again in anger. I want us to start planning a future, and a wedding, but I will not do any of those things until we have at least a year of counseling, both separate and together. If it happens again, I am gone."

"If it happens again, I will go of my own accord," Kai said. "I refuse to be that person."

Bethany, breaking her silence, spoke, "I think we made some progress today."

23

"Where are we going?" Eleanor asked as she pulled up next to Kai on her bike at a stoplight. It had been two weeks since their counseling session, and things had been going exceptionally well. Eleanor was still approaching everything with cautious optimism. She wanted things to continue going well, but she was going to keep all the bad that had happened in the back of her mind to act on it if necessary. She'd forgiven, but she was not going to forget.

"You will see," Kai said as the crosswalk light turned green and he continued down the road. Eleanor followed him at a slight distance until he pulled up to a familiar store, Bee's Flowers.

Eleanor looked at him questioningly. She didn't know if he'd pieced together that this was the place she was picking up her fairy garden supplies. He knew that it was a new obsession as there were now succulent and air plant fairy gardens scattered throughout their apartment, but they'd never really talked about it.

"We aren't even close to a place where we are planning our wedding," Eleanor commented.

"I understand and am respecting your request," Kai said, "I'm trying to open up to you. Just wait and see; trust me." He opened the door, causing a familiar jingle, and guided her in.

Kai walked inside and gave Stacia and Rachel a nod. "Good morning ladies," he said simply, "I want to get another tulip bouquet today, please. I also wanted to introduce you to my fiancé…"

"Eleanor?" Stacia interrupted, looking confused as she glanced at the couple.

"You all know each other?" Kai asked, looking equally confused.

"She is our best fairy garden customer," Rachel interjected, "We even had her help us on our last order after she showed us pictures of the gardens she has completed."

Eleanor nodded sheepishly, "I should have skipped nursing school and had a career in fairy gardening, apparently. It would have saved me quite a bit of money on student loans."

"We just got a new shipment if you guys want to go look at the fairy garden supplies we just stocked while I grab you some new tulips from the back," Stacia said. "Rachel, will you help me in the back? I don't think I can manage without you holding the step stool." Stacia gestured towards the back. Rachel nodded and followed Stacia to the back.

"We don't even have a step stool back here," Rachel whispered as soon as they were out of earshot.

"I know," Stacia hissed, "I just can't believe that Eleanor is Kai's fiancé! He used to be such an asshat, and I can't imagine our sweet fairy-garden-loving Eleanor ever dealing with that!"

"Need I remind you, dear sister, that you can never know what goes on behind closed doors. Eleanor has always seemed pretty normal, and you have to admit that he has gotten less asshatish in the last several months. Last time he was here, he laughed three times, and he left us a $15 tip!" Rachel walked to their small cold-storage area and began pulling tulips of various colors out and arranging them in a bouquet that they would wrap in paper for Kai. A colorful tulip arrangement had been his flower of choice over the last several months. She could not remember the last time he'd gotten a dozen roses and a card.

"Well, for his sake," Stacia said, "his asshat days better be behind him because I like her a hell of a lot better than I like him. I will 86 his ass if I ever see him writing her an apology card again." Stacia replaced her sassy expression abruptly with a smile before exiting the storeroom as the sisters took the flowers out to the couple.

"Could I get a bag for these please?" Kai asked as he paid for the flowers as well as some fairy accessories that Eleanor had picked out, "We are mobile today. We rode our bikes."

"No problem," Rachel said as she gestured to a customer walking in the door, giving Stacia something to distract her. Rachel was slightly afraid that her sister would say something that neither of them could repair.

"See you soon!" Eleanor said a few moments later as they left the flower store with merchandise in tow.

"Now can you tell me where we are going?" Eleanor asked as they unlocked their bicycles from the bike rack right next to the flower shop.

"I actually need you to stay out here with the bikes and flowers for about ten minutes," Kai instructed as he went a few doors down to the closest sandwich shop. A few minutes later he came out with a paper bag.

"Okay, I can smell that, and it smells amazing," Eleanor said as her stomach growled audibly.

"I promise we just have a five-minute ride from here," Kai said, and carefully placed the brown paper bag and the flowers in the backpack he'd brought with him.

She nodded, curious as to where they were going. She followed him down city streets for a few more minutes until the cemetery came into view. They pulled in and parked their bikes on a sidewalk, out of the way of traffic. Eleanor wasn't quite sure why they were in the graveyard, but she knew there must be some sort of purpose. Kai grabbed her hand, walking determinedly towards a grouping of tombstones. He walked with a purpose as if he knew where he was going.

Eleanor looked at him confused when they reached their destination. The tombstone read: *Lanie Milburn, January 22nd,*

1994-January 25th, 2017.

As it had in the counselor's office, it clicked suddenly for Eleanor. Lanie had been the last victim of the Halloween masked predator, Mitchell Pierce. She'd just turned 23-years-old when she was assaulted and beaten to death.

She saw a vase buried into the ground, and in the vase were slightly wilted tulips of various colors. Kai bent down and removed the old flowers from the vase, unzipped his backpack and perked the fresh tulips for a few seconds before placing them into the vessel.

"I came here for the first time the day after I threw the salt-shaker at you," Kai informed her. "I was so angry that day, after the dismissal, I don't really remember driving home after the trial, and I wasn't even drunk. I am beyond sorry that I hurt you that night. I'm not sorry that it sparked something in you, which in turn sparked something in me."

Kai took a deep breath before continuing. "I stayed up that entire night and, at first, I was mad. I was mad at Bill for being such a horrible stepdad. I was mad at my mom for turning a blind eye to what he was doing to me and not stopping him. I was mad at my sisters for being treated like perfect princesses, and I was mad at them for constantly checking up on me. I was mad at my boss for passing this case onto me, and I was mad at myself for accepting. I was mad at myself for hurting you, and I was mad at you for not leaving the first time it happened, and every time after that. I was mad at Mitchell Pierce's parents for enabling him, and I was mad at Mitchell Pierce for not even trying to conceal his guilt with me in private. I was mad I let Lanie and all the other victims down."

Kai grabbed her hands and squeezed them tightly, "Let me be clear that I'm well aware that none of this is your fault. I made a promise, the day I came here, to change. It has come slowly, and not always seamlessly, but every time I doubt who I truly am inside, I come here and focus on the person I want to be. The person who will quit letting myself and others down, especially you."

Eleanor looked at Kai, emotional and fragile Kai. She'd not really seen this much vulnerability from him in the past. Without a word, she took out the tiny beach towel from Kai's backpack and patted the ground next to her. They sat on the beach towel and ate their sandwiches, content and hopeful.

24

Scarlett had taken to appreciating everything in life. Her husband joked that someone could run a red light and blatantly crash into her, and she would somehow find a way to thank them for doing it. She knew that having them all together was all that mattered from this point on.

She'd learned not to sweat the small stuff and to enjoy every second they were able to spend together. She could not remember ever having this much contentment at any other time in her life. Food tasted better, flowers smelled more potent, the sky appeared bluer.

Scarlett loved the mornings when they would wake up to find their daughter sandwiched in between the two of them, head covered in downy soft peach fuzz, only interested in cuddling with her parents.

She loved the afternoons they would spend in the garden, covered in dirt, sweat, and organic matter. Eating a leisurely lunch outside with the sun shining on their faces and sometimes napping in the outside hammock.

She loved the nighttime when they would read *Harry Potter* and *Peter Pan* books out loud, all of them taking turns reading in funny voices, reenacting scenes when the moment struck them.

She loved that they'd made some new friends and acquaintances. She loved that they had so much to laugh about and look forward to. She loved their life as it was right now and would not take it for granted.

25

"**M**ommy, Mommy, Mommy," Molly came into her room, zipping this way and that as if a Tasmanian devil were her spirit animal, "I can't find my gardening gloves. We have BeeKeepers this morning! I need to find my new gloves so I can show Stella and Marie!"

Scarlett extended her hand, holding the gloves out to Molly, "Remember we found them last night and laid them out?"

"Oh yeah, I totally forgot," Molly said as she grabbed them from her mother and ran out of her parent's bedroom to continue getting ready.

Scarlett had taken Molly into Bee's Flowers a few weeks after her release from the hospital, as soon as she was comfortable with her being in public, mask securely in place for her safety. They happened to be at the store at the same time as Rachel's husband, Chad, with their 8-year-old twins. The twins had complimented Molly's wig and inquired curiously about her mask. They'd nodded when Rachel explained that Molly had cancer, in that nonchalant way that children deal with serious things. They then asked if they could show her around the store and that sealed the friendship.

Bee's Flowers had officially been turned over to Rachel and Stacia for operation, and they'd been working on branching out the business by offering classes on a variety of things both indoor and outdoor. On Saturday mornings, they had BeeKeepers, which was a class for children about gardening. Today they were going to paint flowerpots and plant a flower of their choice to take home.

BeeKeepers was one of those activities where the adults were entertained by the efforts of the children, and sometimes the adults. Watching the children and their parents interacting together on the projects was fun and entertaining.

Last month there had been a birdhouse disaster when Rachel's husband was demonstrating how to put together a birdhouse and had somehow accidentally stabbed himself in the thigh with the bird perch. He'd thought it was just a tiny scratch until one of the children started running around in circles, screaming while pointing at Chad's leg, "Blood! Blooooooooooood!" This had caused multiple children to react, following suit by also screaming and pointing.

Chad had looked down at the red spot on his jeans that was slowly expanding before quickly wrapping duct tape around it as a tourniquet and hobbling out of the line of sight of the screaming children. Scarlett and Tevin had assisted in calming the screaming children, including the twins, as Rachel had loaded him into her car. They'd taken him to the local emergency room and gotten him patched up.

Scarlett finished getting ready and went out to the kitchen where Molly and Tevin were flipping pancakes and dancing around to Katy Perry's "Eye of the Tiger."

"Y'all are funny. I love the dance moves though! What is today's pancake combination?" Scarlett asked. Tevin and Molly loved to make pancakes in different flavor combinations and had even joked about one day having a father/daughter pancake food truck.

"Bananas and peanut butter. Not a new combination, but one of the best ones," Tevin said as he scooped a few fresh pancakes onto a plate for Scarlett.

Molly slid next to her, her tiny notebook and pen in hand, "My name is Dorothy, and I will be your waitress today. Would you like water, juice, milk or coffee? Would you like Nutella or syrup?"

"I would love coffee and syrup please," Scarlett said as Molly wrote it down on the notebook.

"Coffee and syrup coming right up," Molly responded as she whipped the top of the pad down, mimicking a busy waitress, apparently by the name of Dorothy.

Tevin smiled at Scarlett from across the room, and when she smiled back, he put the pan on the back burner and came over to give her a kiss. Molly returned with the syrup, delegating the coffee task to her father.

They ate together, and Scarlett took the task of dishwasher since her husband and daughter had cooked and waitressed. She even left two dollars on the counter for "Dorothy."

They all grabbed their gardening gloves ready to spend the morning at the shop and then possibly run errands later.

The flower shop was a bustle of activity with excited children and parents. Molly immediately spotted Stella and Marie and ran to them, new garden gloves in hand. Molly had become slightly fixated on the mermaids in *Peter Pan* recently and had bothered her parents non-stop until they purchased her not only shiny scaled mermaid gardening gloves but also a long, multicolored blue and purple wig. The twins had screamed in delight as they each tried on a glove and fingered the wig in fascination.

Scarlett and Tevin walked over to Rachel and Chad, exchanging casual greetings. "How is your leg?" Scarlett asked. Chad and Rachel looked at each other and laughed.

"I should have known, given my combat training, that any injury to the thigh is a big deal. I just didn't know how big of a deal they would make of it until we walked into the emergency room triage area," Chad said with a smirk.

Rachel continued telling the story, "They saw that the injury was to his thigh and swooped him into a wheelchair. We heard a full trauma announcement overhead, and as we were walking back, I commented on how we were fine and could wait in the lobby while they dealt with the trauma."

Chad and Rachel both started laughing. Between chortles, Chad managed to finish the story, "The nurse looked at us like we were crazy and said, 'You are the full trauma.' We thought she was joking with us until she wheeled us into a trauma bay and about thirty people came into the room. Thankfully, they quickly determined that there was no arterial bleed, and then it was just us and a few nurses and doctors. But, for a few minutes, I thought I might actually bleed out given the amount of attention I was receiving."

"It has kind of been our inside joke for the past month," Rachel said, trying to calm the laughter. In succession, she and Chad looked at each other and said, "You are the full trauma!"

Scarlett and Tevin looked at each other with smiles on their faces as the shared laughter between friends added to the organized chaos of the event. They'd never had trouble making friends as they both were friendly and relatively outgoing. It had become trickier maintaining friendships when Molly had been diagnosed, and they'd both transitioned to more at-home work to make money while still supporting the family emotionally. Some of their old friends just didn't know how to deal with Molly and cancer. They seemed to feel guilty that their own children were healthy and eventually several friendships just fizzled out.

They appreciated the Bee sisters and the fact that they'd easily let them in, treating them like old friends, not just customers. After meeting the girls' grandma, Betty, they could see it was a family trait. They appreciated the fact that Stella and Marie treated Molly just like a healthy child. They weren't sure if it was typical 8-year-old behavior, if it had to do with their upbringing, or if the fact that they'd dealt with the difficulty of having a parent deploy had helped with compassion. They knew Molly wanted nothing more than to be a normal kid and do "kid things." With the BeeKeepers, and Stella, and Marie, Tevin and Scarlett saw her doing kid things. It was beyond refreshing.

"I would have loved to see all that unfold," Scarlett said, picturing the emergency room scene in her head. "Can we sit with y'all or are you teaching today?"

"We would love to sit with you guys. Marco and Stacia are taking this one on after the literal trauma our family incurred last time," Rachel said with a snort. As if Stacia could sense her sister speaking about her, she waved from across the room, and she and Marco came over to say hello.

They exchanged more casual greetings, catching up on the last few weeks. "How has work been going?" Chad asked Marco. "Rach said you had been doing more weddings."

Marco nodded, "I have been, and I must say that I will be pretty relieved when the wedding season rush is over. I have about reached capacity when it comes to brides."

"Bridezillas you mean," Stacia interjected.

"Well yeah, I was trying to be nice. I don't want your family and friends to know how jaded we as wedding professionals are," Marco said with a smile.

"It is how we cope with the drama," Stacia informed them. "Thanks for letting us be cynical around you."

"Y'all are welcome to be sarcastic and cynical around us any old time," Scarlett said sweetly.

"You about ready to help herd these kids outside so we can get started?" Stacia asked Rachel. "Marco, you ready to snap some pictures? These kids move quickly, so you have to be ready."

Marco lifted up his camera, which was around his neck, "Ready!"

Stacia put her fingers in her mouth and whistled shrilly, causing all the parents and children to look at her. "Will all BeeKeepers and parents please make their way to the alley out back? We have set up some tables with planters and paint on them. We will paint first, and while the pots are drying, we will discuss the planting and caring of our plants."

Marco quickly started snapping pictures as there was a mad rush of children out the back door. Scarlett and Tevin hung back, letting the children exit before heading to the alley and joining Molly, Rachel, Chad, Stella, and Marie at a table. Stacia walked around assisting as needed while Marco continued taking candid pictures for the Bee's Flowers website.

Molly began painting her pot with mermaid scales, using her gardening gloves as her point of reference while Stella created an abstract pot and Marie painted hers a solid green. Once children started finishing their pots, Marco took posed pictures of them next to their piece of art.

Stella asked if she could borrow Molly's wig for the picture, which Molly agreed to immediately. She didn't seem embarrassed at the fuzzy down that covered her scalp, about ¾ inch in length. She smiled at Marie and nodded sheepishly when Marie asked if she could touch her hair. "It is just as soft as it looks!" Marie exclaimed with a giant smile, minus her missing front tooth. "I wish my hair was soft like yours."

"I wish mine was fluffy and curly like both of yours!" Molly stated. Marco picked this moment to come over for their photo, and the girls put their arms around each other's shoulders and grinned, Stella's curly hair peeking out under the mermaid wig.

The twins leaned towards each other whispering before smiling and nodding at each other. Marie walked over to her mom and whispered in her ear. Rachel then gave Tevin and Scarlett a "bear with me" grin as she then whispered into Chad's ear. Chad nodded, Rachel nodded, then Marie and Stella nodded again before asking, almost in unison, "Can Molly come over and spend the night?"

Tevin smiled and held up one finger, "That is an amazing offer. Am I allowed to have a private conference with my lovely ladies one at a time?"

"By all means," Chad responded as Rachel, and their girls nodded in agreement.

Tevin and Scarlett walked over to a quiet area of the alleyway. "Thoughts?" Tevin asked.

"Conflicted," Scarlett admitted. "Obviously we have gotten to know each other fairly well over the last ten plus months, so it's not that I don't feel comfortable with her being looked after by Rachel and Chad. It is just…"

"The big C," Tevin said knowingly.

"Isn't it always?" Scarlett asked as she looked down sadly. Tevin walked over to her and lifted her chin, so they were looking into each other's eyes. Scarlett continued, "I know she has been doing well, but we both know that can change in an instant. What if something happened tonight and we weren't with her? I don't know if I could ever forgive myself."

"I know how you feel honey, believe me," Tevin said. "I'm scared all the time, too. I know that there's a chance our daughter will be buried before either of us and that eats me alive every day. Do you think it's fair for us to keep her by our side, never getting to pursue friends and friendships outside of our vision?"

Scarlett shook her head reluctantly before Tevin continued, "Why don't we ask Molly what she wants and what she's comfortable with? If she wants to go, great, If not, great. Her going over there and not spending the night is also an obvious alternative."

Scarlett again nodded in agreement with her husband. He started walking back to their table before turning back and whispering in his wife's ear, "There's a lot we could do together without a child in the house if you catch my drift." Scarlett blushed slightly as her body tingled with anticipation. She could not recall having an empty house, in years.

Molly came over to join them, wig askew from being hastily placed back on her head, "Can I spend the night, please please please please…?"

Scarlett cut her off before she could fit in another please. "Your dad and I discussed it and wanted to know what your thoughts are. It is obvious to us both that you'd like to go, but will you be okay staying somewhere that isn't our house for a night?"

"Mom," Molly said primly, "must I remind you that I've also spent a lot of nights away from home and was just fine? There were a lot of kids also spending the night at the hospital, so it's almost like I'm super familiar with sleepovers."

Scarlett glanced at her husband who was sucking his lips in attempting not to smile or laugh. He composed himself and shrugged, "She kind of has a point."

"Okay," Scarlett said in defeat, "I'll talk to Chad and Rachel about the details. If there's ever a point in time that you aren't feeling well and want to come home, it's okay for you to let them, or us, know. Do you remember the code word if you feel like you want to come home, but don't feel comfortable telling them?"

"Justin's Pizzeria," Molly said immediately, "Codeword is Justin's Pizzeria."

"Correct," said Scarlett, "If you don't feel well or don't feel comfortable telling the girls or their parents that you want to come home, you can call me and ask to go to Justin's Pizzeria for dinner tomorrow. Deal?"

"Deal," Molly held her hand out to seal the deal. She squeezed Scarlett's hand three times before she let it go.

"I love you too, bug," Scarlett said planting a kiss on her daughter's mermaid hair before grabbing her hand on one side and her husband's hand on the other. Hand-in-hand they walked back to the table to discuss the plans for the night.

26

Scarlett had only felt slightly neurotic as they had dropped Molly off for the sleepover. She could not count the number of times, "I trust y'all but..." came out of her mouth. Chad and Rachel had been so kind and patient, letting her speak about her concerns without judgment. Rachel had hugged her tightly before she left and assured her that she would call if there were any concerns. Rachel said she would also assist Molly in calling Scarlett before they went to bed.

Molly had been over-the-moon with excitement. They'd attempted to let her pack herself for the overnight visit, but she'd come out with a backpack overflowing with stuffed animals, her entire wig collection, and 3 boxes of Legos. They'd compromised and let her pick one of each to take with her. On their way to Chad and Rachel's house, they'd stopped at the store to get her a sleeping bag. Of course, she'd picked one that resembled a mermaid tail.

Molly, usually quite the talker, talked even more than usual on the way there. On the ride from the store to the Bee-Harper's house, Scarlett was afraid that not even a seatbelt could keep Molly in her booster seat, having to remind her more than a few times that excitement was okay but that safety trumped enthusiasm every time.

Tevin and Scarlett had pulled away from the Bee-Harper house and made it one whole block before pulling over. They'd looked at each other with their own nervous energy and excitement. The air was full of sadness at leaving their daughter for a night, nervousness at a night alone, and sexual tension at the thought of a night to themselves sans Molly.

"Is it strange that I want to laugh, and cry, and make out with you all at the same time?" Scarlett asked, turning to look at her husband.

"I feel the same way, babe," Tevin said, turning towards her and putting his arm behind the car's headrest. "I feel like we are ditching school or something equally taboo. You know that nervous energy that it caused? I always felt excited but bad at the same time."

"I wouldn't know how that feels because I was nothing but sweet and innocent in high school," Scarlett replied with a serene smile.

"Liar!" Tevin exclaimed in return. "At your ten-year reunion last summer, they told me your nickname was Sassy Scarlett The Harlot! You were not only a troublemaker, but I'm also pretty certain that I heard you were the ringleader!"

"Well, that was a different life, my dear! I'm now a very responsible mother and contributing member of society," Scarlett argued with an innocent grin.

"Yeah you are," Tevin said huskily as he leaned forward and gave her a passionate kiss. "What do you say we get out of here, go home, get snazzed up, and go on that date we have been talking about before someone around here calls the cops on us for steaming up the windows?"

Scarlett was looking forward to a romantic night with her husband. It was all she could think about as she slipped on a casual, yet sexy sundress and a pair of flats. They'd been intimate more often since Molly got home, but it was always hurried and cautious. They were never sure if she would become ill and need assistance, or want to cuddle and crawl into bed with them. She was trying to focus on the potential of the night and not how

Molly was doing. She had to remind herself that Molly deserved some alone time without her hovering, but she'd already had to refrain from calling Rachel, and it had only been an hour.

She was just accentuating her lips with some bold red lipstick when Tevin came up behind her and slipped an arm around her waist from behind. "Damn, Miss Scarlett The Harlot, you are beyond sexy this evening," Tevin said into her ear before bending forward and planting a kiss on her neck. "You ready to be a delinquent with me tonight?"

Scarlett, tingling all over, swatted him away from her neck. "You aren't looking too shabby yourself, handsome pants." She turned around and gave him a passionate kiss, wiping away the red lipstick off of his lips when she was done. She could see that he was tempted to take advantage of her right then and there on the counter in the bathroom, but she teasingly sauntered out of the room, purposely swaying her hips, hoping to prolong the anticipation of the night.

They'd decided not to drink anything alcoholic on the off chance that they would need to pick Molly up from the sleepover, but they chose to still walk to the restaurant so they could enjoy the warmth of the Colorado evening. They started towards the restaurant, her arm tucked into the crook of his elbow, "This is so nice."

"I agree," Tevin said in return. "I obviously never expected cancer to become a part of our lives. I love that we have been able to be so available to Molly, but all of this has definitely taken away from us being available to each other. I miss my wife." He stopped suddenly and swung her in front of him, enveloping her in a full body hug.

Scarlett hugged him in return, taking in his scent and the shape of his body. "I've missed you too." They broke apart when a vehicle full of teenagers drove by them and shouted, "Get a room!"

"We will! We're adults and have worked hard for that right..." Tevin yelled back jokingly as they drove away before kissing his wife again. They laughed as they broke apart and continued on to the restaurant.

They enjoyed their meal, simply taking their time. They talked about grown-up things, and though Molly was always in the back of their minds, they tried to focus on each other and how, despite two years of hell, they were still incredibly in love with each other. They ordered dessert, bananas foster, to split as well as fancy dessert espresso. They left stuffed, feeling more connected as a couple than they had in a long time.

They walked home, hand-in-hand, again enjoying the freedom of taking their time and not needing to rush anywhere. "So, what are your thoughts on staying in Colorado versus moving back home?" Scarlett asked as they walked.

"Well, if you had asked me a year ago, I would have said home was in Louisiana," Tevin answered honestly. "But now that we know some more people, and Molly has some friends outside of the hospital, I think Colorado is seeming more and more like home. Even though we have only been here two years, the house is finally up to your standards. I would hate to have to sell and move somewhere and start all over."

"I know that the original intent was to stay here as long as we needed to access Children's." Scarlett said. "We still have some follow-up appointments we need to think about before we make a decision. I say that we stay here for now and not make any rash decisions either way. Maybe if all works out, we could try to transfer schools so Molly and the twins could all attend the same school."

"I agree," Tevin said, "I really like how they all interact together, and I obviously also enjoy their parents."

Tevin and Scarlett had decided to move to Colorado pretty quickly after Molly's diagnosis. The amount of time and money required to go back and forth from Louisiana to Colorado had become overwhelming. They'd purchased their ranch-style house at the perfect time, and had gotten it at a great price, right before the real estate in Colorado became less affordable.

Molly had initially been enrolled in school but had to be in and out so much that they'd eventually pulled her out and enrolled her in private tutoring. Tutoring had gone okay and had served its purpose, but now that she was doing fairly well, they knew she was wishing for school experiences and friends. It wasn't easy being "the sick kid," and Molly didn't tend to deal well with overwhelming sympathy.

"Let's keep all of it in mind," Scarlett said, squeezing Tevin's hand in hers. "Let's enjoy as little stress as possible in the last ten minutes home." They continued holding hands, enjoying the beautiful night before arriving home.

"So…. sex?" Tevin said, a look of excited horror on his face as soon as they got in the front door.

"I can tell by the look on your face that you are just as full as I am," Scarlett said with a giggle. "How about we recover for a while while we call Rachel and Chad and find out how Molly is doing. Then we could sit outside and actually use our fire pit."

"Oh, thank God," Tevin said, "I'm SO full. I didn't know if you would be super tired by our usual whopping 9:30. I promise that is the only reason I just tried to schedule sex with you."

Scarlett answered shyly, unsure of why she still felt like this after eleven years of marriage, "I want to make tonight last as long as we can."

Tevin smiled at her, grinning ear-to-ear, "I'll see what I can do about that." He pulled out his cell phone and dialed Chad's number, placing the phone on speaker.

"Good job guys! You totally got me out of dishwashing duty for the next week!" Chad said excitedly when he answered the phone.

"Chad!" They heard Rachel exclaim in the background.

"I wasn't supposed to tell you, but we made a bet on how long it would take you to call."

Rachel quickly rushed over to the phone and interjected, "Not because we think it is weird to call at any point in time, I just knew that mom instinct on the first sleepover kicks in within the first hour."

Tevin and Scarlett looked at each other over the phone, amusement on their faces. "I wanted to call in the first hour if that counts for anything," Scarlett admitted.

On the other end of the line, they heard Rachel reply, "I told you so!"

They'd talked for a few minutes, Chad giving them the details of the *Peter Pan* play the girls had put on in dress-up clothes and the plan they'd foiled when the girls discussed staying up until 4 am. Rachel had put Molly on the phone, and Molly had told them excitedly how much fun she was having and how she would NOT like to eat at Justin's Pizzeria for dinner the next night. Tevin and Scarlett hung up the phone relieved and happy for Molly.

Scarlett made them iced tea while Tevin lit their porch fire pit. He brought out their speaker and put on some Bon Iver. They laughed and talked, enjoying the warmth from the fire pit and the August night. Around 10 p.m. Tevin dimmed the lights outside, so they only had the glare of the fire for light. He turned the music down, so it was now more of a dull background noise.

"May I have this starlight dance?" Tevin said, slightly fumbling towards her, eyes not having yet adjusted to the darkness.

"Well of course," Scarlett said, "just don't fall! We don't want a full trauma experience of our own."

She stood up and allowed him to guide her in a slow circle. After a few minutes of swaying, she became aware that he was humming what sounded like "A Whole New World" from Disney's *Aladdin* soundtrack. "You are not humming what I think you are humming, are you?" Scarlett asked stopping the dance for a moment.

"I hold this song responsible for us falling in love," Tevin replied. "Of course I'm humming it."

Scarlett chuckled, remembering the slightly intoxicated karaoke night at a bar in New Orleans where she'd drunk too many Long Island ice teas after getting into the bar with a fake ID. Her friends had dared her to ask a man at the bar to sing a duet. She'd selected Tevin as her partner and "A Whole New World" as their karaoke song. They were blown out of the water when Tevin started belting the song with a better voice than the original singer. He'd been hers ever since.

"That was definitely a Scarlett The Harlot night. Wow, thinking back I was kind of a rebel. Please don't ever tell Molly how bad I was as a youth," Scarlett said as she grabbed Tevin by the hand and led him to the hammock stand that was currently located near the garden, "I want to look at the stars and cuddle with you."

"You actually read my mind. Why don't you settle in, and I'll grab a blanket from inside in case it gets cold out?" Tevin first made sure Scarlett was successful in getting in the hammock with only the light from the stars and moon to guide her.

He returned a few minutes later with a few scented candles that were located throughout the house and a soft chenille throw from their couch. He lit the candles, and the faint hue from them added to the glow from the constellations. At first, they lay side-by-side holding hands, enjoying the peace and contentment of a moment of solitude together.

Eventually, Tevin released her hand, carefully turning on his side, propping himself up on one elbow. He started to slowly kiss her, his fingers tracing patterns on her arms before eventually pulling the straps of her sundress down one-by-one. She gasped as the cold air hit her bare skin. His hands slowly and gently expanded their pattern to include her breasts, and then her navel, and then below her panty line.

She gasped softly again and again as his hands continued to wander up and down her body, leaving a trail of goosebumps and want in their wake. He continued to kiss her gently, their lips never apart for more than a few seconds for them to catch their breath, "You are torturing me," she whispered.

"I'm trying to," he whispered in return. "Do you want to lay down somewhere more solid, so we don't fall out of the hammock?"

They scrambled out of the hammock, desire increasing with each moment they were not touching each other. Tevin laid the blanket on the grass next to the garden and, with the scent of the summer flowers adding to their desire, slowly peeled off

Corlet Dawn

Scarlett's sundress and panties before removing his clothing as well. They kissed and explored for what felt like hours before they could not stay apart any longer and their bodies fused together. They started slowly and carefully until it became too much, and they'd become almost frenzied in their need and desire. Scarlett had to shove her mouth over his to avoid screaming out and waking the neighbors when she climaxed.

After, they'd laid there, entwined together, tracing patterns again on each other's naked, sweaty skin.

"Imagine how the HOA notice is going to read on our door tomorrow," Tevin joked as he planted a soft kiss on her temple.

"Whatever, they would be so lucky as to have witnessed that," Scarlett joked with him in return. "That was hot! Hot enough to kill poor Hank that lives behind us if he happened to be stargazing tonight. I'm pretty sure he is 105-years-old."

They joked like that, cajoling quietly back and forth until the mosquitos drove them inside into their bed where they slept naked, in each other's arms, until the sun rose.

150

27

Stacia was unequivocally in love. She'd tried to avoid it at all costs, but it was unavoidable with Marco. He was kind, he was funny, he listened, he was handsome, and he loved her for her.

She could see why other cultures had so many words for love. "Love" in its definition seemed like such a black and white concept; you either loved something, or you didn't love something. In reality, love was black and white and all of the shades between. The way she felt love towards Marco was continually changing, and she was thrilled that it could be so multifaceted.

She felt like Marco had become her best friend in addition to being her boyfriend. She could not remember feeling this way with Luke, although she didn't doubt that they'd loved each other in some capacity. In hindsight, she felt her feelings of love had been more childlike, a friend love. Their relationship had been very black and white; either in-love or out of love. She felt that every time she didn't live up to his expectations of her, he'd been "falling out of love" with her, and when she pleased him, he "loved her so much."

Now she knew what love was supposed to feel like. She belonged with Marco, but it was in a whole-person way instead of half of a whole. They were two people who fit together. Instead of a puzzle with missing pieces that needed to be filled, they were two complete puzzles that complimented each other when placed side-by-side.

She felt like she could still be herself around Marco and he could be himself around her, which is what she'd hoped for. There wasn't a single interaction that they had where they didn't laugh, smile, appreciate, and enjoy each other. If they had conflict, they talked through it, figured it out, and moved on. They'd figured out how to be in love without the constant, unhealthy, negotiation that had occurred in her previous relationship with Luke.

She knew what she wanted for the future and, though it scared her, she was excited.

28

"If I look over the side again, I may just throw up in your car," Marco said weakly as he once again placed his hands over his eyes.

"Do you need some air?" Stacia asked, briefly taking one hand off of the steering wheel to place a comforting hand on his leg.

"Are both of your hands on the steering wheel?" Marco asked, the panic apparent in his voice, raising it by an entire octave.

"Doesn't Guatemala have mountains? Haven't you also lived here half of your life?" Stacia asked, quickly removing her hand before more panic ensued.

"Yes, there are mountains in Guatemala, but they do not have crazy paved roads like this with no guardrail and two lanes. No, I've never been up here as I prefer to drive around mountains, not over them. Plus, I've never driven with someone passing people on the top of said two-lane road on top of a crazy high mountain before. I'm pretty sure my life has flashed before my eyes more than once in the last twenty minutes," Marco answered as he braved a hand down, opening a window and shoving his face as close to the breeze as he could. His eyes, however, remained clamped shut.

"I assure you," Stacia began before Marco interrupted her.

"I know, I know babe. You and Rachel grew up being driven up here as children and were highly encouraged by your parents to drive it yourselves as soon as you got your learner's permit. That does not make me and my need to be closer to the ground any better. Nor does it make me less afraid of hurtling full speed off the mountain," He leaned his head against the window as Stacia put her blinker on and turned into the Alpine Visitor Center.

"You are missing the beautiful view, plus, I'm only going twenty miles per hour," Stacia said quietly under her breath, "and they kind of forced us to drive it, but whatever."

Marco groaned softly. She had to make a few loops through the parking lot as it was quite full of tourists stopping to hike, use the restroom, or grab a bite to eat. She eventually parked and placed a hand on Marco's leg again, "I'm fully stopped and now able to comfort you. Do you need a hug?"

Stacia saw a smile appear that lit up the half of his face that wasn't covered with his hands, "Of course I need a hug... and probably a kiss... and probably a.."

"A kiss is as far as your girlfriend is going to go on the top of Trail Ridge Road," Stacia said with a chuckle as she leaned from the driver's side to the passenger side in an attempt to pry Marco's hands from his still closed eyes. After she was success-ful, she gave him a sideways hug and planted a quick kiss on his cheek.

"What, I don't even get a kiss on the lips?" Marco asked weakly as he slowly opened one eye, and then once gaging his safety, the other eye.

"That solely depends on how likely you are to throw up on me, as you slightly resemble a sweaty ghost at the moment," Stacia said, shrugging her shoulders after he gave her a weak at-tempt at his "Really?" look.

"What do you say we take a quick break and give your body some time to adjust? Want to run indoors and get a coffee for me? A Sprite for you?" Stacia asked as she unbuckled her seat-belt.

"I will agree to anything as long as it does not involve the edge of a mountain cliff." Marco unbuckled his seatbelt but waited until Stacia reluctantly nodded before getting out of the car.

They'd decided to go on a quick getaway to celebrate their ten months of dating. Bee's Flowers had been extremely busy since she and Rachel had taken over. Rachel and Stacia were still able to run the store between the two of them, but they'd been throwing around the idea of a part-time fill-in person so they could both take a little more time off.

Their workshops had become so popular that they were using the overhead money from the classes to turn a section of their storage and floral workshop area into a dual-function space. When they'd booked the renovations for a weekend, both sisters had jumped on the rare chance at a getaway.

Stacia had covered a few extra days solo so Rachel and Chad could surprise the girls with a quick trip to Florida. Stacia and Marco had decided to go on a trip to Estes Park for a night before taking Trail Ridge Road over to Grand Lake for a few days stay at her parent's cabin.

Greg and Cheryl had loved to use Cheryl's parents' cabin in Grand Lake, while the girls were growing up, and the girls had spent a lot of their childhood up there. When her grandparents had passed away, each from cancer, six months apart, they'd left the cabin to Cheryl and Greg, knowing how important it was to them, and to the girls. After her parents moved to Florida, they'd hired a property management company to manage it as an Airbnb.

They'd spent the previous night in Estes Park, Stacia had re-served a beautiful cabin that was adjacent to a river. They'd arrived in Estes early afternoon and had done a short hike to Bear Lake in nearby Rocky Mountain National Park before showering and getting ready for a night on the town. Marco had taken his camera and gotten what he hoped were some beautiful scenery shots. He'd managed to capture both bighorn sheep and elk thus far, both from the safety of the vehicle. He was still getting quite a lot of business from his online store and was looking forward to plumping up the mountain section this weekend.

Marco had reserved spots on the ghost tour at the Stanley

Hotel, which surprised Stacia as he didn't like scary things, but she was excited to go. They'd both decided that it was haunted when on the second floor their hands, which were clasped together, obtained such a massive static shock that they had to let go. They'd decided then and there that they would never spend a night there, and in Stacia's words, "piss the ghosts off further."

They'd picked up a few groceries in town and asked the checker where they should go for a drink later. They were referred to The Barrel, the local craft-beer bar. They'd decided to walk there as they were unsure of the ride-sharing situation in the little mountain town and wanted to be able to enjoy a few beverages on their mini vacation.

The minute they'd gotten there, Marco's eyes had lit up, obviously in craft-beer heaven. They'd sat outside and enjoyed the crisp mountain air while sampling tiny tasters of beer. Stacia had loved how quaint and cozy it was, hoping to take some seating and lighting design ideas back with her to Bee's new classroom area. They'd played corn hole, petted some friendly dogs, ordered dinner from a taco truck, and chatted with some more locals before taking in some live music and dancing in the indoor beer hall until the night wound down and they decided to brave the chilly night air and head back to the Estes Park cabin.

They'd walked back in pitch black, stars popping out in full force without the light pollution from the big city, scaring each other with stories of ghosts and animal attacks until they both had to use the flashlights on their phones to calm their feelings of imminent doom.

After they arrived harm-free back at the cabin, they'd changed into their swimsuits and took in the scenery, sitting outside in the hot tub while gazing at the stars and the moon. They'd laughed so loudly that a nearby neighbor had shushed them through an open window which had caused them to laugh louder. Hands clasped tightly over their mouths, they'd run inside, slightly wet. It was so slippery on the kitchen tile that they'd both almost fallen. Marco had resorted to clutching onto the kitchen counter for dear life as his legs slid back and forth on the slippery floor. At the sight of this, Stacia had laughed harder, and harder to the point where she had to run to the bathroom, one hand still on her mouth and another on her crotch as she was slip-sliding down the hallway, attempting to not pee on the floor en route.

They'd showered off and crawled into the wooden framed bed with a moose quilt on it and started kissing, enjoying the feeling of each other's bodies until eventually they shed their clothing and had uninhibited drunken sex.

Stacia could not help but remember the first time they'd been intimate. They'd been dating each other for about three months and, though they'd participated in their fair share of intimate encounters, they'd started to make a joke of it, each trying to tease each other to see who would cave first.

On New Year's Eve, Marco had gotten them reservations at a champagne countdown. It had been very posh, and they'd both felt a little out of their element, but also excited at the chance to get fancy together. Stacia had looked stunning in a floor-length backless black gown and Marco had looked like a model in his gray suit that accentuated his eyes. They'd eaten fancy tapas and sipped champagne, mingled, and danced together until the countdown.

After the strike of midnight, they'd walked down to their hotel room, and Stacia had gasped in surprise the minute the hotel door had opened. Inside the door was a trail of flower petals of various shapes, sizes, colors, and scents. The path lead to the bed where there were so many petals the comforter resembled a kaleidoscope.

"How did you manage this?" Stacia had asked breathlessly, astonished by the beauty of all of the petals.

"Remember when I said I had some indigestion from all the fancy food and asked if I could run to the room to get an antacid?" Marco came up behind her and had slipped his arm loosely around her neck, kissing the top of her head.

"How did you get all of these different flower petals?" Stacia asked, amazed. She'd heard of a trail of flowers being done with your run-of-the-mill-roses, but never with a variety of flowers like this.

Marco's dimples had lit up as he smiled, "I almost don't want to tell you as it probably won't seem quite as romantic if I say it out loud."

Stacia had looked at him with adoration, "This is so sweet that short of you telling me you robbed my flower shop, I will be impressed."

Marco again, flashed a sheepish smile, "I put a tarp down in my delivery truck for the past week and captured as many petals as I could and then stored them in my refrigerator so they would still be fresh-ish. By the end there, I felt like some of my food was starting to taste like a floral dryer sheet smells."

Stacia had flung herself into his arms, "That is so incredibly sweet! I love it!"

"Well, I love you," Marco had said, pulling her back slightly so he could look directly into her eyes. "I've felt that way for a while, but I wanted to be confident when I said it to you."

Stacia had looked into his blue eyes and felt the butterflies in her stomach so forcefully that she almost felt nauseous with nerves. She knew that she loved him too, but it was hard to say it and risk the hurt the future would hold if she lost him.

She'd gotten better about not blushing non-stop in his presence, better at not having as many clumsy moments and better at not letting the "what-ifs"" freak her out. When she thought about all of the positive things Marco had shown her so far, she'd known that she had two options: to ignore what he'd just admitted or share her true feelings with him. She was so content in his arms, content with his company, content with him.

"I love you too," she said in return, with the same confidence. She couldn't remember ever feeling this sure of herself when she said the same to Luke.

They'd slowly and sensually removed their fancy clothing and laid in the flower petals, consummating their relationship for the first time on the bed, and a second time in the giant jetted tub, as they washed the flower petals off, and a third time back on the bed. Again, letting the flower petals surround them, making a beautiful memory of the night. That New Year's Eve they'd made a mutual agreement that all bets were off, they'd both caved at just the right time.

"Oh. My. Goodness!" Marco exclaimed as they pulled into Stacia's parent's driveway. "Is that a moose?" He quickly turned around and started rummaging in his backpack fumbling around for his camera. He was just about to open the car door and hop out before Stacia placed a hand in front of him to halt his hasty retreat.

"You do know that a moose can kill right?" Stacia asked, holding Marco in place.

"You are kidding, right? Who would be scared of a moose? You are too funny," Marco made a move to exit the car again.

"I'm actually being serious for once. Look at how big that thing is! Do you think your impressive body could withstand a ton of trampling with hoof and antler involvement? Those things are big and can be super mean! It may not gnaw you to death like a mountain lion, but I can assure you that you would be much less handsome, and depending on the damage, there would be a potential for me to have to change your diapers. I would do it without complaint because I love you, but I would prefer to avoid that if possible," Stacia said as she took her hand away and Marco leaned back in his seat.

"You would change my diapers," Marco said with a smile.

Stacia nodded, "Hell yes I would." She smiled back at him as they patiently waited for the moose to exit her parents' yard before sprinting to the porch, Marco with camera in-hand, finger on the shutter, ready to snap a picture of the big creature. Once Marco had successfully snapped about fifty photos of the moose tromping through the trees and brush, they entered the cabin.

Greg and Cheryl's quaint A-frame was located just out of Grand Lake. It had most of its original furnishings and, though not super fancy, it was a perfect little getaway home. In all the time she'd dated Luke, he'd only gone to the cabin two or three times. His getaways revolved around his soccer schedule. He'd never grasped how vital the cabin was to Stacia.

After the moose vacated, Marco and Stacia went inside and put their groceries away before unpacking their belongings. They then sat on the porch swing for hours, talking, sipping beer, breathing in the fresh air, and watching the hummingbirds come and go from the hummingbird feeder. They'd eventually grown tired and went inside for a nap, leaving only the screen door open so they could smell the fresh mountain air and feel the breeze from the master bedroom.

They awoke lazily and slowly after a few hours and decided to head to Grand Lake's downtown. Stacia warned him that it was a simple strip of shops that took up only a few blocks. They went into the quaint shops, and each purchased a cheesy tourist shirt for each other, which they placed over the shirts they were currently wearing. They got an ice cream cone from the little food stand across from the lake, also named Grand Lake and dipped their feet in the ice-cold water.

That night they worked on a puzzle together in front of the fire before falling asleep in each other's arms on the couch, too cozy to walk the twenty steps to the bedroom. They'd not woken up until the sunlight streaming in the giant picture window at the front of the cabin had been too bright to ignore any further.

"Want to hike again today?" Stacia asked as they cleaned up breakfast.

"Yesterday when we hiked in Estes, I didn't know about all of the danger lurking around. I will hike, but I need to do some research first," Marco said as Stacia gaped at him in amusement.

Marco proceeded to look up how to handle each animal encounter so he would not be confused and would know the correct reaction. He wrote down: mountain lion, bear, moose, elk, and deer. He attempted to write down chipmunk until Stacia had shut that one down, assuring him that a chipmunk attack wasn't likely.

"Have you ever heard of rabies?" Marco asked in reply.

"You are more than welcome to write what to do if a zombie-like, mouth-frothing chipmunk approaches you if you want, but I'm pretty sure if you get rabies you die, so there is that......" Stacia trailed off as Marco glanced at her in horror.

On their hike, he initially insisted that they needed to be as silent as possible, which Stacia knew was the exact opposite of what they should do. Stacia decided to sing as loudly as she could, almost causing a panic out of Marco until she made him pull his reference paper out of his pocket. Marco became a chatterbox after that, pointing out different landmarks and stopping intermittently to take pictures.

They walked to the river where they both stripped off their hiking boots and socks and rolled up their pant legs. "Careful Marco, you don't want to encounter a ravenous mountain piranha," Stacia said as they tentatively walked from slippery rock to slippery rock.

She was so busy watching for his reaction that she didn't notice that the depth increased a little, and she plunged part way in, soaking her pants and part of her shirt.

Marco laughed at her, "Serves you right! There are no piranhas though, right?"

In retaliation, she splashed some water in his direction. The sudden movement made her lose her balance, causing her to topple completely in. She stood up, shocked by the briskness of the cold glacial water and again heard Marco's laughter. She sputtered a few expletives before tentatively walking towards shore, laughing under her breath at her clumsiness.

They lay in the sun, letting her clothes dry after eating a picnic of protein bars and trail mix. They talked about everything and nothing, enjoying both superficial talks as well as in-depth conversations. That night, after roasting hot dogs and s'mores on the fire, they sat on the porch again and watched the stars. At that moment, everything felt right with the world.

29

R achel felt at peace. She no longer rolled over in bed to a cold sheet. Instead, when she awoke in the night seeking comfort, she rolled over to a warm body who could interact with her

She was ecstatic to be able to look at him and know that he was okay physically. She would sometimes call him during the day just to hear his voice. She felt at peace knowing he was always within reach.

She loved the mornings when her daughters would wake them up by jumping on the bed or pulling the covers off of their sleeping parents, running with the comforter as fast as they could. The girls would run, laughing the whole time, as she and Chad chased them through the house.

She could not remember the last time she'd felt so whole; her family was back together and stronger than ever. The transition had not been entirely smooth, but they'd all been able to work together to deal with the adjustments that occurred when a family member left, and then returned.

She'd noticed a change in herself as well as the girls, where they used to just function, they now seemed to all be thriving. The girls were doing better in school and arguing less with each other. She was happier at home, at work, and in general.

She was happy to come home to her husband every day. She loved being able to hug him hello and kiss him goodbye and hold his hand while they were watching television. She loved having some romance in her life and the ability to date her husband. She loved the feel of his hands on her body, every touch and every caress remarkable.

She no longer had a death grip on her cell phone, never knowing when he could call. Instead, she made a point of leaving it at home when they were all together so she could focus on being together without outside distractions.

She'd replaced fear and hope with contentment and a sense that all would be okay and work out for the best. She knew that any obstacle placed in front of them could be conquered together.

She had her family back, and she could not be any happier.

30

"**G**randma, watch this!" Stella yelled as she catapulted herself off of the diving board in an attempt at a graceful swan dive. Instead, she succeeded in a belly flop with a splash so loud it caused all of the adults to automatically grimace. Stella surfaced and instantly let out a squeal that was part pain-induced and part laughter.

"Well, I give it a 10 out of 10 on the belly flop scale!" Cheryl shouted in her direction as all of the grown-ups watched to make sure the squealing diver got to the edge of the pool without any problems. Stella somehow managed to get to the edge of the swimming pool without swallowing a ton of water. She waited for a moment before hauling herself out of the pool.

"Look at my stomach, mom," Stella said as she lifted a corner of her tankini, displaying a tomato-red abdomen.

"That makes my stomach hurt," said Greg as he swooped her into a towel, giving her a comforting hug.

"Thanks, Papa," Stella said, snuggling next to him on the lounge chair.

Greg and Cheryl had been unable to accommodate them as they currently lived in a condo and there would not have been quite enough space for all of them to comfortably relax. The daughter of one of Greg and Cheryl's friends happened to have a rental property that was close to their home, with a screened-in pool inside. They'd spent a good bulk of their mornings and evenings there, all watching the girls swim and enjoying the Florida heat.

In fact, spending time at the house with a pool in the backyard had been the girls' favorite activity. They had even asked to go back there and swim after a fairly hot day at Disney World. The girls had enjoyed getting matching rose-gold Minnie Mouse ears with their names embroidered, and had enjoyed the rides, but had appeared to notice their dad's anxiety with the crowds. They had asked to go home and swim, blaming the long lines and the heat, but Rachel and Chad both knew that their girls were doing it for their father's sake.

Chad had been understandably jumpy since returning from deployment. He hadn't been in combat situations this time but was used to the potential for danger to appear at any moment, at any place. He'd done a good job of covering up the bulk of his anxiousness with the girls, turning to Rachel and a counselor to deal with it, but the girls were quite intuitive. When it had all come to light, the twins had been understanding of it all.

They'd done a few family-counseling sessions when Chad first returned, and it had helped them all deal with their feelings. Independently, Chad had gone through EMDR, Eye Movement Desensitization and Reprocessing, with the help of his psychologist. He felt this had been instrumental in helping his fight-or-flight response and equipped him with better management of his anxiety.

The hardest part of the increased fight-or-flight response was that he never quite knew when he would experience it, but crowds and loud noises made it worse. Had they not gotten this chance to have five days off together, they would have probably waited a few years before going to a place jammed with thousands of sweaty, loud people.

Tomorrow they were going to attempt Universal Studios. Rachel and Chad had decided on the code word "burrito" to use in the event that all of Chad's anxiety-deducting techniques were less effective and he needed to leave. They'd gotten fast passes in the hopes that maybe less line time would also be helpful.

"Papa, watch this!" Marie shouted, in an attempt to one-up her sister. She too succeeded in a fabulous belly flop. Rachel and Chad looked at Greg and Cheryl and winced as the second wounded diver now surfaced and started screaming.

"10 out of 10 in the belly flop round, which is now over," Greg said. "Any more belly flops will result in disqualification from finals tomorrow." Rachel nodded thanks to her father, envisioning some sort of freak belly-flop injury resulting in them having an astronomically high emergency room bill.

"Maybe we should take a break for some lunch?" Rachel had asked, hoping to give the girls a bit of a break from the sun and the "diving." They'd both already soaked in so much and become so dark despite the sunscreen that their skin tone was closer to Chad's coffee color at the moment. The Florida humidity made their hair curlier, fuller, and even more beautiful. Rachel could not even begin to imagine how beautiful they were going to grow up to be.

Rachel had been so excited for the chance to get away before the girls started school in a few weeks. They were actually quite excited to start this year since Molly was going to be attending and they were all going to be in the same class. Scarlett and Rachel had requested that they ignore the typical twin rule by allowing them to all be in the same class together so Molly could have as much support as possible.

Rachel and Chad, wearing swimsuits and sunglasses, laid in lounge chairs while the girls laid on the shade of the porch. They relaxed, warm, and content until Greg and Cheryl came out with a platter of sandwiches and fresh fruit. They all ate on their lounge chairs, relaxing and enjoying each other's company and the fact that they could relax without guilt for once.

After lunch they lazed in the sun, jumping in and out of the pool until dinner time, when Chad and Greg fired up the grill and cooked chicken and bratwursts to accompany the salad Rachel put together. The girls then assisted their grandmother in making cookies for dessert. They all watched a movie together, though the girls were out in thirty minutes, exhausted from a day of swimming. Greg and Cheryl went home with plans to meet again the next day after Universal Studios.

The next morning Rachel and Chad were woken up by two excited girls. They brought in a bowl of cereal for each of their parents, balancing the cereal and milk filled bowls precariously in their arms along with some juice and napkins, "We brought you breakfast in bed." They beamed with pleasure at themselves for thinking of this on their own. They'd both dressed and gotten their hair combed on their own and were ready to go.

The walk up to the entrance to Universal was riddled with excitement. Similar to Disney World, there were so many options on what to do and where to go. The girls had been fascinated with the dinosaur unit they had in school last year and jumped on the chance to go on the *Jurassic Park* ride. They all screamed and laughed and held onto each other when the dinosaurs popped out.

They were most excited about the chance to visit *The Wizarding World of Harry Potter* and each girl purchased their own special wand. They sampled butterbeer, which was delicious, and Rachel managed to convince Stella to go on a rollercoaster. Marie firmly declined.

Stella and Marie by far loved the virtual rides the best, especially The Simpsons ride. They requested to postpone lunch in the hopes that they could get some even faster fast pass access while other people were eating their midday meal in order to ride as many times as possible. Rachel and Chad agreed to their plan, and they were able to ride the same few rides over and over until both girls became cranky and it became apparent that food was necessary quickly.

"I think that even though your food proposition was brilliant," Chad stated as he steered them towards the food court area, "You are both cranky and in need of some food ASAP!"

Both girls groaned, whining about the short lines they wanted to go stand in. But after being led to a picnic table to sit down in the shade, they'd both acquiesced. Rachel and Chad walked around the small food court, keeping the girls within sight, trying to find just one place that could satisfy the food needs of all of them.

"I'm in the mood for a burrito," Chad said to Rachel, who in her hyper-focused efforts to take care of her husband's PTSD, only heard the word burrito.

"You want to go? You seem to be doing okay, but we can go now if you're ready. Should we just feed the girls when we get back to the rental? I'm okay with that but they are acting a little bratty from the lack of nutrition in their little brains."

Chad looked at her perplexed for a moment before understanding that he'd inadvertently used their code word, "No babe, I'm doing okay today. In fact, I'm having a blast with my Queen and princesses. Though I do like that burrito is our code word, maybe we need some additional words to make it stick out a little better as we didn't factor in the fact that we love burritos."

"Like unicorn encrusted shrimp burrito?" Rachel asked with a wink.

"In my many travels, I have only encountered a few places where unicorn encrusted shrimp burritos are a delicacy so we may be safe with that addition," Chad laughed deeply.

"Well, it sounds to me like we are safe then. Unicorn encrusted shrimp burritos, or U.E.S.B for short?" Rachel joined in the laughter.

"U.E.S.B?" Chad asked.

"You know, in case we need to abbreviate it. I would hate to offend the unicorn lovers of the world," Rachel informed her husband.

"Oh yes," Chad agreed, "I would not wish to anger any potential unicorn-rights enthusiasts. I was clearly only thinking about my well-being."

Rachel looped her arm through her husband's arm as they stood in line for some food for their cranky children.

Part 4 - Marigold - symbol of loss

~Despair and grief

~Cruelty and coldness

~Remembering and celebrating the dead

31

Eleanor wasn't used to things going consistently well. She was trying to approach life with optimism, but she felt like she was teetering on a tightrope, waiting to either cross the obstacle successfully or be thrown into the void.

She tried to approach life without a sense of imminent doom, but her life seemed to have a tendency to trend that way. Thus far, her situations gravitated towards a series of unfortunate events with intermittent periods of normalcy. She worried that the rope could snap at any time, causing her life to be upended once again.

She was learning how to grieve the period of time Kai had been so mean and cruel, while also trying to grieve the person she'd been during that time. She'd never thought she would be in a situation like that and she'd definitely never thought she would stay in that type of situation. She also never thought she could forgive someone for behavior like that or give them another chance, but that was what she was currently doing. She did, however, love the fact that she and Kai were both working on getting healthy.

She felt like she was a good person with good moral character. She had a great job, and an excellent reputation at work and was hoping, if karma counted for anything, that her life would continue down this positive path.

She knew Kai was day-by-day becoming a better person. She'd seen him grow in leaps-and-bounds in the last several months. He seemed more successful with her, with work, and in his social life. He continued to smile more, laugh more, and seemed more satisfied with all of the opportunities life had to offer them.

They both wanted to focus on the good things that life had to offer and the good things they had to offer each other. She knew that the chances of life going forward without strife wasn't even slightly realistic, but she hoped to avoid it as long as possible.

In regard to the past abuse, she was still keeping all of her options open on the off-chance things didn't work with Kai. She'd given him her line in the sand at the counseling office, and he'd agreed and also verbalized that he would voluntarily leave if he ever put her in that situation again.

Yes, Eleanor wanted to continue to love him and think about a future, but she also wanted to be prepared if she needed to bolt. She was unwilling to sacrifice her morals and change herself for the worse ever again.

32

Eleanor had had some extra excitement leading up to Halloween. Children's Hospital put almost more effort into Halloween than they did into Christmas, causing several weeks worth of chaos and preparation. They did a flash mob every year, which was played on YouTube, and this year they were doing a trick-or-treat area where all of the units were going to do themed costumes that fit in with their display section where they would hand out candy.

The staff on her unit had decided to dress as characters from Star Wars, and Eleanor had been picked to dress like C3PO. She'd purchased as realistic a costume as possible online and had used gold body paint to cover all the remaining areas the costume didn't cover.

She didn't have to work on the floor that day but had volunteered so she would be able to see all the costumes and dress in costume herself. She'd volunteered to hand out candy and, a few days ago, after speaking with Molly and her parents, had volunteered to perform a solo routine with Molly during the flash mob.

She'd randomly run into Molly and her parents a month ago at Bee's Flowers. She'd been gathering supplies to start making Christmas fairy gardens for some of her friends and coworkers. Molly and her parents had been attending a BeeKeepers event there. Molly had immediately shrieked her name and ran full force into her arms.

Tevin and Scarlett had been pretty diligent in stopping by when Molly was at the hospital for follow-up appointments, but she still missed seeing Molly frequently. Certain patients stuck in your mind and in your heart and Molly was that particular patient to her.

In nursing school, they'd emphasized caring for someone without getting too involved, without it becoming too personal. It was hard not to feel that way about Molly. She had the most extraordinary personality and spirit.

Eleanor could not remember Molly ever being anything but upbeat -- even when she threw up every day from the chemo. When her hair fell out, she'd started looking at wigs online with the help of her parents and had worn them with pride. When new children were admitted to the unit, Molly liked to make them feel welcome and always invited other patients to meet her in the playroom. In the playroom, if another patient verbalized fear about being there, Molly would matter-of-factly talk them through it and bossily ask them if they had any questions after.

Molly and Eleanor had clicked quickly after Molly's first hospital admission. Eleanor had been made Molly's primary nurse, so she assisted Molly every day she was working. It had been so rewarding working with such a nice family through a difficult time, getting to see her discharged had been just as satisfying, though Eleanor genuinely missed seeing all of them.

When they'd run into each other at the flower shop, they'd laughed at the Six Degrees of Kevin Bacon that occurred at the store. Eleanor had retold the story of Kai taking her there and how perplexed the sisters had been, not realizing they already knew both of them.

"We had been there several times but always separately," Eleanor had said with a chuckle, "They both could not seem to hide their surprise when they realized I was Kai's fiancé."

"For Denver being as large as it is, I'm always surprised at the amount of connection we all have. To think that we are all connected through a flower shop of all things," Scarlett had commented before asking, "Are you going to the Halloween extravaganza?"

"Of course," Eleanor said. "I wouldn't miss the flash mob for anything. Speaking of flash mobs, I had actually spoken with Dr. C after your last appointment to see if he could get you a message about Molly and me performing our little routine there. What do you think?" Eleanor had not realized Molly was right behind her, listening intently. She'd hoped to ask Scarlett or Tevin in private first, in case they had something else already planned or Molly wasn't feeling well.

"Yesssssssssss! Please say yes, yes, yes, yes! I saw the flash mob last year from the balcony, and I was SOOOOOOOO jealous that I was too sick to perform. Please say yes, please!" Molly had jumped up and down enthusiastically. No wig today, just her hair, which was growing back slowly but surely: short strawberry-blond downy curls springing up and down with every bounce.

"Would we ever say no to a dance performance? Unless you weren't feeling well, that is," Tevin looked at his daughter imploringly.

"Well I would surely hope not, but I know that you are worried about me being tired, and doing too many activities," Molly had said matter-of-factly, abruptly stopping her jumping as if remembering her parents were watching her activity level. She looked at her parents questioningly, and when there wasn't an immediate answer, she shrugged once before giving Eleanor one more quick hug and walking away, briskly, to join her friends in the wind chime-making activity.

All Eleanor had had to do was shoot a quick glance at Scarlett and Tevin for them to fill her in. "Cell counts were a little off at the last appointment, but as you know, this is all a horrible waiting game. This was bone marrow transfusion number two, so again, as you know, it is always all up in the air. Either she will outlive us, or we will outlive her," Scarlett took a giant gulp of air in an attempt not to unleash all of their fears on Eleanor.

Scarlett had learned from experience with other parents whose children had cancer, that just because they lived in that world and understood it didn't mean that she should burden Eleanor with every single fear. "She has been tired lately, and that scares me. Though that could be the fact that she is in full-time school with play dates. On top of that, she is involved in BeeKeepers and Girl Scouts with the Bee-Harper girls. I just worry," Scarlett tried to brush a few escaped tears from her lids casually.

"Is now a good or a bad time for a hug?" Eleanor had asked Scarlett, who had whispered, "Good time," as she'd enveloped Eleanor into a hug herself.

"That girl of yours is special," Eleanor had whispered into Scarlett's ear, "There is no denying that. I'm always here if you need me." Eleanor had taken a few deep breaths before they separated as she wanted Scarlett to have a chance at being upset without having to comfort Eleanor in return.

Scarlett and Tevin had agreed to bring Molly in for the Halloween celebration so she could do some trick-or-treating in a smaller space to minimize her exertion that day. She knew that it would be tempting to go trick-or-treating with friends after that, but she hoped that if she got Rachel and Chad on-board, the twins could come, get some candy, and see Molly perform. Then they could all hopefully call it a night, giving Molly some recuperation time.

"Bye Molly!" Eleanor had said to Molly before she left. Molly had run up to give her a parting hug. "What are you planning to dress up as?" Eleanor asked.

"Well I probably shouldn't tell you as I'm keeping it pretty hush hush, but we wouldn't want to risk clashing our costumes or anything like that, so I can tell you, I guess. I will be a *Peter Pan* fusion character. Part fairy and part mermaid. I can't wait to do our dance, and I love you, and I will see you later!" Molly had said in rapid succession, clearly trying to get back to her friends.

"Her costume is pretty funny," Tevin had informed Eleanor,

"It is seriously a mermaid costume with fairy wings."

"I can't wait to see it. It sounds like a perfect Molly costume," Eleanor had admitted before hugging both Tevin and Scarlett and heading home.

Today, Eleanor was looking forward to getting to perform with Molly. She'd hyped it up to all of her patients upstairs on the unit. Those that could not make it down with a mask would be able to watch it on video later on.

When she thought back about what Scarlett had mentioned about Molly being more fatigued lately, she did notice that Molly had looked a little gaunt around the eyes. She thought back to a month ago when they'd stopped by after an appointment and Eleanor could not recall her looking quite as tired, or frail. Eleanor hoped that Molly was doing okay. She knew, as did Scarlett and Tevin that there were not many other options for treatment for her. She prayed for health for Molly. She knew tragedy didn't discriminate. It could strike at any time and affect anyone. She made a note to pay close attention to how Molly looked in a few days at the Halloween shindig.

The day of the Halloween celebration, she was in the bathroom, making sure her gold makeup was still in place when she received a text from Scarlett: *We are here, where should we meet y'all?*

By the front of the food court? Eleanor asked.

Sounds great, we are on our way, Scarlett replied.

Eleanor briskly walked to the front of the food court and got into a robot position, waiting for Scarlett, Tevin, Molly, Rachel, Chad and the twins to get closer to her before walking up to them with jerky, robotic movements. She stopped with her arms up, bent at the elbows in classic C3PO form, "Please help, I require a dancing partner," Eleanor used a robotic voice as she tilted her head to the right.

"Eleanor?" Molly asked, as she came closer and poked her with her finger.

"My name is C3PO, my owner Eleanor sent me here to do a dance for the people," Eleanor continued in her robotic voice.

She attempted to wink at Molly but could not quite manage that with her mask on, she moved the mask to the side so Molly could see her eye and winked again.

"Well in that case," Molly said blatantly winking at Eleanor with no discretion, "I think I can assist you with that."

Molly looked adorable in her mermaid fairy ensemble with shiny blue and purple scale leggings, a blue and purple wig fashioned into a Tinkerbell bun, fairy wings, and a floral crown. In her hand, she was carrying a wand that had a starfish mounted on top of it. "If merfairies existed," Eleanor commented, "You would obviously be their queen!"

"You may address me as Madame Tinkershell," Molly said regally as she curtsied. Eleanor bowed in return, and Molly touched the top of her head with the wand. "I now appoint you, robot, to be my dance partner."

"How do we look?" Marie piped in, grabbing Stella, so they stood side-by-side. They were dressed like the Super Mario Brothers. They looked great with their fake mustaches and overalls. Eleanor remembered how much Molly loved Mario Kart and wondered if she'd carried that obsession over to the twins.

"I may need some plumbers later to fix one of my leaky fixtures," Eleanor said in robot voice again, not realizing it sounded slightly sexual until Chad snorted under his breath. Eleanor was glad the mask covered up her blushing face and decided to play innocent.

Eleanor led them to the trick-or-treating area and left them to admire all of the different displays put on by each floor. She told them she would give them some time to get candy and play games. She gave them a meetup time shortly before showtime so they could have a brief practice session before performing for the crowd. The flash mob this year was going to be led by a handful of the Broncos cheerleaders, with a few breaks for soloists to perform.

Eleanor went to her floor's booth and helped Chewbacca hand out candy until the meeting time arrived. The group, minus Scarlett and Molly, were in the lobby with bags full of goodies at their assigned meeting time.

"Molly had to throw up," Mario/Marie exclaimed with a look of horror on her face, obviously appalled at the thought of vomit.

Eleanor looked at Tevin with a questioning look. Tevin shook his head slowly, indicating he wasn't sure if she was okay. "Do you want me to go check on them?" Eleanor asked as she heard Molly's voice behind her.

"I ate so much candy I puked!" Molly said weakly, but bravely.

She turned to look at Molly and could tell that she did look fairly pale with some dark circles now appearing under her sparkly mermaid scale makeup. Eleanor wasn't entirely sure if Molly had looked fatigued to begin with and the makeup had covered it up, if it was from throwing up, or if she was getting sicker again, as her parents seemed to suspect.

Eleanor looked at Scarlett with the same questioning look she had given Tevin, and her response was similar to Tevin's, with downcast eyes, a shake of her head, and a shrug.

"Miss Molly," Eleanor said, stooping down, so they were face-to-face, "we don't have to do the dance. You feeling okay and staying well is much more important."

"Tinkershell would like to have this dance," Molly said, pale lips firmly pressed together.

"I wouldn't want to get on Tinkershell's bad side," Scarlett added, attempting to sound upbeat. Looking at Scarlett, Eleanor could tell that Scarlett wanted nothing more than to pick her little girl up and rush her somewhere in the hospital for urgent blood work to find out if she was okay. Eleanor could also see in Scarlett a determination to sacrifice her own comfort so she could allow Molly to live as normally as possible in case her health was declining.

Eleanor didn't have children of her own so she couldn't predict how she would act if she were in the same position. She could only hope that she would be selfless enough to not react to every variance from the norm to give her child a chance not to feel like they were defined as "sick." Eleanor looked in Scarlett's eyes, and a sense of understanding passed through them with one glance.

"I would be honored to have this dance, Madame Tinkershell," Eleanor said as she bowed and took Molly's hand and walked to a less chaotic section of the lobby so they could practice their routine. Molly's smile was contagious. She beamed from ear-to-ear during every hand slap, every turn, every movement of their bodies. Eleanor couldn't stop smiling herself, and her mood was instantly elevated.

Keeping Molly's fatigued state in mind, they performed all of the moves a little slower, and Eleanor told Molly it would be better that way so the audience could admire every single one of their dance moves. Eleanor could tell that Molly was fatigued, her little chest heaving from the effort. She gave Molly one more chance to sit this one out and Molly again, firmly declined, determined to make it through.

The countdown ended for the flash mob, and there was a flurry of activity as everyone got in place. The lobby was packed full of costumed employees and family members. When Eleanor looked up towards the ceiling, she could see the glass walls that lined every floor lined with additional families, patients, and hospital staff, all ready to witness the dance collaboration.

Eleanor and Molly had discussed previously whether or not Molly had the energy to try to dance with the flash mob as well as their routine, and she could tell from Molly's reaction that it was going to be better if Molly only did their routine. Eleanor had tried to play it off as if she didn't personally feel comfortable with the dance moves for the flash mob; she hoped this little fib would help Molly save some of her much-needed energy.

The music began, and the cheerleaders started to lead the crowd in the dance. The music for the dance was composed of snippets of several popular songs and Eleanor and Molly held hands, swaying to the music, mouthing the words to each other. Before she knew it, it was their time to perform.

Eleanor grabbed Molly by the hand, and both of them made their way to the front of the dance line. They counted down, bowed towards each other and began. Eleanor could see how motivating the cheers from the crowd were for Molly as she shimmied and danced, and hand slapped her way through their routine. When it was done, the crowd roared, and Molly added another little victory dance of her own. Raising her hands like a victorious boxer, Molly walked slowly around the floor. Eleanor joined in her victory march before grabbing her hand and walking her back to her parents and friends.

"That. Was. Awesome!" Luigi/Stella proclaimed as they all surrounded Molly.

"I feel like I need both of your autographs," Rachel said to them, beaming from the aftermath of the collaborative energy from the flash mob.

"Well...I could totally... make that happen... on my end," Molly said slowly as she lapped up the attention. Eleanor noticed that she was having to time her talking to breathe better. Eleanor looked at Scarlett who had become slightly pale.

"Baby, why don't you sit for a few minutes and catch your breath," Scarlett said, walking closer to Molly so she could guide her somewhere more comfortable.

Molly motioned for her mom to get closer to her mouth, "Mommy," she gasped. Scarlett had just reached for her daughter to pick her up when Molly collapsed limply in her arms.

Stella and Marie looked on in horror as Scarlett hoisted up her listless daughter and carried her towards the emergency room with Eleanor and Tevin following closely behind. The triage nurse ushered them immediately back, and Eleanor motioned to them to let them know that she would wait in the waiting room, not wanting to overstep her boundaries.

Eleanor sat in the waiting area and tried to process what was going on. Several minutes passed before Rachel came to the waiting room solo, Chad tasked with calming the girls down. She left her phone number and asked for an update when one was available.

Once Rachel left, Eleanor realized she needed to let Kai know what had occurred and the fact that she may be delayed coming home.

He texted simply: *I am so sorry Ellie. I am here for whatever you need.*

She stayed in the waiting room for an hour or so. Tevin and Scarlett both came out, looking scared, and emotional. "Molly is asking for you," Scarlett said as she sat next to Tevin. They both looked shell- shocked. Eleanor didn't ask for any medical update, she'd already discreetly texted Dr. C and mentioned that a favorite patient of theirs was in the emergency room. She, without violating privacy laws, wanted Dr. C to have a heads up so he could collaborate with ER staff as soon as possible.

Eleanor hugged them both and turned her phone on Do Not Disturb mode before walking through the ER waiting room door. She walked into Molly's room and immediately felt tears welling up in her eyes. Molly, who hours earlier had been a magnificent Merfairy, looked like she had declined tremendously. Madame Tinkershell had been replaced by a very pale, sick little girl. She had a mask over her nose and mouth, delivering oxygen. Eleanor sat next to her at the bedside, placing a hand on Molly's arm, she could tell it took a lot of her energy to merely open her eyes.

"We danced so well," Eleanor said to Molly as she took her little hand in hers.

Molly reached up and grabbed her mask, pulling it down slightly so she could speak to Eleanor: "I don't know if I will ever dance again. I'm sick." Molly struggled to take a breath, Eleanor grabbed the mask and placed it back on her face.

Eleanor let out a sob, "You're sick honey. You don't have to be scared, Dr. C knows you're here, and we'll work as hard as we can to get you feeling better."

Molly again, with some effort, pulled her mask up, not even opening her eyes this time. Eleanor could not hear what she said initially, having to move her ear closer to Molly's mouth to listen to what she was saying. "I keep hearing the music, can you hear the music?"

"No, Miss Molly, I can't hear any music," Eleanor said as her heart sank.

"I think it's the angels telling me to come to them," Molly whispered hoarsely. Eleanor placed the mask back on her face as Molly again drifted off to sleep.

Eleanor sat there for a few minutes, trying to allow her brain to communicate what was happening with her heart. Molly was dying. She was dying, and it was going to break them all. Eleanor cried as her heart broke for Molly ... Scarlett ... Tevin ...and for her ...and all of the care team.

She didn't know how long she sat there before the ER nurse brought Tevin and Scarlett back in. They sat there in silence, watching the Merfairy transition back into what she truly was, a pediatric cancer patient.

Eleanor got back to her apartment shortly after 9 pm, after sitting in the hospital room, watching Molly with her parents until the ER doctor and nurse came in again to deliver test results. Eleanor had kindly excused herself at this point, assuming they would need to deal with whatever news they received as a family.

Eleanor stayed in the waiting room for a little while, waiting to see if Tevin or Scarlett had an update or needed anything from her; respite, food, drink, prayer. When neither had come out in an hour, she realized she should get home and get an update tomorrow.

Eleanor walked into a dark apartment, "Kai, I'm home." She walked through, looking and listening for her fiancé. She made a full loop of the condo, seeing no sign of him. She quickly swiped up on her home screen, turning off the Do Not Disturb. Kai should have been home hours ago. It had been his idea to buy enough candy to give the entire neighborhood diabetes. She knew he was excited for the trick-or-treaters as evidenced by the giant bowl of candy on the counter, prepping it even before he left for work.

She heard her cell phone *ding* and *ding* and *ding* catching up after being left off for so long. She felt her heart drop for the second time that night as she looked at her cell phone, 20 missed calls it said on the home screen. She quickly went to her voicemail and saw that there were multiple missed messages. She pressed the play button on the latest voicemail.

She heard the words, "Emergency contact for a Kai Newton, robbery, injured, intensive care unit," before the phone slipped from her fingers.

33

Eleanor had not had time to pick up her phone, in shock, before she heard her doorbell ring. She couldn't remember a time she felt so discombobulated. Everything felt surreal, and, for a brief minute, she almost expected to wake up and figure out that the knock on the door was something she was hearing in a dream. How could things be declining with Molly at the same time as something happened to Kai?

Later, she didn't remember walking to the door but did recall opening it to a tear-stricken Rachel. Rachel immediately enveloped Eleanor in a hug. "I can't thank you enough for what Kai did for my sister. I can't live without her, and if it hadn't been for him, she would have died tonight."

Eleanor sat there for a second, trying to absorb what Rachel was saying, "Rachel I don't know what's going on. I just got back from Children's. I waited with them, and Molly is not okay, and Kai, I think, isn't okay either. I don't know how you found me, and I need someone to tell me what's going on," Eleanor started breathing faster and faster, now sobbing.

"Oh God," Rachel said, "I had no idea that no one had gotten ahold of you. She started leading Eleanor farther into her and Kai's apartment, eventually sitting her on the couch in the living room. "Where should I start?"

"Is Kai alive? What the hell happened? I'm freaking out," Eleanor said shakily, still sobbing, unable to calm herself down.

"Kai is alive. The last update I got was that they were going to admit him to the ICU at Presbyterian St. Luke's," Rachel said calmly.

"Rachel, please tell me what the fuck happened," Eleanor said, suddenly dizzy with worry, sick to her stomach at the thought of what Rachel was going to tell her.

"From the best we can figure out from surveillance footage, and from what Stacia was able to tell us, Stacia was in the back with music playing, trying to get closing duties done early because it is always slow on Halloween. She wanted to try to see the girls in costume later. She heard the bell jingle and went to see if a customer was there. She was leaving the storage room when she was attacked from the side," Rachel took a deep breath, tears falling rapidly.

"On the security footage, you can see a man in a mask holding her down. He punched her..." She paused, finding it hard to get the words out but knowing she needed to get there soon so Eleanor could hear about her fiancé's part in all of it. "He punched her, and you can see Stacia struggling and trying to get away until he punches her hard enough and she doesn't move again. Then he starts to rip her clothes off." Rachel clapped a hand over her mouth, trying again to get the words out so she could spare her friend some agony while covering up her own.

"In the background, you can see Kai sneaking up on the man. He clocked him over the head with a vase. Then you see Kai tending to my sister, he gets her to wake up somehow and is starting to assist her out of the store when the attacker comes up from behind and hits Kai over the head with something. Stacia tries to help but can't reach him in time, and Kai falls," Rachel paused here, obviously not wanting to tell her what happens next.

"What happened next?" Eleanor asked, ready to find out what had caused Kai's injuries.

"In the footage, Kai is kind of tangled with Stacia when he gets hit. It caused him to fall straight back and hit his head on the corner of the counter, hard. The intruder started attacking him again before you see Stacia head towards him and he starts to run towards the front door. The police said this was when they got there, Kai obviously called him. They caught the man right outside the front of the store," Rachel finished her story knowing Eleanor would have a lot of questions.

"Do you know what his injuries are?" Eleanor said, "He wouldn't be going to the ICU if it wasn't serious. I'm going to head there now, but I want to know what I am dealing with."

"They would only tell me where he was. Marco is there and was told that he is stable but will need to be admitted like I said earlier, into the intensive care unit," Rachel said. "I came straight here using the address on Kai's driver's license so I could take you to the hospital."

Eleanor grabbed her purse and followed Rachel outside, still not quite comprehending the night. She knew that, when dealing with her patients, she felt like she knew what she needed to communicate with the providers, but she could not for the life of her think of anything to ask except for whether or not he was okay and if the doctor thought he would live. She didn't know if she should contact his family now or wait; she guessed it was possible that the hospital might have already called them.

They got to visitor parking, and Rachel called Marco to see where to go. Rachel led them towards the emergency room entrance, "They are all still in the emergency room, he should be going up to ICU soon." Eleanor nodded, and they stopped at the front desk.

"They?" Eleanor questioned Rachel.

"Stacia's here as well. Marco has obviously not left the hospital. Chad is with my girls. They're still incredibly upset about Molly and have not been told about what happened at the shop yet."

Eleanor nodded in understanding, not able to discuss Molly at the moment, needing to deal with one tragedy at a time.

"How can I help you?" The man at the front desk asked.

"We are here to see Kai Newton and Stacia Bee-Wilson please," Rachel said as Eleanor shifted her weight from side-to-side, anxious and nervous about what she was going to find. She'd tried not to think about the fact that the police cars parked near the ambulance bay were probably there for her fiancé and her new friend. Eleanor couldn't even begin to imagine how scary tonight had to have been for both of them. She never in her wildest dreams would have thought that she would be in an emergency department twice in one day.

"Can I ask your relation please?" The man asked.

"Stacia is my sister, and Kai is her fiancé," Rachel answered.

"I will have you both sit over there, and I will send someone out in a few minutes to get you," The man picked up his phone and immediately started giving their information to someone on the other line.

Eleanor knew that when she could process every little detail about what had happened, she would appreciate even more all of the things Rachel was doing to make all of this easier on her. She was barely holding it together and having Rachel to help was proving to be very beneficial.

"Rachel, Eleanor," they heard as Marco appeared, disheveled and visibly upset, from a side entrance that led back to the emergency department. He walked over to Rachel and immediately enveloped her in a hug. He started crying softly, causing Rachel and Eleanor to both start crying again as well. He hugged Eleanor next.

"Kai saved her," Marco said. "I can't begin to tell you how much that means to me."

Eleanor accepted the hug and the kind words, but she needed to see Kai. She needed to see with her own eyes what had happened to him, "Did you see him?" Eleanor asked Marco, who nodded solemnly.

"I'm not going to lie to you. I think he's in bad shape. They wouldn't even let me see him until about twenty minutes ago after he was stabilized, and I had to beg for that." Marco held her hand and squeezed, "My guess is that he's going to fight. He seems scrappy."

Eleanor felt a tiny smile pull at her mouth. If Marco only knew how affected Kai was by everything, he would know that Kai was a fighter. Most recently in a healthy way, previously in a sick way. She felt in her core, in her soul, that he would fight, that he had a lot to look forward to in life.

"Excuse me," they were approached by a woman in her mid-thirties in scrubs, "I'm looking for Kai's family."

"I'm Eleanor, his fiancé," her heart dropping, tears again welling up. If a doctor was coming out to speak with you, that was never a good sign.

"I'm Dr. Hartman, you can call me Ana. I'm not here to scare you. He's currently stable, but we have some things to discuss in private." Eleanor followed Dr. Hartman, and Rachel walked with them as far as the side entrance, letting Eleanor lean on her for support.

"I'll come find you after I see him?" Eleanor questioned.

"We'll find each other. We're all here for you," Rachel answered.

Eleanor was led into a tiny conference room with chairs and a few boxes of Kleenex. She wondered how many family members had heard about the deterioration or death of a family member in this room.

Once they were sitting, Dr. Hartman began. "Your fiancé was assaulted, as I'm sure you have heard by now. He was struck in the head, which caused him to fall, causing a second strike to the back of the head. The good news, though it may not sound that way, is that on the second strike there was a little skull fracture to the back of the head along with a laceration. Because of this, the extra fluid and pressure to the brain were relieved through that open area."

"So, no need for a burr hole or craniotomy?" Eleanor asked, surprised that she was able to dust off the cobwebs of her ICU rotation in school, allowing her to ask the correct questions.

"It sounds to me like you may have some medical knowledge?" Dr. Hartman asked.

"I'm a nurse," Eleanor admitted, reluctantly, not wanting to seem like she was trying to make that known. "I do pediatric oncology, so I'm not too familiar with adult trauma patients, nor patients that I'm engaged to. I feel like I hardly know my own name right now, to tell you the truth," Eleanor admitted.

"It's common that you find it hard to be objective when a friend or family member is on the stretcher. We intend to treat you as a person today, not a peer. We'd honestly be more worried if you could hold it all together right now," Dr. Hartman handed Eleanor a Kleenex as the tears started falling again.

"Now onto the not-so-great news," the doctor said. "We did have to intubate him. He had a Glasgow Coma Score of 6 upon arrival here, and they were not able to nasally intubate him in the ambulance because of the head trauma."

Eleanor started crying, knowing that this could mean many things. He could be okay ... or he could be brain dead. The pendulum swing was extreme when it came to the brain.

"Just to clarify, we intubated him to keep his airway, and give his brain some rest," Dr. Hartman continued. "He was able to breathe on his own, but with his altered level of consciousness and head trauma, we felt it better to give his body some time. In the ICU it will be a waiting game for a while. They will continue to monitor his neurological status constantly. He will be closely watched. If the swelling in the brain increases, we'll probably need to transport him to Swedish, or another neuro specialty hospital. If we do end up needing to do that, he'll possibly require surgery. The open area should be enough for now, as long as it continues to drain without too much loss of cerebrospinal fluid. He should heal on his own with time." Dr. Hartman paused, giving Eleanor time to absorb all of the information.

"Wow," Eleanor sat for a moment. "Either he will be okay in time, or he will be brain dead or severely brain damaged."

Dr. Hartman nodded solemnly, "It really is a waiting game when it comes to the brain, and it's not always a fast answer. Concerning other injuries, he does have a chest tube on the right side of his chest as he suffered some trauma to the ribs, subsequently breaking them and causing a hemothorax."

Eleanor shuttered, thinking of someone kicking Kai so hard that his ribs broke, and his lungs filled with blood. She felt sick. She felt shattered. She couldn't remember ever feeling this crushed.

"Can I go see him?" Eleanor asked, feeling that she could deal with it better if she could see Kai with her own eyes.

"Of course, from one health care professional to another, I just need to warn you that you can't ever really prepare yourself for the moment you see someone you know lying on that stretcher. If it's someone you love, it's that much harder. If you need us to call anyone, would like to speak with a chaplain or just need a quiet spot to sit, please let us know," Dr. Hartman gestured for Eleanor to follow her. She escorted her into Kai's room.

Eleanor took a deep breath before she entered. She tried to focus on picturing Kai as he normally was and not on injured Kai. The deep breath didn't in any way prepare her for what she saw when she walked into the room.

She was hit first by the iron-like scent of blood. She tried not to focus on that. Instead, she focused on trying to hold it together so she could be his support right now. She thought maybe if she went through the injuries systematically, from head-to-toe as a nurse would, she could then focus on being a fiancé.

Kai's face was significantly swollen with black, blue, and yellow bruises around his eyes and cheeks. They had his neck in a straight position, held by some towels on either side of his neck. They were secured on his forehead and stretcher with tape. Dr. Hartman had mentioned that they did rule out any spinal cord injury after his CT scan, but Eleanor assumed they wanted to just protect his neck for a while.

He had blood caked around his nostrils, though you could tell someone had tried to clean it up as best as they could. In his mouth was the endotracheal tube that was attached to the ventilator that was breathing for him currently. He had a smaller tube right next to the endotracheal tube, decompressing the contents of his stomach and providing a way to give nutrition and medications if needed that was attached to a suction canister on the wall.

He had an IV in the crook of both of his arms, giving him fluid and, she assumed, some sort of sedative. He had an occlusive bandage to his right chest that had a canister attached to it, helping to repair his blood-filled lung. She knew that he would have a urinary catheter in to drain his bladder. She pulled the blanket from side to side to just look at his legs and feet and make sure they were without trauma.

His legs and feet were the only things on him that looked at all like Kai. She'd joked with him after they first met that he could be a male foot model as he somehow had reasonably beautiful feet with perfectly angled toes.

She hoped he would be okay. She knew day-by-day the bruises would become less visible and the extent of the damage would be known. For right now she wanted to just hold his hand and be there for him. She hoped he could sense her presence and that he would feel comforted.

She sat there for what felt like hours but could've been minutes, watching the monitors on the wall that showed his heartrate and rhythm, his blood pressure, his core temperature, and his pulse and oxygenation. She tried to will him to wake up, though she didn't really want him to wake up and be in pain. She just wanted to hear his voice.

She was interrupted in her thinking state by a light knock on the door. Kai's emergency room nurse, Lane, came in and checked to make sure his vitals and his tubes were okay. "Your friend is wondering if she could come in and see you both. Stacia, I believe it is? I can push her over in a wheelchair if you are okay with that?" he asked.

"I'd be okay with that," Eleanor agreed. Lane left to grab Stacia, and in a few minutes- Stacia entered in a wheelchair.

"Hi," she said weakly to Eleanor, "I really hope I'm not interrupting anything."

"I'm just trying to let him know I'm here," Eleanor said, motioning towards their joined hands.

Lane pushed Stacia closer, and Eleanor saw how battered and bruised Stacia was. She had multiple bruises on her face, a cast to her right arm, and an angry blue bruise surrounding her neck.

Eleanor felt sick seeing the physical evidence of what she'd been through. She placed one hand on Stacia's arm. "I'm so glad that you're alive. I can't say I'm glad that you're okay because I know that you aren't okay. I don't think any of us are okay at the moment, in fact."

Stacia spoke quietly, Eleanor assumed because it hurt to talk after the neck trauma. "He saved me. I used to think he hated us. Though he did seem to be a little nicer recently. Anyway, he risked his life to save me. He saved me. I could feel myself dying, and then he was there...he saved me, and now nothing seems okay." Stacia broke down, sobbing quietly. Eleanor kept her hand on Stacia's arm, trying to comfort her.

"I'm glad that he did what he did," Eleanor assured Stacia. "We just have to take it one day at a time. I happen to know that he can be a stubborn ass, and whatever happens, he will fight to make it better. All we can do is wait and hope."

Stacia nodded, using the blanket covering her hospital gown to dry her face. "They caught the guy," she said quietly. "The police officers who came and interviewed me said that they'd been looking for him for a while. Apparently, he always wears a Halloween mask and only targets small businesses. He must not have done his research though; we have security cameras."

Eleanor felt the hairs at the back of her neck stand at attention, "What did you just say?" She asked as her blood froze in her veins.

34

Scarlett hurt so badly she couldn't breathe. She could not breathe, she could not speak, she could not focus. Everything hurt. She couldn't remember ever feeling this destroyed.

She couldn't believe that she was losing her little girl, her baby. She sat in the corner of Molly's hospital room in a daze, feeling the cold tile floor under her, focusing on the coolness beneath her so she could feel something that was more than all-consuming pain.

She felt like her body was being torn from the inside out. She could not breathe, she could not speak, she could not believe what was happening. She wasn't ready for this. She didn't want to do this. SHE DID NOT WANT TO DO THIS!

She wanted to stand up and scream … at Molly's body for not cooperating, at her husband for not being able to stop it, at herself for not being able to fix it. He was the father, he was supposed to protect his daughter, and he could not even do that. She was the mother, she was supposed to fix her when she was sick and hurt, and she couldn't even fix it.

SHE COULDN'T BREATHE, she wanted to SCREAM, the HURT was so severe she could not stand it.

She felt her heart BREAKING. She felt her soul SHATTERING.

35

S carlett could not function. She knew that no matter what she was thinking and feeling, time was still ticking by one second at a time and each second that went by was a second less that she would have with Molly. She was trying to hold it together, but she was hanging by the frailest of threads, mere strands from breaking apart at any given moment.

She quickly grabbed a Sprite from the refrigerator in the galley room and walked back to Molly's hospital room, back on the Bone Marrow Transplant Unit, the one with an angel pin on it, signaling a hospice patient.

She thought back to two days ago when they'd first gotten news of pneumonia from the emergency room doctor. He'd started her on heavy antibiotics, but he'd let Dr. C give them the news the next day after they were admitted upstairs. She thought about hearing the news, how their lives had come to an abrupt halt; how it had all transpired:

Scarlett and Tevin had grasped each other's hands, fear coursing through both of them. "She has severe pneumonia, as you know." Scarlett had gripped Tevin's hands harder, knuckles white, heart pounding, as they listened to Dr. C. "She is requiring less oxygen than she was initially, and they have given her some broad-spectrum antibiotics, which is good."

Scarlett had nodded, as Dr. C continued. "Now we need to talk about the serious stuff. The cancer is back." He'd looked at them both somberly as they'd both broken down together. They'd clung to each other, hoping to give each other some of the grief while also taking some of it away, the emotional news of what they'd heard, too much to handle. They'd sobbed in each other's arms, trying to release some of the grief that threatened to break them into pieces.

Robbi, from the social work team, had spoken first, "Has anyone talked to you about hospice or the Angel Program before?"

For now, Scarlett and Tevin were keeping her inpatient, hoping that with some antibiotics and oxygen she would become stable enough to get her home, where she would spend the last of her time surrounded by friends and family.

Support had been offered to them in droves. Chad and Rachel had gotten in touch with the school, and thus far she'd heard that there were meals lined up for an extended period of time. Today they'd been notified that there was going to be a delivery for them that Molly's class had organized.

Scarlett had heard about the attack on the flower shop from the local news she'd been watching while Molly and Tevin were sleeping last night. She didn't blame them for not bringing it up to them, but she was upset that it had happened and hoped there would be a good outcome.

Their new friends had been in contact regularly, checking on them to see if there was any news and to find out what their needs were. Rachel had volunteered to act as a contact person, so they didn't feel like they had to continually update a lot of people. She'd given Rachel the news via text, unable to say the words out loud yet: *Molly is going to be put on hospice.*

She knew that there could not be any happiness associated with a hospice meeting for a 9-year-old. She'd however felt a slight sense of hope, given the situation, after her meeting with the Angel Program case manager.

The case manager had informed her that hospice didn't always mean that death was moments away. Hospice, in its definition, suggested that death could be inevitable in six months or less. She assured Scarlett that the dying process was obviously outside of their control. Molly, if she miraculously got better could be on hospice for six months before they reassessed the need.

Scarlett felt out of control. She felt like she'd felt the denial, anger, bargaining, and depression stages of grief simultaneously. She couldn't believe that her daughter, who had been healthy enough to attend school this year, was now facing end-of-life care. She was pissed; pissed at the doctors and nurses, pissed at herself, pissed at Tevin, pissed at God. How could he have given her a child that she didn't even know she would love this much, just to take her away when she meant everything to her! She tried to bargain, offering herself up instead, if it meant her daughter living. She knew there was nothing she wouldn't do if it meant her daughter would live longer than her.

Molly had been more lucid after the antibiotics and oxygen, no longer mentioning the angels calling her to heaven. She was now on a nasal cannula, and they'd been able to wean her down on the amount of oxygen she was requiring, which was a good sign.

They'd sat down and talked to her with the Angel Program staff. They'd talked about the possibility of her going to heaven soon. Molly, ever the strong soul, had simply smiled and said, "Okay."

Her cell counts were still declining, and Scarlett knew that that would eventually be what caused her demise. Scarlett thought about how she'd created Molly and Molly's cells in her own body, carrying her and nurturing her for nine months. Scarlett knew that feeling like it was her fault was irrational, but she needed someone to blame, and she was willing to take some of the blame if that would help with the pain.

She walked into Molly's room, Sprite in hand. Merely walking into her room had been extremely nerve-wracking since she'd been admitted. She was deathly afraid that she would step in and find Molly having already passed on, without her being there. Neither Tevin nor Scarlett had left the room for more than a few moments since the discussion yesterday. Eventually, they were going to need to either ask someone to bring them clothing from home or one of them was going to have to drag themselves out of the hospital room and away from Molly, which she didn't see happening.

As if Rachel had read her mind, her phone dinged with a text. She sat down next to Molly, who was still sleeping and looked at her phone. *Chad and I have volunteered to bring you the gifts from school. We wanted to try to bring you guys something to eat as well, let me know if there is anything you would like me to pick up. Do you need us to run to your house for anything? Are you still in Halloween attire? If the answer is yes, please allow us to run to your house for you.*

Molly looked down at her shirt and realized she was still wearing a Wonder Woman shirt. She'd taken the cape off in the emergency room, not feeling very festive. She noticed now for the first time that Tevin was still wearing his Jack Skellington shirt. She handed her phone over to Tevin so he could read it.

"We need them right now. We need as many people in our corner as we can get. Speaking of which, when should we contact our families?" Tevin asked.

"I know we need people," Scarlett admitted. "I also know we need to get some wheels in motion, but I can only handle one thing at a time right now."

The truth was, often times Scarlett didn't have the energy to deal with either of their families. They were all very nice and cared about Molly. However, they just didn't understand how difficult all of this was. In this current situation, Scarlett didn't know if she could handle any additional stress yet. She knew, deep down, that she owed it to them to contact them as soon as possible so they could make the necessary travel arrangements.

"Let's work on figuring out if we can get her healthy enough to get her home first and then decide how to proceed with our families. Dr. C said that they'll repeat some blood work today to see if her condition is improving or deteriorating, and that may help us with directing family members."

Scarlett reached her hand out for Tevin, and he handed the phone back to her. She constructed a quick text: *First, I heard about the robbery. I know y'all are just trying to protect us, but I want to make sure everyone is okay and to let you know I'm sorry it happened. Second, we have a key hidden in the little birdhouse on the corner of the porch. If you could just stuff whatever is in the laundry basket on the kitchen table into a bag for me, I would really appreciate it. Last, I hope the girls are okay. I can't imagine they, like all of us, have any idea how to wrap their brains around all of this. Thank you for everything, y'all are amazing, and we are so thankful to have you.*

Scarlett and Tevin sat, staring at their little girl, a sense of unconditional, parental love surrounding them with a hint of the loss that would be inevitable. Molly was sleeping a lot, but she'd slept a lot previously when she had pneumonia, so it was hard to tell if her body was healing or failing further. "I will never be ready to not see her every day," Scarlett choked out a sob.

Tevin motioned her over, and when she got closer, he pulled her into his lap. He began to cry as well, and they sat there together, staring at the child that they loved more than anything and grieving for all that they would miss about her when she was gone.

After a few minutes, Molly stirred and opened her eyes, "Are you guys crying?" she asked hoarsely.

"Yeah baby, we are," Tevin answered.

"Is it because I'm sick again?" Molly asked.

"Yeah baby, it is," Scarlett answered. She stood, grabbed the water pitcher from the tray table, filled it with some ice and went to sit beside her. She made sure Molly was sitting up a little so she wouldn't choke and fed her a few ice chips. Molly slowly let the ice dissolve.

They heard the ding of the cell phone, and Scarlett looked down to see a text from Rachel: *We should be there in about ten minutes. We brought you some clothes and some food for this evening. We also brought a lot of gifts from the school. Should we meet you down here, or can we meet somewhere closer for you?*

"Where should we meet them?" Scarlett asked Tevin.

"Meet who?" Molly asked weakly.

"We needed to get some clothes and things from home, and Rachel and Chad are going to bring it to us," Tevin answered.

"It would be easier if we could just go home. I want to go to our house, Mommy and Daddy," Molly said. Using Mommy and Daddy was abnormal for her at her much more mature age of 9, but they knew when she used it it was because she needed something.

"You're still sick baby. Remember we talked about heaven?" Scarlett answered. Inside she again wanted to break apart. She hoped that heaven existed so this beautiful girl of hers would be well taken care of somewhere else. She couldn't imagine a world where a spirit like Molly didn't exist. She was still pissed at the thought of a God allowing a beautiful girl like her to be dying.

"I do actually hear singing sometimes, it seemed to freak you guys out a little bit, so I don't always tell you," Molly admitted. She closed her eyes for a second, "I can't hear it right now though, I just checked."

Despite their sadness, Scarlett and Tevin each let a tiny smile appear, even sick, their girl was sweet and sassy. Scarlett texted back: *We can meet you in the visitor's lobby on the unit. Let me know when you get there.*

"I'm dying, aren't I?" Molly asked matter-of-factly.

"We are all dying sweetheart, but we are afraid that cancer has taken over the good cells in your body," Scarlett said, trying to leave the conversation fairly superficial, so she didn't breakdown moments before having to see her friends in public.

"I want to die at home," Molly said, again matter-of-factly. "Also, the Discovery Channel is full of lies. They said in seven years…. or maybe it is because it hasn't been seven years…. or maybe." She shut her eyes again, exhausted. "I may just need to take a nap right now. Can you tell Stella and Marie to come see me at home? They are my best friends after you two." She then closed her eyes.

Scarlett choked back a sob, then took a few zen-level breaths.

Tevin went in for a hug, and she swatted him away temporarily. He didn't take offense but quietly backed off, giving her some breathing room. They collected themselves for a few minutes, pacing back and forth in the room together. Holding themselves together in their silence. Scarlett knew that if she sat and thought about all of the things that Molly had just said to her, she would completely lose it, though she knew that she needed to lose it sometime soon in order to start dealing with the past few days ... and the seemingly bleak future.

They walked to the lobby and were greeted by quite a sight. There were countless stuffed animals. The room was crowded with containers of bright, cheery colors of various animals. Chad and Rachel looked at them sheepishly. "We actually dropped some of them by the front office so they could be donated," Rachel said. "I hope that you know the whole school is rallying behind you guys. We have meal trains lined up and people volunteering to clean the house and mow the lawn. Anything you need, we've got you covered."

Scarlett and Tevin smiled weakly. It wasn't until Rachel enveloped her in a hug that she lost it. "Thanks," Scarlett said tearfully. Why was it way more emotional to have help and support, she wondered?

They started to gather up the gifts for Molly. Among the stuffed animals were cards, books, and toys. Once they had everything a little more organized, Scarlett ran in to check on Molly and, when she found her still sleeping, ran out to visit with her friends. One of the CNAs had seen Scarlett peeking in the room and said she would sit in there and chart just so Scarlett could get some time. Scarlett once again almost lost her composure at the offer of assistance.

"How is Stacia? How are Eleanor and her fiancé?" Tevin asked.

"Stacia was released yesterday. I don't know if Marco will ever leave her side. I tell you what, I liked him before, and now I think I'm in love with him," Chad said attempting to crack a joke.

"I'm so glad they're okay. Does anyone know about Kai?" Scarlett asked, again hoping that Eleanor was coping okay. She truly appreciated all that Eleanor had done for them, and she was sad that she could not give time and effort right now to help her. She assumed that Eleanor felt the same way. Scarlett made a mental note to at least text her so they could stay connected.

"Kai is still in ICU," Rachel said. "They're just watching the pressure in his brain to make sure it's staying at an acceptable level. He hasn't needed surgery, and I believe they're going to start trying to wean him off of the breathing machine soon to see if there is the potential for him to be able to breathe on his own." She paused, "I think we're going to stop by there next. We dropped the girls off with Grandpa David. My grandparents came back from their latest adventure to make sure Stacia is okay and to get the store put back together."

"Speaking of the girls," Scarlett said. "How are they? Have you told them about Molly being on hospice?"

"They're shaken up, they understandably didn't like seeing their friend feeling so ill. We've shown them a few videos that talk about hospice, and we got a book from the library. I think they get it as much as third graders can. They just really want to see her. I know that's probably not possible, but maybe we could FaceTime or something when she's ready?" Chad asked.

"I'm sure Molly would love to FaceTime them; I hadn't thought of that. I'm so sorry that they had to see her collapse like that," Scarlett said. "I also can't imagine it is easy having to talk to them about a friend being this sick, about hospice, especially after all that just happened with their aunt in their family store."

Rachel put her hand on her arm, "I can't even begin to imagine what you're going through. I just need you to know that we are here for you. We have your backs, and as I texted you previously, there is nothing we will not do to help you all out. I almost forgot; do you have family coming? My grandma asked me to ask you. We would be more than happy to stay with my grandparents so we can open our house up to guests."

"I'm having a hard time with all the kindness y'all are showing us, to be honest," Scarlett said shakily. "Thank you so much for being our friends."

"We didn't know how much we needed friends until we met you," Tevin chipped in unsteadily.

"Well, we're always happy when we meet people, we can consider family," Rachel said. "Oh, that reminds me of two quick gifts I wanted to give you, and then we will leave you alone. First, here is food. I know you like Thai food, so we got some to-go for you. Second, the kids at school wanted to make Molly some flowers, so we had a flower making day at school." Rachel pulled out a few gallon size Ziplock bags, inside were hundreds of crepe flowers of various sizes and shapes.

Scarlett smiled, knowing Molly would love another version of a flower garden. She'd loved the flower collage, her paper flowers, and her new fairy garden so much that she'd insisted that Scarlett and Tevin put the flower collage on her bedroom wall at home in a corner by the window. She'd arranged her large beanbag chair there and placed her mesh canopy above it. She'd surrounded the area with her paper flowers. It looked like a cozy little life-size fairy garden habitat by the time she was done with it. They would often find her there, reading *Peter Pan* to her stuffed animals.

"She will absolutely adore these," Tevin said. "We should get back to her. Please let your sister know we are wishing her well, Eleanor and Kai too if you talk to them. They caught the guy, right?"

"Yeah, they caught him," Chad said. "The strangest part of it all was that Kai had defended the guy about a year ago and charges were dismissed. Crazy if you ask me."

"Wow, that's crazy," Tevin agreed. They all stood and hugged, exchanging thank yous and goodbyes.

Molly woke up when they got back into the room, "Oh my!" Was all she could manage when she saw the bags of animals. Her eyes lit up with the sight of her new crepe paper garden, and she insisted on decorating some plastic solo cups like vases so she could arrange them.

They gathered some supplies for her from her room, and the craft room, and let her get to work. After a few minutes, she motioned them both over to sit on the bed, "I have thought hard about this. I would like to pick two animals to keep, and the rest I want you to give to the other kids. I don't think I have the energy to give them all enough love."

Scarlett, feeling like she was spending most of her time fighting off tears, felt them flowing again at her daughter's statement. How could this world be okay without a soul like Molly? She knew it wasn't fair. She thought of people like the man that attacked Stacia. How could the world need him more than they needed Molly?

"Mom?" Molly asked, "Are you okay?"

"I just can't get over how kind and thoughtful you are. Of course, we can and will give these animals to some kids who can take extra special care of them. You're so sweet," Scarlett enveloped her daughter in a frail hug, wishing that she could absorb her into her own body so she could keep her safe and keep her close. She knew that she would always have the memories of her daughter, but how could she make it through without being able to talk to her every day, without being able to hear her sweet voice and smell her sweet scent?

She broke away, giving Molly room to breathe. She felt her stomach grumbling and realized she'd not eaten much at all in the last few days. She pulled the Thai food out, and the smell was intoxicating, even in its now lukewarm state.

She ate a few bites of the tofu pad Thai and instantly felt better. She'd just opened her cell phone to call her parents when she became incredibly nauseous. She grabbed the pink emesis bucket that they kept next to Molly's bed "just in case" and promptly threw up her food.

"Gross Mom!" Molly said, "It's usually me that throws up."

Tevin looked at Scarlett in surprise, unsure if he'd really just witnessed his strong stomached wife throw up. They always joked that she had a stomach of steel because of her ability to put hot sauce on all food.

"Nerves," she said weakly, grabbing a Kleenex and wiping her mouth. She went to the bathroom and disposed of the contents of the basin. She returned to Molly's bedside and slowly sipped on some Sprite and felt much better.

Twenty minutes later they called their families and made arrangements. They knew that blood work later would tell them some things, but with Molly discussing hearing singing, and a desire to make it home to pass away, they felt it was better to have family come now. They decided to take Rachel and Chad up on the offer of the use of their home, making it easier to get more of the family out. They discussed getting Molly home as quickly as possible so she could live out her remaining time at home, per her wishes.

Molly rested after the flower vase making, and while she was resting, they delivered the remaining animals to the charge nurse who promised she would deliver animals to the children on their floor that needed some comfort and then pass the others on to the volunteers. She even offered to take pictures, with parental permission, of course, of children with their animals so Molly could follow their "adoption" status.

They got back to her quickly and just watched their little girl sleep, enjoying every second they had left.

36

"Have you gotten everything lined up with the home health hospice nurse?" Robbi asked, passing over the packet of material from the Angel Program.

"Yes, she actually agreed to come by this afternoon or evening to make sure we get Molly home okay," Scarlett said, nodding.

"Molly really wants to get home," Tevin said, grabbing the packet from Robbi. "I really appreciate y'all and all that you have done for us."

Scarlett grabbed a tissue, blotting the tears, "We weren't sure that getting home would happen for her, and I will never have the words to express my appreciation."

Earlier that morning, Dr. C had asked what their thoughts were, "She is still her sassy self, but her blood work is getting a little worse every day. We can continue giving her antibiotics and oxygen here, which could potentially prolong her life for a short time, or we can send you home and continue the same things but with home hospice."

They hadn't had to think twice before asking him to get her home as quickly as possible. The whole care team had jumped in full force to get things ready for them, and somehow, before lunchtime, they received the news that it would all work out for them to be discharged that afternoon. They'd texted Rachel and Chad to see if one of them would be available at the house for delivery of a hospital bed before they arrived, and without question, Chad had taken the afternoon off of work to be there.

Molly had looked so frail, every morning aging her. She'd recently started wincing with her movements, which broke Scarlett's heart. She knew that her daughter was tough and for her to show any discomfort was heartbreaking. Scarlett had talked Molly into a little medicine for pain before the drive home, knowing that the bumps would be horrible.

Scarlett and Tevin's family members would be trickling in over the next few days, and Chad had informed them that he would stick around at their house until they got there so he could hand off keys to their home and help get Molly inside if they needed any additional assistance.

Tevin drove just as slowly home as he had the day they took Molly home from the hospital, this time for a whole different reason. Scarlett remembered how frightening it had been driving a newborn home from the hospital. She'd sat in the backseat, staring at the sleeping face of her newborn baby. Scarlett recalled praying the entire way home that Molly would remain safe, the thought of any harm coming to this tiny creature unfathomable.

This ride was so similar, yet so different. Molly hadn't been able to comfortably sit in her booster seat, so Scarlett sat in the backseat with her, holding her in a blanket, trying to absorb every jostle from the car, praying this time that her baby would live a little longer. She could not believe that in 9 years their journey had come full circle.

Both Chad and Rachel met them outside of their house, "They delivered the hospital bed, and I hope you don't mind, we wanted to do something special for Molly. It was all the girls' idea," Rachel said as they greeted them outside the car.

Tevin gingerly picked Molly up from the backseat, still wrapped tightly in the blankets. She made a tiny whimper of pain when he initially picked her up and then commented on it being, "Not so bad," after he started walking.

They walked into the house and were hit immediately with

the sweet scent of flowers. Floral bouquets in various sizes were located throughout the living room. "They're all so beautiful!" Molly commented weakly as she forced her eyes open, taking in the sight.

"Oh honey, those are not even the half of it," Rachel said, "Let's check out your room. Stella and Marie were very specific in what they wanted us to do for you."

Scarlett looked at Rachel questioningly. Rachel whispered, "I promise, it was the least we could do."

Tevin, with Molly in-tow, and Chad entered before Scarlett. She heard both Molly and Tevin gasp. Scarlett stepped into Molly's room seconds later and gasped as well, once again hit with a pungent floral smell. Molly's room had been transformed into a virtual garden. Every available space was covered, almost entirely, in flowers. There were flowers on her desk, flowers on her windowsill, flowers hanging from the canopy, and in a few larger vases on the floors. Her stuffed animals were arranged around the room, positioned as if they were in an outside environment. A few new stuffed animals littered Molly's beanbag and a new pediatric hospital bed. They'd added some pictures to the flower mural on the wall. There were pictures of Molly with the girls and other classmates. Get well cards were positioned on the wall and around the room as well.

"I've never seen anything so pretty," Molly said, crying softly. "I love it. It is beautiful and...thank you so much."

"The girls said to tell you that they wanted it to feel like you were a fairy in your own fairy garden," Rachel said, going over to Molly.

"That is exactly what it feels like; I feel like Tinkerbell," Molly said, more pep in her weak voice than her parents had heard in a few days. "Tell them that I love it and that I love them. When do I get to see them?"

"Well babe," Scarlett began gently, "we're going to have to figure out when you might be feeling up to visitors."

"Mom," Molly said, fighting again to keep her eyes open, exhausted from all of the activity of the day, "I want to see everyone soon. It needs to be soon." She quickly drifted off, leaving the adults in the room to deal with the details of the coming days and weeks.

They all quietly tiptoed out of the room and into the living room. "Once again, y'all are too nice. I can't imagine how much work or money all of this was," Tevin said emotionally.

"Believe it or not," Chad started, "we do have some connections in the flower world. Even if we didn't, it was worth it. The smile on your daughter's face when she got into her room was absolutely priceless. I would do it again just to see how surprised and happy she was."

"She is surrounded by all the things she loves in that room," Scarlett said, "I couldn't wish for a better place for her to be right now. I'm just so thankful we were able to get her home. I didn't want her to have to stay confined in a hospital for the rest of her short time. You guys have made that even more special. Thank you both."

Scarlett hugged each of her friends again, thanking them repeatedly for all that they'd done for them in the past few days. "It's the least we can do," Rachel said. "From the minute we met you guys, you've been great to us. You've dealt with so much, and you don't even complain. We obviously enjoy you all and Molly so much."

Tevin agreed, "We enjoy all of you too. I'm so sad that we just met y'all, and now there is a lot of sadness. It doesn't seem fair that this is the way it's all ending."

"We can always hope that Molly will bounce back," Scarlett said sadly, "but I don't really feel that she can fight anymore. I want her with us forever, but I can't stand the thought of her in pain for even a second. She is so much tougher than me, much tougher than cancer and all of its awful side effects. I ..." Scarlett couldn't go on speaking.

She felt so drained, she was depressed, she was defeated. It was as if the weight of the world was pressing down on her. She felt so conflicted. She didn't want her daughter to be in pain, and it was very apparent that she was. She'd never heard Molly complain and for her to agree to pain medicine was rough. She knew from speaking with the hospice personnel that Molly sleeping more than she was awake could be a sign that death was near. She hated that her urge was to wake her daughter up so she could spend every second with her and at the same time ward off what everyone was saying was inevitable.

"You okay?" Tevin asked as Scarlett became aware that she'd zoned out a little.

Scarlett nodded, not okay, but too mentally exhausted to go into it at the moment. Rachel jumped in, sensing her friend's mood, "Would now be an okay time to go over the house details?"

Chad and Rachel had graciously gotten easy-to-make foods like bagels, sandwich materials, and frozen dinners for the family members that would be staying at their home in the next few days. They gave Scarlett and Tevin the printout of the meals that would be coming to them and informed them that the nighttime meal would be large enough to accommodate quite a few people if they wanted out-of-state family members to come over. They also assured them that there was food for people to eat elsewhere if they needed time and space to be together as a family.

"Once again, I don't think there will ever be a way we can repay y'all for your kindness, especially since you have had some unexpected burdens on top of all of this," Scarlett said again as they walked their friends to the front door.

"What are your thoughts about the girls seeing Molly?" Tevin asked as they all hovered at the front door, not quite sure where to go from here. There was no guidebook for this kind of tragedy.

"I think that it would do them all some good," Rachel said. "I know that it won't be easy for anyone, but I think they will all need that closure. Oh man, should I have said closure? Does that sound awful? I'm so sorry."

Scarlett waved away the apology, looking at her friend's face which had now drained of any and all color, "During the hospice case management meeting, they talked to us about the importance of talking about all of it. The dying process happens to us all, and it is sometimes less scary to talk about it. Believe me, I'm not at all okay with the fact that I have to have these death and dying discussions about my young child. I will never be okay with her leaving before me but..." Scarlett stopped talking, again not feeling like she had the mental energy to deal with much more today.

Rachel nodded, still looking visibly upset but obviously wanting to remain calm, "We're so sorry you three are going through this, and we want to assure you that we are here. I can't say that enough. You let us know when you want the girls here and how that needs to happen, and we'll make it happen. Until then, we are here in spirit, but we can easily be here physically if you need anything."

Once the house was empty, Tevin and Scarlett, without saying a word, walked into Molly's room. They sat together in her large beanbag, surrounded by the sight and scent of beautiful flowers, holding hands, watching their girl sleep, waiting for the hospice nurse to arrive.

Their families started to arrive the day after Molly got home. Molly had been extremely tired but had done well with visitors. They decided it would be better to only allow family for the first few days, giving Scarlett's parents and Tevin's father a chance to get some alone time with their granddaughter.

Annabelle, Scarlett's mother, and her father, Brooks, had been understandably sad but had stayed fairly stoic around them while Tevin's father, Greer had been a little more emotional.

Greer had been widowed five years ago. Though quite a playboy, he missed Tevin's mother, Joanne, so much that he compared every woman he dated to her, always finding the other women lacking. Despite his constant companionship, he remained a bachelor.

Joanne had died in a car crash, and it had been very hard on the family, especially Greer. He'd been more emotional since Joanne's unexpected passing, and they were trying to find that balance; trying to be respectful and allowing him to grieve how he needed to without freaking Molly out.

Scarlett was an only child, but Tevin had a sister, Kathleen. There was always a little bit of drama going on between Kathleen and Greer, but they'd both been behaving reasonably well on that front. Kathleen had always been a bit of a party girl and that bothered Greer. There had been many an argument about it, often in front of others. Tevin and Scarlett were relieved that they were sensitive enough to behave thus far in the presence of others.

Their family members had all seemed to be surviving in close quarters together at the Bee-Harper house as far as Scarlett and Tevin knew, but, of course, they were too preoccupied to really care.

The family days had consisted of eating, napping, and taking turns watching movies with Molly. She sometimes had short bursts of energy where she would ask to go outside. During those times, they would push her outside in the wheelchair hospice had brought over. She loved to sit in the fall sun in front of the garden while a family member read aloud, usually from *Peter Pan*. She'd asked to lay in the hammock as well, which they would accommodate until the pain became too severe.

Annabelle, after hearing about the twins and their adventures with Molly, thought that a tea party in the garden would be a neat activity and everyone agreed to help. Kathleen volunteered to make cucumber sandwiches while Annabelle baked some cupcakes. The men volunteered to be waiters, offering to wear bow ties and aprons. Rachel agreed to bring the girls over in dressy attire.

They set up a table near the garden with the fanciest tablecloth and place settings that Scarlett and Tevin owned. They took the freshest of the flowers and placed them all around the yard. They put her in her Christmas dress, which was long sleeved as Molly had been pretty cold since her hospital admission.

Stella and Marie showed up dressed to the nines with white

gloves, fancy dresses, flower crowns, and hair in updos. They brought a crown of flowers for Molly to wear, along with some artwork from other BeeKeeper members sending their love.

They had a blast, allowing themselves to be waited on hand-and-foot by their "waiters" and delicately eating cucumber sandwiches. They sipped their tea pinky up and acted like children should, keeping the sickness on the periphery. When the time to say goodbye came, Molly had become tearful, hugging each girl and telling them both how much she would miss her best friends.

Stella and Marie both cried but had held their heads high, staying brave for their friend. Towards the end of the visit, they could all tell Molly was becoming fatigued, and they left without complaining, bravely saying what would end up being their last goodbyes.

Molly died peacefully after a little over a week at home surrounded by her friends and family. The time had gone by in a blur. Scarlett had kept feeling like she just wanted time to stop. From the moment she got home from the hospital, she and Tevin had started to sleep only when Molly was asleep, which was often, afraid to miss any moment that Molly was awake. She would have given her own life to make every second slow, lasting years, prolonging her last moments with her beautiful daughter until she was the one who died first, instead of Molly.

She missed her so much. She didn't know how, in a time where so many people surrounded her offering her comfort, she could only focus on the one who could not physically be there with her anymore, her beloved Molly. She felt like she had no more tears to cry. She felt empty. She kept reminding herself that her daughter was no longer in pain and that she could now be an ethereal being, ideally, a fairy.

The day Molly died she asked to go outside in her wheelchair despite the fatigue and the pain that was becoming more constant. Tevin and Scarlett noticed her breathing had become more labored as the day progressed and she didn't show any interest in eating. She did insist on sitting in her wheelchair in the garden and asked that her parents come out and read to her. They sat in the sun together, Molly huddled under multiple blankets holding one of each of her parent's hands. They all intermittently squeezed three times, their unspoken "I love you" to each other.

Looking back, Scarlett could not recall what she was reading the moment her daughter took her last breath, but she hoped that it was this: "'*So come with me, where dreams are born, and time is never planned. Just think of happy things, and your heart will fly on wings, forever, in Never Never Land.*'"

The hospice nurse had been there frequently in the last few days, and when she confirmed the death, they'd pushed her back inside and laid her in the hospital bed, where it just looked like she was sleeping peacefully, allowing the family to come in and say their final goodbyes. Annabelle had taken the reigns, letting Scarlett and Tevin's friends know of her passing so they could worry only about their grief.

The funeral was held two days later after Molly had been cremated and her ashes had been placed in a beautiful wooden box adorned with wooden flowers. Molly had asked that people wear bright colors, "If people are going to be sad, I want them to at least be cheered up by some color. I also don't want sad flowers; I don't want to wreck what anyone thinks about flowers."

Rachel and her girls made bright Gerber daisy crowns for everyone, and every person there donned one in memorial of the spectacular soul. Stacia had provided seed packets with Molly's picture on them for people to plant in her honor. Stella, Marie, and most of the BeeKeepers wore fairy wings as well, which seemed even more fitting. After the service, they had served special pancakes that Kathleen had prepared in all sorts of flavor varieties.

Neither Scarlett nor Tevin felt up to speaking at the funeral. Neither had been eating or sleeping much and Scarlett had been throwing up daily, physically ill from grief. Their families stepped up to the plate, and Greer and Annabelle took turns reading a few snippets from *Peter Pan*:

"*'Did you know I always thought you were braver than me? Did you ever guess that that was why I was so afraid? I knew I'd miss you. But the surprising thing is, you never leave me. I never forgot a thing. Every kind of love, it seems is the only one. It doesn't happen twice,'*" Annabelle read, intermittently stopping to gather her courage.

"*'I like to think that one day after I die, at least one small particle of me- of all the particles that will spread everywhere- will float all the way to Neverland, and be a part of a flower or something like that,'*" Greer read, also having to stop frequently to compose himself. Molly had verbalized wanting to be a fairy instead of an angel, living in a hollyhock pod or an acorn shell. Tevin and Scarlett were planning to hold on to her ashes until they someday found the most beautiful field of flowers to lay her ashes in.

It was easy to see the impact Molly had made on people's lives. There were people from the hospital, from Bee's Flowers, and from Molly's school. Eleanor was there, looking exhausted. Scarlett went over to hug her. "I appreciate you being here. You were so fantastic with her, and I'm so glad that I will have the YouTube video of you on Halloween to look at any time I need to see her dancing."

Eleanor hugged her back, "I will miss her more than you will know; she was such a special soul. I'm so sorry for your loss, and I'm so sorry that I haven't been available."

"How is Kai doing?" Scarlett asked.

"Every day it gets a little bit better, but it's still a little too soon to tell. I want today's focus to be on Molly. Would you have time to go to Bean Juice in the next few weeks and we can catch up?" Eleanor asked.

"I would love to," Scarlett answered, "I'm going to need distractions and people if I'm going to be able to get through this."

Scarlett and Tevin made the rounds, trying to give and receive comfort. There were butterflies everywhere, and Scarlett hoped that maybe one of them was really a fairy named Molly watching and guiding her through the loss.

37

Stacia had a new lease on life. She hated that she felt like a cliché. She felt like a typical survivor who had gone through something traumatic and tragic and now saw life in a whole new light.

She felt hyper-aware of everything in a way she never had before. She felt like a pot of emotions, threatening to boil over at any time. She knew that she would now have to deal with the mental and emotional trauma, possibly forever.

She was beyond happy that she'd walked away with minimal physical injuries, even though emotionally she was up and down. She had guilt that she'd walked away with fewer physical injuries than Kai since she'd been the attacker's original target. She now understood why people who experienced trauma together suffered from survivor's guilt. Though they'd both survived, she felt that she'd not sustained the most damage and as strange as it sounded, she felt terrible because Kai had been merely trying to save her. She was alive, thanks to Kai's bravery. She was well aware that had Kai not walked in when he had, she would most likely be dead.

She hoped that the perpetrator actually paid for what he'd done, not just to her, but to all of the victims. He'd caused irreparable damage to so many families. She was glad that he'd been caught and that, this time, there was probably enough evidence to convict. She didn't know how she would handle it if he were rereleased, which would indicate a lack of justice.

She appreciated the outpouring of support, particularly by Marco, but part of her felt that she didn't deserve any. She felt guilty that many of her friends were going through so much as well, and she wanted all of the support to go to them.

She felt conflicted at the same time, knowing that she needed help now more than she ever had. She was glad that Marco was there when the nightmares took her over at night, holding her tight and comforting her.

She hoped for fast healing for all that had been involved in this tragedy as well as healing for her friends, several of which were currently going through tragedies of their own.

38

HALLOWEEN NIGHT

Stacia wasn't always the biggest fan of children unrelated to her, but something about kids in costumes pulled at her heartstrings. She didn't know if the costumes covered the general dishevelment that seemed to come with childhood. Somehow, she was a sucker for all of them when they were in costume.

Children in costumes and their parents had been trickling in all day as the shops in the area had collaborated the last few years, offering candy to kids and parents who stopped into a specific group of shops. It was convenient for kids and parents as they could get lots of candy in a short time. It was never a bad thing for the business to get that extra traffic either.

Stacia and Marco had made plans to get together later that night to go and see her nieces' costumes. They'd recently become interested in Super Mario Brothers and had decided to dress up as Mario and Luigi for Halloween, which Stacia thought was hilarious. She'd helped Rachel purchase fake mustaches on Amazon, and she'd no doubt that the girls were going to look great!

Stacia was starting to get a little bored towards the end of the night, all of the traffic dwindling down as families were going home to eat dinner before possibly going back out for trick-or-treating in their neighborhoods. There had been at least an hour without any traffic. She went to the back and turned the music up, intent on listening for the sound of the bell as she started to clean the cold- storage area. She deadheaded the flowers and refreshed the water in the vases. She'd just finished cleaning the classroom area when she thought she heard the bell jingle.

She didn't have time to turn down the music as she started to head quickly to the main display area so she could catch the customer before they left. She was fumbling to get the remote for the overhead speaker out of her apron when she was slammed from the side, going from standing to being suddenly airborne.

Days later, when she was in a place where she felt able to think back on the attack, she recalled thinking, as she was knocked into the air, that there had been an earthquake. She remembered falling and wondering how that had happened in Colorado. She remembered not realizing until she looked into the masked eyes of a stranger that there was a potential that this someone had knocked her to the ground on purpose.

Stacia landed hard on the cement floor. The wind was knocked out of her as she felt a sharp pain to her right arm.

"What...." she started to say, hoping that maybe she was wrong and the man wearing the plastic pumpkin mask had accidentally knocked her over. The intentions of the pumpkin-masked person became all too clear as soon as she felt the heavy pressure of another person holding her down.

She could not remember ever feeling this frightened in her life as she saw the looming face of a man in a grotesque pumpkin Halloween mask hovering over her, hand smashed brutally against her mouth in an effort to suppress any sound. In the back of her mind something sparked. She recalled this man coming in a few times today, always in the mask. She remembered thinking that is was a little strange that he'd come in more than once. She recalled him being with people every time, but hanging on the perimeter, appearing to be part of the group without actually being part of the group.

Stacia knew she had to act quickly and immediately started

to wriggle, trying to get out of the masked man's grasp. She tried to reach both arms up to try to get him off of her, but the pain in her right arm was excruciating.

She tried to move her mouth in the hopes that she could attempt to bite him through the thick gloves he wore, but he seemed to be putting all of his weight into keeping her mouth covered. Before she could free herself at all, she felt like a ton of bricks was dropped straight onto her head. She tried to scream again, straining her voice with the force. One of his hands wound around her neck as he used his free hand to punch her again in the head once, and then twice, a whole new set of pain exploding through her head before everything went black.

Stacia was upset. Her head hurt so badly, and she needed some medicine for it. She'd just been driving in a car when a purple child-sized cow had jumped out of a spooky looking pumpkin patch landed directly in front of the vehicle. She'd never seen a purple cow before and didn't want to be responsible for harming it. She swerved to miss it, hitting a tree instead, before sliding down the hill into a pond. She shivered with cold, as she floated in her car with cold water slowly trickling in causing her to feel colder and colder. She felt a jostle and wondered if there was some rough water ahead, she needed to get out…

"Stacia," She heard a whisper and felt a jostle. "Stacia please wake up."

She tried to open her eyes, but her head was pounding with pain, and everything felt foggy, she must have gotten something in them when she crashed. She felt another jostle, and another, and another.

"Stacia, wake up," She heard the voice say, more forcefully this time. She wondered why this person was so bossy. She hoped that maybe if she opened her eyes, her head would quit hurting so badly.

She tried for what felt like a long time to get the weights that were sealing her eyes shut off, each time getting closer to successfully getting and keeping her eyes open.

Stacia opened her eyes and immediately felt like her head

could potentially explode. It hurt so badly that she felt bile rushing up her throat. Before it could exit, she felt someone turn her on her right side while trying to stabilize her neck as best as they could.

"My arm!" She exclaimed, but it came out in a throaty whisper, her throat hurting so badly she could barely utter two words.

She threw up a little which didn't do much to dampen the throbbing in her head, the stabbing pain in her arm, or the ache in her throat. She looked to her side and could see the body of someone lying close by.

"Stacia," she heard the bossy voice again. "It's Kai, I need you to get up, and we need to get out of here. I need you to wake up and listen to me NOW! I don't know how much time we have until he wakes up."

"I AM trying to wake her up," Stacia heard Kai say frantically to someone who was obviously not her, maybe someone on the phone? She could now identify Kai as the source of the bossy voice. "Please get here quickly! He is out right now, but I don't think I can fight him off while I'm trying to take care of her."

In a flash, it came back to her. She recalled being attacked, she recalled trying to fight someone off, and she recalled feeling like she was asleep or dreaming after he'd punched her. She sat still and quickly attempted to inventory some of her injuries. Her head hurt, and her throat was on fire, her right arm felt broken. She felt cold, she shivered as she looked down and figured out that it was because her clothing had been partially ripped off and she appeared to be laying in some water. She looked down and verified that her bra and pants, though ripped, were both on her body still. She choked down more vomit as she thought about all that could have potentially happened while she was unconscious.

"Stacia," Kai said more insistently, "we have to get out of here. I hit him over the head with a vase, and the police are on their way, but I don't think I can get you out of here and fight him off. Let's go, I can help you!"

Stacia groggily got to her feet with Kai's assistance. She tried to focus on what would happen if they didn't get out of there quickly instead of the pain that was ripping through her body.

Kai slung her uninjured arm over his shoulder as he tried to half carry, half drag her out of the store. They made it a few steps when Stacia heard Kai yelp and felt him falling towards the ground. They were tangled together, and she watched in horror as, despite her efforts to keep him upright, he hurtled towards the ground.

She screamed in horror as, on the way down, his head struck the corner of the counter. The masked man pushed past her and began kicking Kai repeatedly in the ribs. Kai didn't move or so much as blink, as a puddle of blood started to expand from the back of Kai's head. Stacia heard the first sound of sirens and knew that, though help was closer, she was still in a difficult predicament.

"Help, we're in here," she bellowed at the top of her lungs, almost sick again at the pain and the burning in her throat, hoping that the police would get in there in the next few seconds. Adrenaline kicked in as she saw the man go to kick the motionless Kai again. She started limping towards him, every tiny step feeling like it was a mile long, before she could fully comprehend the danger.

"Don't think I won't come back and finish what I started, I'm untouchable," the masked intruder said menacingly as he pulled his foot all the way back for a kick.

Stacia screamed again, in rage, which seemed to startle him enough to make him barely make contact with this kick. Adrenaline covering up any discomfort at the moment, causing Stacia to be running purely off of fight instinct. "Oh yeah, asshole? That pot right up there is a camera, and it's just one of many that you were too stupid to notice when you canvased us earlier. I also noticed your little gloves are gone which means my friend must have yanked them off. DNA evidence makes you a little more touchable, asshole. Oh, and you hear those sirens right outside the door? Those are for you!" She looked at him with pure hatred. She knew predators like him got off on fear, and she wasn't going to give him the satisfaction of knowing how scared she'd been, and still was. She picked up the closest hard object that was within her reach and advanced towards him.

"Bitch," was the only word he had time to say as he headed towards the front entrance in the hopes of exiting before the police pulled up.

"You are going to have to call me something much worse than that if you want to fuck with me," Stacia said quietly to the retreating man's back. Stacia continued to hold the stone statue that she'd picked up from the counter menacingly in her hands as adrenaline continued to course through her body. She waited until he'd left the building, the sound of the jingle confirming his exit before she dropped to her knees, all adrenaline gone, fear and pain taking over. She crawled as best as she could over to Kai and tried to rouse him, without jostling him as she was worried about how hard his head and neck had hit the counter.

The police began trickling into the store and it seemed surreal. They'd come in guns drawn, which she understood was necessary, to make sure that there were no other perpetrators inside.

"Please help him!" She'd urged hoarsely, adrenaline continuing to wear off, causing panic and nausea and pain all simultaneously. Once the police had done a quick sweep, emergency medical personnel entered the store and began examining them both.

Stacia had refused an exam until Kai was taken care of. She promised she would stay seated and not move until they assessed her thoroughly. In a panic Stacia called her sister, telling her to get to the store immediately.

She had Eleanor's information stored on her phone as well and attempted to call her a few times before the pain and panic became too much, and they assisted her onto a stretcher and loaded her into the back of the ambulance so she could warm up. They placed a temporary splint on her right arm and a soft neck brace on her neck after the paramedic saw the bruising.

Given her neck trauma and the fact that she admitted to being choked until she lost consciousness, they told her they would take her to the hospital for a complete work-up. They assured her that Kai was being taken care of and that the ambulance carrying her battered savior was already heading to the same hospital.

The EMT in the back of the ambulance sat next to Stacia and held her hand as Stacia cried. She didn't try to reassure her that things were going to be okay, she just sat there and comforted her without saying a word until they pulled up to the hospital.

PRESENT DAY

Stacia was running through a maze, she didn't know what she was running from, but she knew that if she didn't give it her all she would die. She heard something behind her, and she attempted to pick up speed. She turned the corner and ran smack-dab into a man wearing a pumpkin mask, but when she tried to push away from him, he disintegrated into dust. She turned around again, trying to find her way out of the dead end when she ran into another man wearing a pumpkin mask. She didn't panic until she realized that the man was really a man and not an apparition. She screamed loudly as he grabbed onto her and snaked an arm around her neck.

"Babe," Marco said, gently, stroking her hair as he tried calmly to get her to wake up. "You're safe, I'm right here."

Stacia opened her eyes, trying to shake off the dream that felt so real. She took a deep breath, allowing Marco to hold her until she calmed down. She did the deep breathing exercises her counselor had been encouraging her to do, smelling the proverbial roses and blowing out the proverbial birthday candles. In 1, 2, 3, hold 1,2,3 and out 1,2,3. Marco, spooning her from behind, started breathing right along with her until the slow, deep breathing lulled them both back to sleep.

She wasn't sure when during the night the nightmare occurred, but she was relieved that she'd been able to go back to sleep and that she hadn't kept Marco up all night, as she had a few times since the attack a few weeks earlier.

They were still all in the process of recovering. Her grandparents were not allowing her to go back to work for another week, and even then, some things would need to be modified because of her broken right arm. Though she appreciated the time to come to grips with what had occurred, she was irritated that everyone was treating her like she was made of glass.

Being home also caused more time for fixating on the bad things that had happened. Though Stacia loved redecorating her apartment, there were only so many times it could be done in a short span of time.

Her Grandmother had insisted that she see a counselor before she returned to work. She'd been so thankful for the social worker and the case manager who had helped get her information on a counselor after her overnight stay at the hospital, but she hadn't initially planned on needing to go. She'd ended up making an appointment a few days in, after her first nightmare.

The CT scan of her brain and neck had been normal, but the doctors had decided to keep Stacia overnight for observation. She didn't find out until she looked at the news report on the attack a few days after Halloween that the perpetrator, Mitchell Pierce, had been taken to the same hospital as she and Kai were in for a few hours, getting medical clearance before going to jail.

She appreciated that the emergency room staff had not disclosed this information to her and had eased her anxiety about being there in general by having security stationed close to her room. The care and compassion that all of the hospital employees showed, coupled with the sweet EMT, Zoie, had made a very tough situation a little bit easier.

Upon discharging, she'd verbalized how impressed and thankful she was to her family, and the day after, her sister and Chad had brought flowers for all the first responders, the emergency room staff, and the floor nursing staff as a collective Thank You.

Stacia had spent the first day after getting home on the couch at her condo with Marco never leaving her side. She felt so loved, having him there taking care of her, but she felt horrible that everyone was having to change their lives and schedules in order to dote on her. A few times she'd used the desire for a hot bath for relaxation as a way to get some alone time, locking the door in case Marco or a family member decided that checking on her was more important than her privacy.

Her family had not updated her on Molly until she discharged, and even then, provided only tiny details at a time until it became clear that she would pass away soon. Stacia had felt horrible for them all and was in constant contact with Rachel about what she could do from home to help.

When Molly had passed, Stacia had ordered seed packets for people to plant and had assisted Rachel in getting the word out to the BeeKeeper community. The funeral had been really difficult, but Scarlett and Tevin had done a great job at making it a celebration of Molly's life.

She knew that Eleanor had a lot to deal with while caring for Kai, so she tried to refrain from contacting her too frequently for updates. From the updates she'd gotten, it appeared that Kai was breathing on his own but was still not awake, meaning he wasn't out-of-the-woods yet.

She constantly flashed back to a few weeks ago and how had he not been trying to get her out by slinging her arm over his shoulder, he would not have been facing sideways, and he may not have fallen at such a strange angle, hitting the corner.

Eleanor had continued to call her intermittently, assuring her that Kai would have wanted it this way. That he knew what the potential was for harm when he assisted her. Eleanor passed on the information that the emergency room doctor had told her; that it was the open skull fracture that may have saved his life, preventing extreme swelling to his brain. Yet, none of it made Stacia feel much better about the situation.

Her grandparents had come back immediately from their latest RV vacation when they heard of the attack. They wanted to make sure Stacia was okay and to assist in assessing the store for damage, as well as the investigation. Grandma Betty has been running like a chicken with her head cut off between Stacia's house and the store since they'd returned.

Each day that went by inside her apartment caused Stacia to feel a little bit more overwhelmed at the amount of attention she was receiving from friends and family. After the news story aired about the attack, she'd gotten calls from high school friends who had not bothered to contact her when she moved back more than two years ago.

She'd even gotten a get-well card from Luke and Amber, who she could tell had gotten married as they had the same last name on the return address on the envelope. Stacia had appreciated the gesture, though a part of her was slightly annoyed. She didn't love Luke anymore, and she sometimes missed her friendship with both Luke and Amber. But what they'd done to her had still been completely unacceptable and heartbreaking. She hoped that someday she could maybe forgive their betrayal, but she wasn't quite ready for that yet.

"What do you want to do today?" Marco asked as they made breakfast.

"Rachel texted me this morning, sounds like the girls are still kind of having a hard time. I was thinking about maybe seeing them for lunch or something," Stacia answered.

"Do you want me to come with you?" Marco asked as he sweetly came over and wrapped his arms around her from behind, giving her a chaste kiss on the cheek.

"Why don't you go into work for a bit?" Stacia advised. "I really am starting to feel guilty that you have been with me so much." Marco had not really left her side for more than a few hours which, once again, made her feel loved, but she wondered if not being alone was making it a little more difficult to process what she'd been through.

"I really don't want to leave you, baby," Marco said as he pulled her out of the chair and pulled her in closer for a hug.

"Really, I need some time to decompress and be alone, I think. I'm so sick of being cooped up in this house. I'm just going to throw on some running clothes and hope that it helps me get back in the groove," Stacia squeezed him tightly. "I'm fine."

"But you still have a cast on. I can come with you in case something happens. Really it isn't a big deal, Benny is okay with covering for me for a few hours. He needs some extra money so he can try to move out of his parent's house next semester. I'll go get changed. I brought gym clothes last time I ran home in case you were up for some outside activity," Marco went into the bedroom to put on his running attire.

Without realizing what she was doing, Stacia impulsively grabbed a pair of tennis shoes by the door and left. She sat on the curb outside of her apartment building and tied the laces, which proved to be slightly tricky with her casted arm. She'd slept in a long sleeve shirt, with one arm pulled up to accommodate her cast, and a pair of Denver Broncos pajama pants, which she would not usually run in, but it would do.

She started slowly, letting her muscles warm up a little before picking up the pace, the fall air crisp but not too cold. She wanted the run to cause a little bit of a burn, wanting the pavement to punish her so she could suffer the way so many of the people she cared about right now were suffering. She started to run faster and faster until her legs and her lungs burned, and her arm throbbed from the constant motion.

She ran through the light at a crosswalk and into the park, running on the trail, passing a couple pushing a stroller as well as a group of speed walkers. She slowed slightly as she turned a corner and ran down into a dim tunnel with the overpass overhead. She was winding a somewhat blind corner when she stumbled into someone who was kneeling next to the edge of the tunnel, and she sprawled onto the ground, somehow managing not to cause further injury to her right arm. The man came over and tried to assist her up.

"Stay the hell away from me!" She shouted, instantly on the defensive, ready to attack if provoked.

The man stood up, startled, "I was just tying my shoe, lady. I wasn't trying to hurt anyone. I really am sorry!"

Corlet Dawn

"Why did you stop in the tunnel? You scared the shit out of me. Why would you do that to me? Why the fuck would you do that to me!" Stacia exclaimed, getting louder with each statement. The man looked at her shocked at first, and then the shock turned into concern. He once again tried to help Stacia up, but she pushed his hand away. She burst into tears, "Why can't you all just leave me alone! I can hardly think!"

It was then that she heard Marco's voice, "Stacia?"

She looked up and saw Marco approaching them. He was sweating profusely, now in his running clothes. "I can handle it from here," Marco said to the man, "she has had a tough few weeks."

"I'm sorry," the man said again as he started a slow jog out of the tunnel, a look of relief on his face.

Marco bent down to Stacia's level. "You followed me? Do I have to buy a cat to get some space from you? Geez!"

Marco ignored the cat comment, "I was looking out the window while I was getting dressed, and I saw you running like a bat-out-of-hell. I was planning on following you from a distance to make sure you were okay and get home before you realized I was stalking you. Finding you like this tells me two things: One, I can see now that you really do need some alone time, Two, your fight-or-flight system still seems pretty elevated." Marco said, holding out his hand to assist her up.

Stacia refused his hand, instead stubbornly struggling for a moment before managing to get herself upright. "I'm fine. I told you I AM FINE. Everyone needs to start treating me like I'm not capable of anything. I'm fine." She took two steps forward, attempting to take off at a sprint again when the tears started coming full force. She ran out of the tunnel before the tears blurred her vision and she stopped, collapsing on the grass nearby.

Marco walked to her cautiously and sat down beside her, giving her some space but letting her know that he was there. They sat in silence for a few minutes before her tears slowed down and she was able to speak.

"I feel a lot of things right now. I feel guilty that I'm more okay than Kai. I feel guilty that I lived when his last victim didn't. I'm pissed that everything seemed fine and now nothing feels fine. I feel bad that I'm even bitching about anything when Scarlett and Tevin are dealing with things so much more horrible. I hate everything right now and I don't know what to do," Stacia buried her face in her hands, frustrated and mad.

"I'm here if you need me," Marco said quietly. She could tell his feelings were hurt, stung by the hate comment.

"I know," she said as the sting in his voice instantly took her frustration down to a more manageable level. "I'm so sorry Marco, I obviously don't hate you. Hating you would be impossible, in fact. There's just a lot going on right now. I want to do this with you by my side, but that does not mean I literally need you by my side 24-7. I need some time to process some of this by myself."

Marco simply put his hand out and she placed hers on top of his." I love you, Stacia. I love you more than I can communicate with you. I wasn't looking for love when I met you, but once we started down the romance path, it didn't take long for me to fall for you. I can't imagine not being in your life, but I will do whatever you need me to do. I will be here for you physically or from across town. I can handle you asking for space, and I will try to be respectful of that, but please don't push me away. Getting a call from your sister that you had been attacked just about killed me."

Marco, who Stacia had never seen even mildly sad, started to get a build-up of tears in his eyes. "I cried the entire way to the hospital. If I had found out that Mitchell was in the hospital while I was there, I would be in jail right now because I would have made him pay for what he did to you. I knew I loved you before that moment but thinking that I could lose you..." Marco paused, taking a few deep breaths. "Thinking I could lose you made me never want to leave you again. It made me realize that you are the woman I want to spend the rest of my life with and one day, when the time is right, I will ask you to marry me."

Stacia sat on the grass, dumbfounded, a million emotions running through her. She'd just unleashed anger and frustration on this man. She'd hurt his feelings intentionally, and he'd turned around and told her that he respected her space, that he'd been scared to lose her, and that he wanted to marry her someday. "I can't even attempt to be a smart ass right now. I know all of these feelings I'm suffering from are normal and that the counselor will help. I love you, I'm sorry I scared you, and you are the man I have been looking for. I would be the luckiest woman alive to someday be your wife. Oh, I thought of something slightly smart-assy. I love you more than coffee, which says a lot!"

Marco chuckled, dimples flashing, as he helped her off of the grass and gave her a giant hug and a steamy kiss. He said, "Would now be a good time to mention that you look like a crazy person."

Stacia looked down at her pajama pants (which now sported a hole in the knee), her cast, and her running shoes. She was sure her tear-streaked face made her look even crazier.

"Yeah well, it is very fitting of the mood I was in. Shall we head home?" She asked as she started slowly running back in the direction of her apartment, Marco firmly by her side.

39

Rachel felt overwhelmed, like a circus performer juggling several plates on a stick. One or more was always in jeopardy of flying off and crashing to the ground. She felt that she had a lot of people depending on her for comfort right now. Although she was good at being the one in charge of managing the stress, it felt like the grief was piling on and consuming them all.

She'd had to figure out how to deal with her own grief and pain while also actively dealing with her girls' devastation. She'd constructed a plan with Chad, when he'd been deployed, to make it as easy as possible on their girls. Those monthly boxes had been nice to focus on on a month-to-month basis, and their monthly assignments had given them a nice distraction, especially because it focused on doing something nice for a stranger. Though they'd tried to prepare the girls for Molly's passing with books, videos, and extensive conversations, it was still a daily struggle. She knew that her girls needed her badly right now, and she was doing her best to give them what they needed while still understanding that they may experience grief differently because of their ages.

She thought back to Chad's stress when he first arrived home and how they had gotten through that as a family. They had obtained outside help from a counselor who helped them agree to plans for positive change. But this stress felt different. She also knew that grief triggered her husband by reminding him of all the people he knew who had been taken too soon. She was worried that he would have a regression in his progress because of this.

She felt horrible about the attack on her sister and wondered if her presence there, too, would have prevented the attack.

Rachel was the older sister and knew that her sister was having a hard time but had support from Marco. If only she could take her sister's pain and guilt away.

It would continue to be a bumpy road for all of them, but she was confident they would survive the difficult journey to recovery.

40

"**M**oooooooom! I want the Star Wars Legos! Why can't I have them?! I NEED THEM!!!!!" Stella was throwing a full-blown toddler-like tantrum in the middle of Target. Rachel could not remember it ever being this bad, even when Stella had been an actual toddler. Rachel could see the heads of passersby turning to stare at them.

Marie, usually the more vocal of the two looked absolutely mortified. "Stella, you don't even like Legos and Mom said..."

"Shut up, Marie!" Stella screamed, which caused even more glances their direction.

"I HATE YOU BOTH!!!!" Marie screamed at the top of her lungs, tears streaming down her red face.

Rachel knew that this was going to soon turn into more of a losing battle when sister turned on sister. She could not remember ever being this mortified. She grabbed each girl's hand firmly and marched towards the restrooms. She tried to give everyone looking in their direction the sympathy-inducing mom smile, the one that said: "Yes, I'm aware that my 9-year-old children are acting inappropriately, but I assure you I'm trying to deal with it. Don't you remember those days?"

The emotional breakdown from both of the girls occurred the moment they walked in the door to the restroom, both girls instantly starting to cry. A woman washing her hands looked at

Rachel sympathetically, which was all it took for Rachel to also become teary-eyed.

The woman finished washing her hands quickly, leaving them alone in the bathroom. Rachel started: "I'm trying to be patient, I really am. I know that the last month has been really hard, but I need to know what is really going on with you so we can talk about it. I know this has nothing to do with Legos."

Stella, sobbing, attempted to speak, "Molly..is..dead...and Aunt..Stacia...could..have...died, and I DON'T WANT TO DIE!"

Marie, hearing her sister's jumbled speech, started crying harder. "I don't want to die either! I miss Molly!"

Rachel, whose heart was already heavy, felt her heart become more broken for her girls. "So, what I hear you saying is that you're sad about Molly."

Both girls nodded, moving closer to each other for support, their latest insults to each other forgotten, "Why couldn't they save her?" Stella asked as she wailed into her sister's shoulder.

Rachel sat there for a minute, letting the girls cry in the middle of the Target bathroom before attempting an answer. "Molly was sick and in pain. I know that all of this is hard to understand for both of you and it is just as hard for me to understand as an adult."

"I'm sad, but I'm also really mad! We just met Molly and now she's gone," Marie said.

"It's normal to be sad and also to be mad. When things like this happen, it's hard to understand why it happened. I would be worried if neither of you felt those things. What are some things we could do to honor Molly's memory?" Rachel asked the girls, drawing both of them into a group hug.

"Well, something with Peter Pan maybe," Stella said.

"We could bring it up at the next BeeKeeper meeting and figure out some potential ideas, "Rachel said. "But I like your thinking. We need to also continue looking at the material the Angel Project gave us. I bet there are some ideas of things we can do to honor her memory. There's also some information in there on positively dealing with grief so we can take good care of ourselves and our feelings, so they aren't coming out inappropriately when nobody expects it…"

"Like in the middle of Target," Marie chimed in.

"What about Aunt Stacia?" Stella asked, going back to one of her initial concerns.

"What part of it do you need to talk about?" Rachel asked as she stooped down to look at her daughter.

"What if he comes for us? What if he gets mad that he got caught at our store? What if he kills us?" Stella asked, slightly panicked.

Rachel opened her mouth and was about to provide reassurance when Marie chipped in, "It said on the news that he is a killer."

Rachel shot her a look that implied she wasn't helping the situation, "Okay. Let's address this, one subject at a time. He is in jail, surrounded by guards that make sure he stays there. The judge is currently not going to let him out until he has had a trial. He may be mad that he got caught but, obviously, he should only be mad at himself for the choices he made."

"Yeah, horrible ones!" Marie chipped in again, which resulted in her mom shooting her another look. "What? He did make horrible decisions! He is a horrible person!"

"I think we can all agree on that, Marie," Rachel agreed. "Maybe we can wait for any additional comments until I have finished speaking so I can help your sister calm down."

"Sorry," Marie said, grabbing her sister's hand in support.

"I'll address the last comment, and then we are going to get out of the bathroom," Rachel said. "It's not the ideal spot to be having a heart-to-heart. In fact, it's kind of gross." The girls laughed in agreement, forgetting, if only temporarily, their distress.

"Your dad and I will always protect you. We love you and aren't going to let anyone hurt you. We would gladly give our lives to keep you safe. They probably have enough information to keep him locked up for a long time. Stacia was hurt, but she will heal. She was frightened, but she is seeing a counselor to help her. A counselor is an option that we always have as well, and I think as of today we should maybe look into it again. The option that does not work for us would be bottling it in and lashing out at each other. We need each other right now, and our friends and family also need us. It doesn't work for us to turn against each other when we are all hurting right now." Rachel paused for a moment, letting it all sink in.

It only took a few seconds for Stella to apologize. "I'm sorry, Mom. I don't think I even want to know what I looked like out there. I'm embarrassed."

"I'm not in the habit of kicking a person when they are having a hard time, but I must admit, Stella, that this wasn't one of your finer moments. When you're having a hard time from here on out, please come to me, come to your dad, your aunt, your sister, your grandma, a friend at school, anyone!!!!!!! You have options."

The restroom door opened, and one of the women who had been looking at the spectacle earlier walked in. "You girls ready to go try this again?" Rachel asked as she held the door open for the girls as they walked out. Rachel and the woman exchanged polite smiles as they passed each other on the way out.

Rachel knew that Stella and Marie would both need some time to heal, each in their own ways. Molly had been in their lives for a short time, but she'd made a huge impact on all of them. She'd been as close to an angel on Earth as Rachel had ever seen. She'd been spunky and playful and fit in so well with the girls, never causing them to compete against each other. Molly would never be forgotten. Rachel would need to brainstorm with Stacia ideas for BeeKeeper activities that would honor Molly.

They were walking back to find their abandoned cart when she got a text message on her cell phone: *Kai talked to me today. I think he is going to be okay.*

Part 4- Plumeria- symbol of new beginnings

~New life or birth

~Creation

~Beauty

41

Eleanor was focusing on taking it one second at a time, one minute at a time, one hour at a time, one day at a time. If she focused on the here and now, she knew that she could get through. She knew that there was hope, and she also knew that the road to recovery would be slow.

She knew that she was resilient, and she knew that Kai was a fighter. They'd stayed afloat through a lot, like a pair of castaways on a boat trying to weather the constant turmoil of the storm. She knew that they needed to lean on their support system to help them during the times they could not stay above the surface.

She knew that time was going to be the determiner of their fate. She wasn't naive enough to think that he could walk away from something like this unscathed, but she felt that there was a chance that she could get the Kai back that he'd been determined to be before the attack.

She was sad that they'd made so much ground over the last several months that had it been destroyed in the span of a few minutes, a few seconds, a snap of the fingers. She was proud of Kai for the decision that he had made. He'd unselfishly jumped into a situation that very well could have been fatal to Stacia. She could not remember ever being so proud of him.

Along with the feeling of pride came a touch of resentment.

She was sad that he'd been so severely hurt when Stacia had walked away with less physical trauma. She felt horrible for admitting that, even to herself, as Stacia obviously would be dealing with the repercussions of what occurred that night, possibly forever.

She wished it was like it appeared to be in the movies where a character in a coma wakes up, flutters their eyelashes and asks for a hot breakfast and a newspaper. She knew that there would be a need for a lot of rehabilitation. She knew that with a Traumatic Brain Injury (TBI) there was the potential for personality changes and a decrease in the ability to care for himself. She was aware of her baseline medical knowledge, but it was once again hard to be objective when taking care of someone you loved. When she'd said yes to marrying him, she meant it, and she meant that she would love him no matter what happened.

She knew there was the potential that the broken part of his brain, the part they'd been working so hard to repair with counseling, could be broken again or more damaged than before. If this were the case, though she would love him from afar, she would have to leave.

Now they played the waiting game.

42

"Kai," Eleanor whispered gently in his ear as she had consistently for the two weeks since the attack. She'd held his hand tightly, trying in every way she could think of to let him know that she was there. Hoping that she could coax him faster out of his current vegetative state with voice and touch.

A week after the attack he'd exhibited some movement. Kai had been breathing on his own after a week on the ventilator. After he was taken off of the ventilator, he'd also been taken off of sedation, and from there, they watched and waited. A few days after the ventilator was no longer in use, he fluttered his eyes open for a few moments. Eleanor had not been there, having run home for a shower and a change of clothing. The nurse had called her immediately to let her know, and Eleanor had driven back there as quickly and safely as she could.

By the time she got up to the ICU again, he was unconscious once more. Still, Eleanor had hope. If it had happened once, there was the potential that it could happen again. She'd posted herself right beside him, enveloping his hand in hers and staring at him, barely blinking, willing him to open his eyes yet again until eventually, she fell asleep next to his bed, holding his hand.

The next day he'd opened his eyes again, and Eleanor had

been ecstatic. She couldn't believe that she'd ever taken for granted something as simple as the ability of her fiancé to open and close his eyes. He'd opened his coffee-bean colored eyes and blinked, looking around for what felt like hours to her, but was most likely less than a minute.

The intensivist doctor had been hopeful. "It is a good sign that he is showing some signs of wakefulness, but we will not really know the extent of the damage until he fully wakes up and we trial daily things like eating, walking, toileting. The most recent MRI looked promising with no additional swelling. I know the waiting game is never easy, but let's see what happens in the next week."

Eleanor had nodded in agreement, knowing that there was indeed nothing more that they could do but wait. She had seen the waiting game frustration in families of her patients before, and now she was experiencing just how frustrating that could be firsthand.

Eleanor had not immediately texted Kai's family or her friends after the two days of eye opening. She didn't want to give his family false hope and she didn't want to get encouragement from her friends in case he didn't end up being okay. She knew that false hope would do nothing positive for her. She would rather be pessimistic in this case. If he ended up being all right, she would be ecstatic. She had to protect herself and the only way she knew how to at this point in time was in planning on him not returning to his completely healthy state.

After three days of blinking, Kai started squeezing her hand, hard and with intention. The first time it happened, Eleanor had thought he was just suffering from involuntary body movements, but when she went to drop his hand, he'd grabbed harder, preventing her from letting go. This had happened not just once, but twice. Eleanor had passed the news on to the ICU nurse who had agreed that it was most likely intentional.

The day after the hand squeezing had been even more encouraging when Kai had simultaneously, opened his eyes, grabbed her hand, and wiggled his toes when asked to do so. Eleanor had reassured him that she was there, and for the first time, he was able to keep his eyes open longer.

"Let's try something," Eleanor had said. "If you can hear me squeeze my hand three times," She'd sat there for a few moments, hoping and praying for a squeeze. After she felt like there was no hope, she'd felt three weak squeezes. "I'm here Kai, I'm not going anywhere. You rest, and we can try this again later. I love you."

Two weeks after he started showing signs of movement, Kai spoke. The first time he spoke, Eleanor was sleeping on the pull-out bed next to his, her home for the last few weeks. Work had helped get her shifts covered under the Family Medical Leave Act, and she was able to use her paid time off bank to supplement her time off of work. Her coworkers had been very supportive, constantly calling and texting to see what she needed. They'd started a paid time off donation at work in case Eleanor ran out and needed more.

"Ellie," she heard in a hoarse whisper. She woke up from a dead sleep. She assumed it was similar to the mom state of sleep that she'd heard her friends with children described. She once had a friend tell her that if one of her children so much as stepped foot out of bed, she could hear it with her supersonic-mom ears.

She jumped out of the sleeper chair and went to his side. "I heard you, baby, I'm here." She grabbed his hand and stroked the side of his face. His eyes flew open, which startled Eleanor as it seemed to take a lot more time and effort than it normally did. He blinked and looked at her for a few minutes before his mouth started to contort, "Ellie."

Tears streamed down her face as she continued to stroke his face and squeeze his hand. "I'm here, Kai. I'm here. Stay with me. Can you stay with me?" She could see his mouth straining to work again before he fatigued. He squeezed her hand in frustration. Eleanor could not imagine how frustrating it would be trying to communicate but barely having the energy to.

She moved a chair next to his bed like she'd done when he was first admitted to the ICU, at first afraid that he may die during the night, and now fearful that she may miss a second of him trying to communicate. The next morning, she awoke to him again, calling her name. It was then that she sent a text to everyone she knew: *Kai talked to me today. I think he is going to be okay.*

He seemed to be able to talk more easily as the day went on, but he also needed periods of rest in between.

"What day is it?" Was one of the first full sentences he managed. Eleanor had lost track of the days, living inside an ICU version of Groundhogs Day where each day she'd hoped for progress in leaps and bounds, not the baby steps that had occurred.

"You don't need to worry about that," Eleanor said. "Do you remember what happened?"

"Stacia?" Kai managed to whisper, concern on his face.

"You saved her," Eleanor said, stroking the side of his face. His eyelids fluttered involuntarily, his body telling him already that it was time for another break from both recalling the trauma and exerting so much energy.

"We're all so thankful and proud of you," Eleanor said as she wiped a stray hair off of his forehead, watching him slip back to sleep.

His sisters, Adrienne and Alex, hadn't been able to fly out immediately as they were just finishing some things for school before Thanksgiving break. They'd chosen to fly to Colorado from California to see Kai and spend time with Eleanor for Thanksgiving. She'd been invited to spend time with various friends in the area but didn't feel right leaving Kai's side.

They'd gotten there a few days before Thanksgiving and had been staying at Eleanor's condo, occasionally trading out with her but overall giving her the one-on-one time with Kai that they knew she needed.

Kai's mother and stepfather had been informed of his attack the day after it occurred, but true to his stepfather's personality, he'd demanded updates via phone as he had not wanted Kai's mother to fly out there solo.

The twins spoke candidly to Eleanor about how frustrated

they were with Bill's control issues. Even though he was their biological father and had provided everything for them that he had not provided for Kai, they were very aware of how unacceptable his behavior was. "We keep trying to get her to leave, but she is just so codependent she can't," Adrienne said.

Eleanor thought about the situation Kai's mom and stepdad were in. She thought about how close Kai and she had been to living that same cycle of abuse.

When Kai continued to progress with his speech, Eleanor texted Adrienne and Alex, and his sisters drove there immediately and posted at the bedside with Eleanor. He slept for a while before attempting to speak again, "... catch him? ... I think ... Mitchell Pierce?" Kai asked somewhat unintelligibly.

"They got him, Kai," Eleanor said. "You caught him. He would still be out there if it weren't for you, and Stacia would be dead." She added, "What were you doing there anyway?"

Kai swallowed, took a moment to let his voice rest, before answering, "Flowers for Molly."

Eleanor started sobbing, having to walk away for a moment. When she thought back to that night, she recalled texting him to let him know where she was. He'd gone to the flower shop to get flowers for Molly. Eleanor walked back to Kai after composing herself.

"Molly?" Kai asked. Eleanor shook her head, crying softly. Kai squeezed her hand, "Sorry."

As the week went on, Kai was able to do more and more. They'd been giving him nutrition through the IV and were able to wean him off of it when he could eat and drink without throwing up. They had physical therapists, speech therapists, and occupational therapists working with him daily to make sure he was getting stronger. By the end of week one, he'd successfully started eating meals and doing stand-to-pivot transfers onto a bedside toilet. Eleanor was trying to let the nurse handle some of the things that Kai still seemed embarrassed about, which was okay with her. She knew that some aspects of the whole process could be humiliating.

When he asked who had come from work for visits, Eleanor let him down gently, telling him they had sent flowers but had not been able to send anyone given he was in the ICU. In reality, they had barely even reached out to Eleanor for updates.

When work had inquired about visits, she'd informed them that family only was allowed on the unit, but there hadn't been an effort to see him once he moved to the step-down rehabilitation unit.

"I have been thinking it's maybe time for a more fulfilling job anyway," Kai said in response. "I kept having work nightmares while I was asleep. I feel less stressed out waking up after a trauma than I did going to work there every day. I think it may say a little something about the type of group I've been working for."

Eleanor nodded and couldn't help but think back on the first counseling session they had been to together when it had become apparent that work was a huge stressor for Kai. They had also inappropriately forced him take the Mitchell Pierce case. In the back of her mind, Eleanor sometimes wondered if he had been given the case to fail as the Pierces' pockets ran so deep. Who really knew who all could have been involved with getting Pierce off on his charges last year?

"What was it like when you were asleep?" Eleanor asked.

"A lot of it felt like I was dreaming," Kai noted. "Some of the dreaming took place the night of the attack and just replayed over and over. Sometimes it would end with the same results and sometimes with different results. I didn't honestly know which version was correct until you talked me through it. The strangest by far was when I was trying to wake up. I could hear what you were sometimes saying and yet could not get my body to cooperate. I felt like my brain was normal, but my body wouldn't cooperate at all."

"I can't imagine what any of that was like. Were you scared at all?" Eleanor asked.

"Terrified," Kai admitted. "I didn't know if I would ever make it back to you. I didn't know if I would be stuck inside my brain with no cooperation from my body. I didn't know if years had gone by. I didn't know if you would move on. I didn't know if I would lose out on my chance to prove my worth to you."

Eleanor patted his hand and said: "I didn't know if you would ever make it back to me either. I was so scared. I honestly didn't know who you would be when you woke up."

He replied: "I don't blame you for being afraid. And I know I had been a jerk in the past. I want to continue to show you who I truly am and the man I want to be for you. I will respect that you want a full year of counseling before we start planning our wedding. I plan to spend that time showing you the Kai I want to be. I really was serious about my job, too. I wouldn't mind a drop in pay to be less stressed and actually enjoy my career."

Eleanor nodded in agreement, "Well, we obviously figured out that your job has been a major stressor in your life. I'm beyond okay with us reducing stress. What would you like to do instead?"

"Maybe work for a non-profit where I can help others?" Kai smiled at the thought and Eleanor returned the smile. They were interrupted by the physical therapist who was going to work with Kai on his walking today. It was one of the last steps required to get him out of the hospital.

A few days into his stay on the step-down unit his sisters flew home with promises to connect again during winter vacation. The step-down unit allowed visitors, so Eleanor invited their friends to come see Kai.

Stacia and Marco were the first two to arrive and it had been emotional. Stacia walked in with a get-well bouquet in hand. "I was going to try not to cry but as you can see, I'm failing at that," Stacia said through tears. "I can't even begin to thank you for what you did. I think it would only be fair if you get free flowers for life."

Eleanor and Kai laughed at the free-flowers comment. "No, really. You step foot in our store, you get free flowers," Stacia said.

Rachel and Chad also came to visit a few days later, bringing a get-well bouquet of their own. "You saved my sister," Rachel said tearfully. She handed Kai an envelope.

Kai opened the envelope, reading the words inside. "You don't have to do that," Kai said. "I was just trying to do the right thing."

"I talked it over with my grandmother and we insist. When you guys get married the flowers are on us. It's the least we can do. Oh, and I believe Stacia already told you about the free flowers for life, right?"

"You really don't have to do that," Eleanor said. In her head, she was thinking about just not going into the store again for flowers before Rachel read her mind.

"Don't think we won't notice if you all of a sudden aren't coming in anymore," Rachel said knowingly.

"Only if we can compromise," Eleanor said, "I'm still paying you for the fairy garden supplies."

"Deal," Rachel agreed.

A few days after their pleasant visits and therapy progress, they were informed that Kai could discharge with outpatient services. They were ecstatic. They had been in the hospital for a little over a month. It felt like time to face "normal life" again.

"Do you have absolutely everything?" Terry, the nurse going over discharge instructions with them, asked a few days later.

"I double checked," Eleanor reassured her.

"Okay," Terry answered. "Do you folks have any questions?"

"I think we have it all covered," Eleanor had said reassuringly.

"Case coordination got the first appointment scheduled for you with your primary care provider and from there they can get you scheduled with physical therapy and neurology if needed. Until then, lots of rest. Living with a nurse to baby you will help, too." Terry removed the tape from the IV catheter on Kai's arm. He winced as some of his arm hair came up with the tape.

Eleanor looked at him with one eyebrow raised. "The baby-ing stage is done the moment we walk out the door," Kai looked at her as she winked at him and added, "Now is the time for tough love."

"It's not easy having a nurse as a close family member," Terry had said with a wink of her own to Kai as they got him loaded into the wheelchair.

His walking had improved significantly, and he was now able to provide his own self-care for the last few days.

Kai had been excited about the prospect of some life changes and had been working on his resume over the last few days from his hospital bed. He was ready to turn in his resignation as soon as he had spent time at home pondering the future.

Eleanor was going to work just one day a week at first as she transitioned to full time slowly. One of her coworkers agreed to peek in on him during the day when Eleanor was at work. She was excited to tiptoe back to her job. She had missed her patients and the satisfaction she got with her job.

She was also excited to have the time to try to reconnect with Scarlett and Tevin. Rachel and Stacia both had mentioned some ideas for keeping Molly's memory alive. Kai had even volunteered to help with the legal advice if that was needed.

They weren't going to wait before getting set up with their counselors again. Before discharge, they'd both had some pretty extensive discussions about the need to be extra vigilant.

They'd agreed that there was the potential to try to rush things with wedding planning because they'd been of the traumatic event that occurred. Going through the trauma had made them, in turn, realize how much they wanted to be together, but reinforced the need for counseling.

They were staying firm on their decision to finish a full year of therapy before discussing the wedding planning. They were going to give themselves time to think and heal in order to make smart decisions about the future.

Mitchell Pierce was still in prison awaiting his trial. Kai had written a letter while he was in the hospital to Mitchell's parents pleading with them to not interfere this time. Kai had told them about the guilt that had eaten him up from the inside out from not preventing Mitchell from attacking someone again.

He'd disclosed to them that he felt responsible for anyone being attacked after the dismissed charges and how strange it had felt to be the one to stop the assault.

He described the screams of helpless Stacia and how hard it had been to recover in the hospital. He didn't know if it would help at all, but he knew that he had to try. He would do everything in his power this time to remedy the wrong that Mitchell Pierce had done.

43

I t had been three months, and everything had been slowly returning to normal. Eleanor was working full time again and Kai had found his dream job working as a staff attorney for a Child's Advocacy Center based out of New York with a branch in Denver. He had flown to New York twice already and Eleanor had timed her work schedule to be able to travel with him. She had never had the chance to travel much and she loved her first taste of it.

Eleanor had taken Molly's death to heart. When she returned to work, she had joined the Sunny Committee, designed to bring joy to the children hospitalized at the facility. She had brought up the fact that the oncology patients could not have real flowers and with the help of Stacia and Rachel, they had started a Molly's Flowers campaign.

Customers at the flower shop could purchase a book flower, a crepe flower, or a glass flower for a recipient on the Oncology Unit at Children's Hospital. Bee's Flowers had graciously offered to turn over all proceeds over to cancer research, and they were currently working on getting other flower shops in the area to follow suit. They'd been able to get the gift shop at the hospital to start carrying flower-like flower alternatives, so that was a start.

Kai had helped them start a foundation in Molly's name, and in two days, Molly's Foundation was sponsoring their first 5k race in Molly's honor. They'd gotten a lot of interest, and they hoped if it did well, they could make it a yearly event.

They were only taking the Bee sisters up on the free flowers every three weeks when they would bring fresh flowers to the graveyard. Eleanor and Kai now both participated in maintaining the gravesite.

They'd not yet decided if they would take the Bee sisters up on the free flowers for the wedding. If they did, they were planning on keeping it very simple. Simple had been the main focus of their lives since Kai discharged home. It was amazing what a reduction in stress had done for Kai's recovery and overall well-being.

Today, in preparation of the race, Eleanor was supposed to meet a slew of volunteers at Bee's for the assembly of the race packets. She'd not had to do too much coercing to get volunteers to help her assemble the packets. Between her coworkers, the parents of the children Molly attended school with, and BeeKeeper members, they had more than enough people to help the race run smoothly.

Eleanor entered the back of the store per the sisters' request as it was not quite opening time. She walked in and was inundated with a loud Missy Elliott song. She assumed that both sisters were probably a little jumpy since the attack a few months ago, even though they all knew Mitchell Pierce was still locked up securely in prison. She wasn't sure if his parents had heeded Kai's advice, but from Kai's inside sources, Mitchell hadn't had any visitors for a long time, finally being held accountable for his actions. Kai hadn't heard yet when he and Stacia would be testifying, but he was more than ready when the time arrived.

She lurked slowly through the store and, as she always did, tried not to imagine the scene that occurred the night of the crime. Eleanor was startled when her hip was bumped somewhat aggressively from the side. She squealed loudly as Stacia grabbed her hands and twirled her around, forcing her to join their dance party.

Eleanor thought about the fact that Stacia, who had been brutally attacked there seemed to still always be in good spirits, letting the good win over the bad. She decided that if Stacia could let the good overcome enough to have a dance party in the same space she had bad memories in, she could also continue to fight hard to let the good overcome. Eleanor started to sway and shimmy in time to the music. Rachel came out of the back room a few seconds later and wordlessly danced over to them. For a few minutes the three women let the music enter their ears and take over their bodies and souls.

They danced together, not caring what they looked like or the potential that someone could walk in at any moment. It was as if, for a few minutes, all their worries and stresses just faded away, carried away momentarily by the sound of the music, the pulsing of the bass, and the movement of their bodies.

After the song ended, they all took a moment to catch their breath, "Geez girl, you can dance!" Stacia exclaimed. "I think I assumed that you could dance well, but I was not quite expecting that."

"Well, former gymnast, if you must know," Eleanor informed her. "I still have a few skills apparently. You girls are not too bad yourselves!"

"Why thank you," Rachel said. "We get our practice in twice a day. Moving on to the serious stuff, what do we need to help you with before people start showing up?"

They unloaded Eleanor's car, getting all of the donated coupons and free samples out. Stacia and Rachel oo'd and ahh'd over the race t-shirts, which were pretty whimsical. They were bright yellow with Molly's Race printed on the front and a pair of fairy wings printed on the back, along with all of the sponsors.

"I just have to say that it's so cool that you got this all organized," Stacia said as they finalized the stations in the work area. "I am so happy that she is being honored and remembered in so many different ways."

"It was nothing. All I did was mention it as a possibility and people were jumping at the bit to volunteer," Eleanor said, wiping the sweat off of her forehead. "When is Scarlett coming? I haven't seen her for way too long."

"I think she had a check-up this morning, she's looking so adorable these days! I can't wait to see her! On a different note, how is Kai doing?" Rachel asked. "Is he enjoying his new job?"

"He's doing really well, actually," Eleanor informed them. "He has time off now and less stress. He helped me plot this race out, and he took it WAY too seriously. But I now know the race route like the back of my hand because I am fairly certain he made me run it with him over a hundred times in the last two months."

"I'm so glad that he's not such a dick anymore," Stacia said before clapping her hand over her mouth in shock. "Oh my goodness, I am so sorry. My mouth sometimes has a mind of its own. Please don't..."

Eleanor interrupted her: "He was an asshole for a while there, wasn't he? I'm not mad that you pointed out the obvious." Eleanor gestured for them to sit down, "I know that you ladies are both smart. I know that you have noticed that he does not buy roses anymore. I know that you probably also noticed that his coldness has slowly improved. I don't know that I feel comfortable speaking about all that happened right now but know that we have both seen counselors separately and together. Let's just say if he ever comes here to purchase roses, know that I will be at home packing his things and leaving them outside."

Stacia gulped in shock: "I'm so sorry. I'm sorry I brought all of this up, it wasn't intentional. I don't blame you for not wanting to talk about all the details, especially if you're trying to make it work together, but just know that we are always here for you."

Stacia stood and motioned for Eleanor and Rachel to stand as well. Stacia hugged Eleanor and her sister followed suit. "Just don't forget, we like new Kai, but we like you better. If he does anything that requires roses again, I will personally kick his ass. Speaking of ass, I require more coffee STAT. Does anyone want anything from The Bean Juice?"

"We still have fifteen minutes until go-time. Let's just all walk over there together," Eleanor said as she headed towards the exit with her friends. "Thanks again for everything you guys have done for me. I appreciate all of it more than you will ever know."

"I promise you, the feelings are mutual," Stacia said as she opened the door and held it open for her friend and her sister, excited for her next coffee fix.

44

Scarlett could not quite believe where life was taking them now. She woke up each day trying to cope with the loss of her child. Some days she did this better than others. No matter whether it was a good day or a bad day, she felt like one of the most significant pieces of her was missing.

She was thankful that she had Tevin and that, despite their grief, they seemed to be turning to each other for support instead of turning away from each other. She was glad that they had a supportive group of friends and that their families were helping them in ways they never expected.

She knew Molly would always be with her. Sometimes, when no one else was around, she thought she heard the hint of her daughter's voice in the wind. She sometimes found herself waking up and feeling like she needed to check on Molly. She would sometimes make it all the way to Molly's empty bed before she remembered she was gone.

She had felt like they were coping, like they were dealing with the grief on a day-to-day basis when the rug had been pulled out from under them in a way that they had never expected.

45

Scarlett could not quite bend over far enough to tie her shoes. "Tevin!" She exclaimed down the stairs. "I can't bend over to tie these shoes. Help!" After a minute she heard the sound of Tevin's feet coming up the stairs.

"Geez, little man," Tevin said, stopping for a brief moment to rub her protruding belly. "You aren't even born yet and are giving your mom a hard time."

"Please just help me with my shoes. I have to get to Bee's to help with the race packets!" Scarlett said as she thrust the shoes in his direction. "I seriously could tie these yesterday!"

Tevin dutifully grabbed them from her and began to place them on her feet. While he did this, she thought back to five months ago when she found out she was pregnant.

"Well, Scarlett," Dr. Colif had stated as she walked back into the examination room. "It turns out I don't need to wait for all of the lab work to come back. I ran a urine pregnancy test just to rule it out, and it was positive."

Scarlett had promptly burst out laughing, "Wow, please don't mess with me right now. You are kidding, aren't you?"

"No," Dr. Colif had replied immediately, shaking her head. "The tests are 99% accurate. If you think about the symptoms you described to me -- nausea, fatigue, increased urination-- all of them can be contributed to pregnancy."

"You have to be participating in certain activities to become pregnant, and that hasn't really been on our minds with the loss of my child...there is no possible....... Wait," Scarlett had stopped what she was saying as she tried to do the mental mathematics that would either convince Dr. Colif that she had run the test on someone else's urine sample or convince herself that she could indeed be pregnant.

She thought back to her last period. She thought for a minute: It had been....it had been around the time Molly had been put back in the hospital... but it had been light.... In fact, it had been light since the Molly overnight... when she and Tevin had sex in the backyard.... without a condom.

Scarlett had grabbed the trashcan and promptly thrown up.

Scarlett had driven to Bee's Flowers in shock. She didn't even really remember parking her car or walking to the store. All it had taken was her seeing Rachel's face for her to start crying. Both of the sisters had been there for Scarlett in her grief, so it was not entirely abnormal for her to show up to talk to them. However, sudden tears were unusual enough for Rachel to question what was going on.

"I need a bouquet and some cards," Scarlett had said borderline hysterically.

"Sure, sweetie," Rachel had said, putting a reassuring arm around her friend's shoulders. "What occasion?"

"Something I can give Tevin to tell him I'm pregnant," Scarlett had managed to say between the sobbing.

Rachel, not quite sure she had heard correctly, looked at Scarlett, concerned. Stacia, hearing the crying from the back room, had ventured in their direction. "I'm pregnant y'all. I'm having a baby. I can't believe this is happening."

Rachel and Stacia had then looked at each other with concern. Rachel had ushered Scarlett into the classroom area, and Stacia had gone next door to get herself a coffee and some decaf tea for Scarlett. They had all sat in the back and let Scarlett talk through her feelings.

"I have a million feelings running through me right now. I was pregnant before Molly died, but she never got to know that there was going to be a sibling. I don't know if that would have been good or if it would have been bad, knowing her she would have been over the moon excited. Either way, I feel like she deserved to know. Losing her is still so fresh, and my heart still hurts so badly sometimes I can hardly stand it. How can I take care of a new life when the first life I brought into this world didn't survive? How can I love this baby when I used all of my love for Molly?" Scarlett paused to wipe her nose with a tissue and take a sip of her tea.

"Y'all, I feel so awful saying any of this! I know that there are people who can't even have one baby, and I was lucky enough to have one, but our time together was far too short. Now I am having another one. I know I should be happy to have another baby, but I just lost her... I just lost Molly. Plus, I can't eat without throwing up, which I now know is the damn baby's fault...freaking baby." Scarlett had thrown her head down on the worktable sobbing. "Now I'm already insulting the new one. What is wrong with me?"

Stacia and Rachel had taken turns rubbing her back as she sat there crying until, exhausted and red-eyed, she had raised her head up. "I'm a mess," Scarlett had said honestly.

Scarlett had agreed to let the sisters' text Tevin so he could take her home, and in less than a half hour, he had shown up. They had asked Scarlett if she wanted to disclose the news to him at the store, and Scarlett had shaken her head, "I don't think you need the two of us in shock at your store."

But the minute Tevin had walked into the backroom Scarlett had gone back on her original plan. Instead, she had impulsively said, "I'm pregnant. We're having a baby."

Tevin, in shock, had sat at the worktable, not speaking, pale as a sheet of paper.

Rachel had pulled Stacia aside at that point, "Okay, now I really don't think either of them should drive. I'm calling Kathleen."

Kathleen had decided to stay an extra week after the funeral. She had initially wanted to stick around and help with the aftermath of the funeral before she went back home. An extra week had turned into two weeks and then a month. They were okay with her being there and had found that it had helped process Molly's death.

Kathleen had admitted she felt like she had the potential to go downhill again if she went back to Louisiana. Molly's death seemed to have made her realize how short life truly was and Kathleen finally seemed like she was at a point where she was ready to go to college and progress in life. She wasn't sure what she wanted to do yet but was excited to explore. It had been decided that she could start school at the start of the next semester here and, in the meantime, had gotten a job at The Bean Juice. She had been living in the renovated basement, so she had her own space, and it had been unexpectedly lovely for them to have her there.

Rachel had called Kathleen and told her about Scarlett's unexpected news. Kathleen, though shocked herself, verbalized joy at knowing there would eventually be a baby for her to assist with. Kathleen had driven the shocked and emotional Tevin and Scarlett home, where they had started the journey of accepting the course their life was heading in.

They had been seeing a counselor since Molly's death and had gotten an appointment immediately. The counselor had been invaluable in helping them slowly process the grief, but they had barely brushed the surface. Knowing there was going to be a new baby made both Tevin and Scarlett feel like they needed to deal with the grief as effectively as possible.

The counselor had been assisting them with grieving Molly first, while still acknowledging the pregnancy. Once they talked through the grief process, they were able to start each day with sadness for the daughter they lost and hope for the new life they would bring into the world.

At the 20-week ultrasound, they had found out that they were having a boy. They had been overjoyed. A part of both of them felt like boy territory would be a whole new world. Scarlett had voiced in counseling that she had been fearful that if she had a girl, she had the potential to compare them, and she did not want the new baby to grow up already competing with the sister he would never meet.

Molly's room was still untouched and neither Scarlett nor Tevin felt ready to tackle that quite yet. They had another room upstairs that they had turned into a nursery. Kathleen had helped paint the walls with Colorado mountains and had added cute nature decor throughout the nursery. They had added a little section of wildflowers to the wall and labeled it Molly's Meadow. With only a few months remaining in the pregnancy, they were starting to feel more prepared every day.

"You look so cute!" Eleanor exclaimed as soon as Scarlett and Tevin entered Bee's to assemble the race packets. "Can I touch your belly?"

Scarlett nodded, allowing Eleanor to feel the rounded bump beneath her dress. Eleanor looked up with a smile. "How're you doing with all of it?"

"I miss her every day. I try to keep the missing her separate from the baby. Molly deserves to be missed and this new one deserves to be celebrated. Some days are easier than others. Kathleen helped me get the nursery together and it is adorable!"

"Do you have pictures?" Eleanor asked. Scarlett nodded as she pulled her phone out, handing it to Eleanor to swipe through. Scarlett could tell she was looking at Molly's Meadow as her smile widened, and her eyes got a teary sheen to them.

"Thanks again for all you have done to help honor Molly's life. I didn't have the energy to do any of this alone. I appreciate you. Molly would have loved all of this."

"It was the least I could do. She really was so special to me, to all of us," Eleanor said as Scarlett pulled her in for a hug.

They were interrupted by the sound of a stampede as Marie and Stella burst into the workroom and hugged Eleanor and Scarlett. "How are my little running ambassadors doing?" Eleanor asked. The girls had been quite the promoters, making posters and calling school friends and recruiting other Bee-Keepers to run and volunteer.

"We can't wait!" Marie said excitedly. "We made special head-bands!" With that, the girls both pulled out what had been standard gray headbands that they had painted with flowers, fairies, and mermaids. In the middle, it said: Molly's Run.

"You guys make more of these?" Eleanor asked.

Chad came into the room and answered, "It's all we've been doing for the last few days." He held out his hands where there were still remnants of sparkly fabric paint.

"We're going to display them at one of the tables for dona-tions," Stella chimed in.

"You guys could have a career in marketing, I think," Eleanor said.

The girls both giggled before turning their attention to Scar-lett. They both put a hand on her belly. "What're you naming him?" Marie asked.

"It's going to be a surprise," Scarlett said, crouching down so she could face both of the girls. "I think Molly would've ap-proved though." She hugged each girl before standing up with some effort. "You guys ready for the race?"

"We can't wait!" Marie exclaimed before she and her sister ran off to help with the preparations.

46

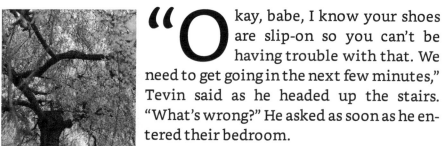

"Okay, babe, I know your shoes are slip-on so you can't be having trouble with that. We need to get going in the next few minutes," Tevin said as he headed up the stairs. "What's wrong?" He asked as soon as he entered their bedroom.

"This just feels even more final," Scarlett said sniffling into a tissue. "It seems like every time I feel like the pain is tolerable, something happens, and it knocks a whole new hole into my heart that was Molly. Do you remember what a wreck I was last week?"

Last week they had gotten a mailer from the school district addressed to the parents of Molly Cline. Scarlett had not dealt with it well. She understood that there would always be reminders of Molly everywhere, and she wanted to have reminders of Molly. The wound was still so fresh that every time it happened, she felt like someone was taking salt and rubbing it continuously over the open wound.

Today they were having an unveiling at the cemetery of Molly's memorial plaque. They had gone back and forth about what to do with her ashes and whether or not she should be buried in Colorado or Louisiana. After much discussion, they had decided Colorado would be a better place as she had spent the last few years there, and Scarlett and Tevin had decided it felt the most like home.

Molly had always said that she wanted to be with flowers. They had considered many options where her final resting place should be. They liked the idea of her being in a field of flowers but did not like the idea of not having a place to visit her. They had eventually decided to purchase a plot within the cemetery where they could plant a tree. They had purchased a special urn where the ashes could be placed, and a beautiful pink dogwood tree would grow and flower. They had picked a scenic, remote area in the cemetery and had chosen a beautiful plaque to be displayed by the tree so friends and family could come and visit her. Scarlett and Tevin had decided to keep some of her ashes in the urn she had been placed in, knowing that their house would not be the same if a physical piece of Molly did not exist there.

Tevin walked over to Scarlett and helped pull her up from the bed. "Molly will always be a part of our day-to-day life. She lives in our hearts and she sends us signs all the time that she is close by."

Scarlett looked at him apprehensively.

"It wasn't until I got past some of the sorrow that I was able to start seeing all the signs," he said. "Have you seen that bird outside that seems to never leave? Have you walked outside and seen the hammock swaying when there is barely a breeze? Have you woken up and just felt like she was around? Have you had dreams where she tells you she is not in pain and that she loves you? I have had all of these things happen. I choose to believe that they are all Molly speaking to us. It is in the process of looking for her in all of the things that she loved that gives me peace and helps me know that she is a permanent part of our lives." Tevin looked at Scarlett, not sure what type of reaction he would get from his pregnant wife.

"Okay, okay," She wiped the tears from her eyes and plastered a weak smile on her face. "Trying to find peace is a daily struggle. I'll work on looking for her in the unexpected."

Tevin gave her a kiss and a hug before also planting a kiss onto her belly. He grabbed her hand and together they walked down the stairs. Scarlett made a point to glance out the window as she passed through the kitchen. Sure enough, the sparrow was perched on the fence. The sparrow seemed to turn its head as she walked by and, for a second, it did bring Scarlett some unexpected joy. She decided she could make it a point to start seeing Molly in her daily routine.

They got to the cemetery a few minutes before everyone else, wanting some time to be alone before others came to participate in the tree planting. The spot that they had picked was beautiful. It was situated in a slightly raised portion of the cemetery, which offered a better view of the town. They stood there with only the sounds of the city and the chirping of the early springtime birds in the background, admiring the view until one-by-one their friends had shown up.

They tried to make the celebration of life brief, playing a few songs that Molly had loved and giving friends a chance to say something. Tevin, Chad, and Kai each grabbed a shovel and dug in, creating a large hole for the tree. Scarlett could not bend over to help place the tree in the ground so she had asked in advance if Marie and Stella would be interested in doing it. They took their job very seriously, talking to it the whole time, giving the tree urn loving words before carefully placing it in the hole. They all cried, but it had been a different type of sorrow from the funeral.

"We have a few more things that we all thought would make Molly's spot a little more special," Rachel said, nodding to Chad and Kai. They jogged down the hill towards the parking lot and returned a few minutes later carrying a bench. The bench appeared to have been painted by children, Scarlett assumed possibly by the BeeKeepers, in various bright colors.

When it got closer, she noticed that on the bench was a plaque with some engraved words, kids' drawings of flowers and fairies, as well as different writing and sayings. Some of the writing was simple statements: "We miss you, Molly. We love you, Molly."

Someone had elaborately written a statement from *Peter Pan* on the back in elegant script: *So come with me, where dreams are born, and time is never planned. Just think of happy things, and your heart will fly on wings, forever, in Never Never Land!*

Tevin and Scarlett clasped hands. "It's perfect," Tevin said, choking back tears as he gestured to the bench. "I can't express how thankful we are for y'all and for this."

Afterward, Scarlett and Tevin sat on the bench and talked to the tree that was also Molly. They told her about how much they missed her, they told her how she would be in their hearts always. They told her about her baby brother who would be born soon and what his name would be. They told her they were there whenever she wanted to make her presence known. As they were leaving, one lone sparrow perched next to them on the bench for a few moments before flying away. She could not remember ever being this at peace since Molly had died.

47

Stacia was healing. She was becoming the person she felt she had always wanted to be. She felt like she had been through hell and back emotionally, mentally, and physically and had come out stronger and more powerful than ever. The person she had always wanted to become was within reach.

She felt like the world was her oyster, that she could go anywhere and be anything. She was not sure what was in store for her but was excited about living out that mystery. She had felt this way before and then the attack had occurred, slowing her forward progress temporarily. The florist now felt that the good days far surpassed the bad days.

She felt closer to her family, to her friends, and to Marco. No matter how hard she had tried to push them away in her hurt, they had not let her, giving her distance and space but always staying within reach. She was so thankful that though she had not always known how to feel and how to cope with the stress of the situation, they had all been there on the periphery.

She had started focusing some of the hatred she had towards Mitchell Pierce into more positive outlets, and she felt like hate was no longer eating her from the inside out. She knew that there would never be perfect justice for her and the other victims, but she also knew that living a successful life without constant fear was one of the best punishments she could dole out to her attacker.

She felt alive, aware, and awakened.

48

"**O**h my goodness Rach, there are fancy robes in the closet here!" Stacia said. "We'll totally have to wear them later when we get back!" Stacia removed the plush robes from their hangers, pulled them out of the closet, and placed them on the bed so they wouldn't forget when they got back in their rooms.

Two days ago, Chad and Marco had surprised the sisters with a spa day and night at a swanky Denver hotel. They had been training Tevin's sister Kathleen in the last month, and she had been showing promise not just in the merchandise part but also with the floral arranging. She was even thinking about going the design route in college. Grandma Betty had also happened to be in town for a few days and volunteered to help cover the day with Kathleen.

They had both been giddy with anticipation, neither having done anything like this before. Chad and Marco had gone all out, scheduling them for mud baths, massages, facials, manicures, and pedicures. They had been surprised when checking in to find that they had also been signed up for a champagne sunset dinner on the terrace.

"I bet they have robes for us to wear all day," Rachel said, turning around to find that her sister had already slipped into her robe. Stacia pressed a button on her phone and dance music began to play.

Rachel sighed, ever the older sister, before donning her robe and prancing around with her sister. They shimmied and shook, doing their usual hip bumps and butt shaking. "I hope this hotel can handle our music," Rachel said after Stacia bumped it up a notch.

"Let's hope they can handle the flower sisters! Flower... sisters... Flower sisters... " Stacia pranced around in her robe, and it was only a few seconds before Rachel joined in. They danced around chanting "flower sisters" loudly together for a full song before they turned the music off, ready to go downstairs for their first spa treatment.

Stacia was in the bathroom brushing her teeth when Rachel opened the door. "Oh... my... God." She said between clenched teeth. "I just heard every single word of our hotel neighbor's conversation about their cat being constipated."

"What?" Stacia asked, "That is super strange. Why would they talk about..." Stacia was hushed when her sister clamped her hand over her mouth, which resulted in Stacia shooting her a disgusted look.

"It means that our neighbors on both sides heard our lovely dance party, and our chanting," Rachel hissed as she removed her hand from her sister's mouth.

Stacia started laughing before whispering, "Well at least we are fun and not talking about how often our animal does or does not shit."

Rachel laughed quietly as she pushed her sister towards the door. "Let's go relax."

Stacia could not remember ever being so relaxed in her life. By the time they got back to their hotel room they had been pampered to the max, "Is it bad that I just want to go to sleep? How is it that relaxing like that just made me want to sleep?"

"Don't worry, I bet you'll get your second wind," Rachel said as they had headed back to their hotel room.

They unlocked the door and both sisters gasped. On the bed were two dresses. Both were calf-length and silky black. One had a note that said it was for Rachel and the other had a note saying it was for Stacia. "Our men have outdone themselves!" Stacia exclaimed as she ran to try it on. It was even more breathtaking on than it was on the bed with a long dipping V in the back of the dress, accentuating her back.

"Wow, you look amazing!" Rachel said as she twirled around in her dress, which was a beautiful halter-style, accentuating her shoulders.

They had just gone into the bathroom to start doing their hair and makeup when there was a knock on the door. Rachel went to the door and saw two women standing there. "We are here to do your hair and makeup."

Stacia looked at her sister. "Wow, they have outdone what I previously thought could not be outdone."

An hour later both sisters headed to the sunset dinner, hair perfectly styled and make-up perfectly in place. They checked in with the hostess and were led to a private area outside on the terrace. "Your table is right over here," the hostess said as she rounded the corner and headed towards a solitary table. Stacia had just about approached the table when she saw someone approaching with a large bouquet of flowers, she assumed was a centerpiece.

She couldn't see that it was Marco until he lowered the bouquet and handed them to her. "What are you doing here?" She looked behind her and saw that her sister had slunk back and was standing with Chad, camera at-the-ready. "What's going on?"

She turned back around and saw that Marco was on one knee. "Holy shit," she whispered, in shock.

"Stacia, I knew from the moment I met you that you were something special. I had the bruise on my arm for a full week. Every time I looked at it, I smiled thinking about the sassy girl from the flower shop. When I got to know you, you became more than my girlfriend. You became my person. If something happens during the day, you're the person I want to turn to. If there is a fun activity that I want to do, you're the person I want to have fun with. Despite your sarcasm and the fact that your blood is possibly 70% coffee at all times, you are the person for me. I want to experience life with you, I want to have a home with you, I want to be your person forever, and I want you to be my person forever. Stacia Bee, will you marry me?"

"Yes," Stacia said, sucking in the tears threatening to fall, barely keeping them at bay, "but just know I am going to refuse to cry right now because I am pretty sure I look way hotter than usual."

Marco stood up and swept her into a giant hug and then gave her a passionate kiss.

Stacia laughed, "Do I get to see the ring? Or is it just a piece of string? Or a Twizzler? I would be okay with all of those. I don't need a ring."

"Hush, my love," Marco said as he put a finger in front of her mouth to hush her. He opened the box, and Stacia gasped in delight. Inside was a rose gold band with a yellow colored diamond. Around the band were little vines interweaving with bead-like detail. The way the diamond was positioned on the setting made it resemble a sunflower.

"It's perfect!" Stacia exclaimed as he slipped the band onto her left finger. "Did you know about this?" Stacia asked her sister as Rachel and Chad walked over to them. They hugged the newly engaged couple and Rachel grabbed her hand to admire the ring.

"I only knew about part of it. The men did not inform me about some of the pampering," Rachel said jokingly swatting Chad.

"Well, I wanted you to still have some surprise pampering, my Queen," Chad said as he pulled his wife in for a hug.

"Well thank you, my King," Rachel said as she planted a kiss on her husband's cheek.

"Sounds like we have some flower planning to do. I even promise to stay at a level of three or less on the bridezilla scale. Not to be too sassy right now, but I'd love to sit and eat with my family and fiancé. All of the pampering I had today has left me starving!" They all laughed as they walked to their table, excited to celebrate together in front of the beautiful Rocky

Mountain view and the Colorado sunset.

A few days later, Marco had come to Stacia's apartment, after work, to give her some exciting news.

"Oh my goodness, Marco, that is amazing. It is exactly what you'd been hoping for!" Stacia exclaimed, pulling him off of the couch for a hug. "This is so unbelievably crazy! What does this mean for us?"

Marco hugged her back and then motioned for her to sit back on the couch. "We need to talk about what we realistically can do from here. I want you to come with me, but I understand what that flower shop means to you and what your family means to you. Will they be okay if you are gone for several months?"

"My family will always be there for me no matter if I am gone for several months or not. If we can find a way for me to go, I want to go," Stacia said.

Marco had been working on his photography portfolio aggressively the last few months. A month ago, he had had a new publishing company inquire about his website and some snippets of writing that had been attached to each photo. When Marco had informed them that it had been his writing, they had asked for a sample piece.

He had gotten a phone call from the publishing company this morning. They were looking for someone to travel and write about it for a travel guide they wanted to put out. They had offered to pay him a small stipend and pay for 100% of the travel. When the book was published, he would get a portion of the proceeds.

"There is something else I should probably tell you. I didn't want to tempt you with further details until I knew if you had any interest in traveling. You haven't ever even left the country," Marco said as Stacia looked at him inquiringly.

"Well, when they first contacted me, I told them I was newly engaged. I asked them what I would need to do to have you along for the ride, free of charge. They laughed at me until I assured them I was serious. They asked what you do for work, and when I sent them your website, they thought your flowers were beautiful. They agreed to send you with me as long as we're covering local flowers and arranging some flowers in each location. They will plan on paying you as my travel assistant until they see the finished product. If they're unhappy with the results, they'll leave the flower portion out of the book."

"We have to do this! I want to do this! How can we make this happen?" Stacia flew off the couch, jumping up and down excitedly. She couldn't remember ever feeling this excited and intrigued about something.

"This seems crazy. We just got engaged. I have the flower delivery job and freelance work, and you have the flower shop. Maybe I should tell them now is not the right time," Marco said. "If they want me, they can wait for a better time, right?"

Stacia sat down next to him. He turned so they were face-to-face. "Marco," Stacia began, "we are young and currently have nothing tying us down. The world is beckoning to us, and through some unheard-of twist-of-fate, we are essentially being offered a golden ticket! Benny has wanted to work more, and you can make that happen. Kathleen has wanted to work more, and I can make that happen. Why would we not go?!"

"They want us to leave in a month. Do you think we can get work squared away, get our affairs in order, and throw together a wedding in less than a month?" Marco looked at her questioningly.

"Wedding?" Stacia said shocked, "What do you mean wedding?"

"I want to go on this journey with my wife. I want to watch the sunset in different countries knowing that it'll be the start of many sunsets to come in our marriage. I want to be your partner in every way possible. If that doesn't appeal to you then I will of course wait," Marco said as he grabbed her hand and, glancing down, subtly admired her ring.

"What about your family in Guatemala?" Stacia asked.

"They sent me a tentative itinerary this morning and it turns out that Guatemala is one of the stops in South America. I bet

my family would love nothing more than to do a little ceremony down there as well."

"I feel like this is either a book or a movie; it just doesn't seem
real!" Stacia said. "Last night I went to bed excited about the future, but not in any way, shape, or form thinking that we could
be facing a different life all of a sudden. I'm excited, but it is
crazy!"

"I agree. This is all super sudden and I don't want either of
us to take it lightly. Why don't you grab some coffee from The
Bean Juice and think about it? I'm committed to you any way
you spin it. I can go solo, I can ask for an extension, we can go as
an engaged couple, or we can get married and embrace all of the
craziness."

Stacia threw on her running clothes, knowing that if she ever
needed to thoroughly think about something that pounding it
out of the pavement was the best way to clear her mind completely. She took the extended loop that would take her by the
shop first so she could wipe herself off in the employee break
room before heading to The Bean Juice for her coffee fix.

She walked into Bee's to find her sister there, "What're you
doing here? We closed a few hours ago last time I checked."
Stacia motioned for her sister to come to the breakroom with
her so she could wipe off the sweat from her face and arms with
a towel.

"Chad took the girls to a movie, so I just came here for
some peace and quiet. I come here sometimes to be around the
flowers.... and the silence. I love the silence," Rachel said as she
stood up and followed Stacia to the back. "What're you doing
here?" Rachel asked again.

"Well, Marco sent me on a coffee mission so that I could do
some pondering. I decided to ponder whilst running and then
come here, so I'm not a sweaty beast when I go to get my coffee,"
Stacia opened her locker and pulled out some deodorant and
swiped it under her armpits. She then sprayed herself with some
body spray.

"Do you need some older sister advice on whatever you are

pondering?" Rachel inquired as she waved a hand in front of her nose to dispel the strong odor of the body spray.

"So, you know how Marco feels about his photography, right?" Stacia said, and Rachel nodded. "Okay, so a few months ago a new publishing company reached out to him. They are just starting and have a pretty hefty budget to start. They want to do a travel guidebook with pictures and writing. He sent them a writing sample about a month ago, and he hadn't heard anything, so he figured it wasn't happening…"

"He heard from them and he got the job?" Rachel asked, excitement in her voice.

"Yes, but there's more," Stacia said. "He showed them our website and they now want me to go and include a flower section. They might not include it in the travel guide, but I will get to travel as his assistant either way."

"Holy crap! Really?" Rachel exclaimed.

"Wait, there's more," Stacia said, pausing to fill up a glass of water. She took a big gulp before answering. "He wants us to get married this month and then leave for several months of traveling."

Rachel looked at her for a moment, "And the problem is…."

"I'm scared. I've never been out of the United States. I never thought I would get engaged again. I'm not only engaged but engaged to the man of my dreams and facing a potential marriage coauthoring part of a book, which is crazy. It is all crazy." Stacia flung herself dramatically into the chair next to her sister.

"Once again," Rachel said, "What is the problem?"

"It's crazy, who are you and what did you do with my sister?" Stacia asked, dumbfounded that her practical sister was not arguing about why she shouldn't go.

"Life is so short, and I thought the trauma you went through, and Molly's death taught you that," Rachel said, grabbing for her sister's hand. "You need to take advantage of every adventure that presents itself to you."

"What about the store?" Stacia asked, fully expecting this to change her encouraging sister into a doubtful sister.

"Kathleen is doing an amazing job!" Rachel exclaimed, "She was born for this type of job. She wants to possibly major in floral or interior design. Either way, she wants to work here while in school so she can get a portfolio put together along with a lot of experience before she graduates. She is highly motivated and a reliable, hard worker. What more could we ask for?"

"I didn't know I was so easily replaceable," Stacia said, rolling her eyes at her sister. "Okay, so the store would be covered. What about the wedding part of his request?"

"You said earlier that he is the man you have always seen yourself with? The perfect partner for you?" Rachel asked.

"He is perfect for me. We laugh all the time and I can be myself around him. I love him," Stacia said dreamily.

"Well, then it sounds like we have a wedding to plan," Rachel said as she stood up and pulled her sweaty sister into a hug.

49

Rachel felt so proud of the people in her life. She was seeing progress in the lives of the people who were near and dear to her. She had seen a lot of highs and lows in the last few years She felt like they had all walked away from hardships bruised and beaten but with a strong bond. She had met some incredible people and they had changed each other's lives.

She had a husband who was no longer deployed but safe at home. Chad had some emotional damage as a result of his military service but was always willing to talk about it and work on it. She had her partner back, the father to her children.

She had two beautiful, spunky girls who had befriended a beautiful little girl with cancer. Her daughters were proving to be braver and proactive in memorializing their friend. She had witnessed her daughters turn their sorrow into something positive and she was beyond proud of them.

She had a sassy sister who had thrived despite many hardships. Through it all, Rachel's sister had met the perfect partner, her soulmate, and they were going to get married and travel the world.

She had Scarlett, who had been a friend she had not even known she had needed. She had seen what a parent's worst nightmare looked like and had seen her friends continue to celebrate the life of their little angel while preparing for a new baby.

She had Eleanor, who was such a sweet, kind person and an

unexpected friend, and Kai, who had literally saved her sister's life.

She could not remember a time she had felt so blessed.

50

"Y ou aren't going to throw up. Calm down, Stacia," Rachel said as she zipped up the simple rose-gold halter sheath dress that Stacia was going to wear down the aisle in less than an hour.

"I could throw up," Stacia said, sounding more and more panicked.

"You need to sit down and do some deep breathing for a few minutes," Rachel said before muttering under her breath, "or take a few shots of tequila."

"Tequila will definitely make me throw up!" Stacia exclaimed, suddenly looking a little pale.

"You weren't supposed to hear that," Rachel said as she guided her sister into a chair. "Did you eat today, or did you have a Bean Juice liquid coffee breakfast?"

Stacia looked at her sister guiltily. "Now that I think about it, I only had coffee this morning."

Rachel draped a large throw from the couch over her sister's dress and forced her to eat a few crackers. As Stacia ate, Rachel decided to run to the backyard and check on the decor and the other members of the bridal party.

Her mother and Grandma Betty had just finished putting up the mason jars full of flowers that were stacked at the front of each aisle. At night, when dusk started to fall, they would move the mason jars with flowers onto the tables for guests to take

279

home and place mason jars with candles in their place.

Stacia and Marco had decided to get married in Grandma Betty and Grandpa David's backyard. It had an elegant garden and space for chairs and a small tent. They had decided to go small, especially after tossing around the idea of possibly doing a little ceremony in each country they visited after reading an interesting article about a couple who had done that online. They had invited their families, their close friends from the flower shop, a few friends from high school, and Marco's indoor-soccer league friends.

Rachel had been the wedding planner, giving Stacia and Marco time to find renters for their apartments, pack, and shop for materials they would need for an extended travel period. Rachel had really enjoyed it and wondered if it was a service they could one day offer as an expansion of the flower shop.

She straightened up the sunflowers in the mason jars when she felt her husband's embrace from behind. "You look lovely, my Queen." She did look lovely, sporting a muted yellow strappy sheath dress. She was her sister's only bridesmaid. Marco had Benny as his best man. Stella and Marie were flower girls -- though Marie had verbalized that flower girls sounded kind of babyish, so they changed the official title to junior bridesmaids.

"You look handsome, my King," Rachel said as she kissed him seductively on the lips, causing his mouth to erupt into an equally seductive smile.

Rachel stared into his eyes for a moment, thankful and happy to be there with him, "What time is it?" she asked her husband.

He looked at his wristwatch and said, "Ten minutes till go time." Rachel gave him a quick peck and an eyebrow waggle, letting him know the seduction was not done, just temporarily on hold.

She gathered Marie and Stella, who looked absolutely beautiful in their yellow-gold junior bridesmaid dresses. She grabbed the beautiful sunflower bouquet from Grandma Betty, who had insisted on doing all the flowers as she was currently suffering from flower withdrawal and Rachel had been focusing on the wedding planning.

Rachel hooked her arm into her father's arm, and together they all went into the room where Stacia was standing, looking much better after eating something, ready for the ceremony to begin.

"You look so beautiful, sissy," Rachel said as she fanned her eyes.

Stacia fanned her own eyes in return. She walked over to her sister, pulling her in for a hug, "Thank you for everything. I love you so much."

Rachel gave her sister a kiss on the cheek and handed her the sunflower bouquet, "Go make that handsome dimpled man your husband."

Stacia looped her arm through her father's arm as he kissed her on the cheek and told her how beautiful she looked. Flowers in hand, she started her walk down the aisle, towards the man of her dreams … and towards a new adventure.

epilogue

"How is it possible to forget how painful this is.... AHHH-HHHH!" Scarlett grabbed Tevin's hand as another contraction waved through her belly.

"Push!" the labor-and-delivery nurse and Tevin screamed together.

Scarlett pushed with all her might, hoping she was getting close to the last contraction.

"I see his head," the nurse informed Scarlett after the contraction had stopped. She was given a temporary reprieve. "You can get this on the next contraction."

Scarlett nodded weakly, not feeling like she had the energy this time to even speak. Tevin squeezed her hand three times, and she weakly returned the I-love-you gesture.

She felt another contraction building and she bore down with all her might.

"He's out!" She heard Tevin exclaim as she heard the cry of her newborn son. They dried him and laid him on her bare skin.

"Hi, Peter," Scarlett said through her tears, "I'm your mommy."

∞∞∞

The subject of abuse is a tough one. I work in a busy emergency room and see patients who are going through some very tough things. I've found that though never okay, abuse doesn't ever seem to be very black and white. It was hard for me to write about this subject, but I think that tough topics are essential to discuss.

In this book, I tried to leave the ending open-ended for the reader. Will Kai continue to work on himself and never hurt Eleanor again? That is for you to decide.

If you or someone you know is being abused, please call 1-800-656-4673, this is the National Abuse Hotline. You deserve to talk to someone about your options.

I also tried to reinforce throughout the book the need for counseling.

Once again, working in a busy emergency room, I see that there is a lack of mental health services and understanding in the United States. It is okay to be having a tough time. There are a lot of resources out there.

Know that you are never alone and there are people out there whom you can talk to. 1-844-549-4266 is the Mental Healthline; this number can help you find resources in your area.

If you have overwhelming feelings or are in a state of crisis, please immediately call 1-800-273-8255 which is the National Crisis/Suicide Hotline.

Lastly, mental health affects all walks of life, sexes, ethnicities, religions, political affiliations. We need to stand up for the rights of people and continue to educate ourselves and others about the lack of these services. Make your votes count, educate, and most of all, have the tough discussions with your friends and family.

Thanks!

About the Author

Corlet (Cor-lay) lives in Colorado with her husband, Mark, and her daughter Serenity. They have two dogs, Allie and Clay. She is an emergency room nurse by trade. She has always had a love of reading and writing, rumor has it when she was young, she was grounded from the library once as a punishment. This is her first novel and fulfills a lifetime dream of hers. When she isn't at work or writing, she enjoys spending time outdoors running, hiking, and gardening. She also enjoys kickboxing with her family.
Her dream job would be to travel the world and write.
Please follow her on Instagram (@corletdawn), Twitter (@corletdawn), and her Facebook author group (Corlet Dawn).
Stay tuned for more adventures with the Bee's
Flowers friends and family.

56615909R00171

Made in the USA
Columbia, SC
29 April 2019